LESSONS IN GRAVITY

A Study Abroad Novel

JESSICA PETERSON

ALSO BY JESSICA PETERSON

THE SEX & BONDS SERIES

An outrageously sexy series of romcoms set in the high stakes world of Wall Street.

The Dealmaker (Sex & Bonds #1)

The Troublemaker (Sex & Bonds #2)

THE NORTH CAROLINA HIGHLANDS SERIES

Beards. Bonfires. Boning.

Southern Seducer (NC Highlands #1)

Southern Hotshot (NC Highlands #2)

Southern Sinner (NC Highlands #3)

Southern Playboy (NC Highlands #4)

Southern Bombshell (NC Highlands #5)

THE CHARLESTON HEAT SERIES

The Weather's Not the Only Thing Steamy Down South.

Southern Charmer (Charleston Heat #1)

Southern Player (Charleston Heat #2)

Southern Gentleman (Charleston Heat #3)

Southern Heartbreaker (Charleston Heat #4)

THE THORNE MONARCHS SERIES

Royal. Ridiculously Hot. Totally Off Limits...

Royal Ruin (Thorne Monarchs #1)

Royal Rebel (Thorne Monarchs #2)

Royal Rogue (Thorne Monarchs #3)

THE STUDY ABROAD SERIES

Studying Abroad Just Got a Whole Lot Sexier.

A Series of Sexy Interconnected Standalone Romances

Lessons in Love (Study Abroad #1)

Lessons in Gravity (Study Abroad #2)

Lessons in Letting Go (Study Abroad #3)

Lessons in Losing It (Study Abroad #4)

FOLLOW ME, Y'ALL!

- Join my Facebook reader group, The City Girls, and hang out in one of the coolest spots on the internet. I'm biased, but I'm also pretty thrilled by how awesome the people in my group are.
- Follow my not-so-glamorous life as a romance author on Instagram @JessicaPAuthor
- Follow me on Goodreads
- Follow me on Bookbub
- Like my Facebook Author Page

Published by Peterson Paperbacks, LLC
Copyright 2022 by Peterson Paperbacks, LLC
Cover by Najla Qamber of Najla Qamber Designs

All characters in this book are fiction and figments of the author's imagination.

www.jessicapeterson.com

❀ Created with Vellum

PROLOGUE

Maddie

August
Atlanta, Georgia

I crank my cranky old Volvo into park on the driveway. Looking up, I see my dad's BMW parked in front of the garage, gleaming beneath the hot stare of the Georgia sun.

That's weird. He's supposed to be at work. Dad rarely, if ever, gets home before seven on weeknights. What is he doing home at three o'clock on a Thursday afternoon?

I look at our house through my grimy windshield. It looks the same as it always does: an enormous, graceful sweep of limestone, shutters, and cedar shake. The prettiest house in the neighborhood. A dream house, where my parents made their dreams come true. It's actually what spurred my interest in architecture. I dream of designing a smaller but just as perfect house for the family I'll raise here someday.

Everything *looks* fine. But as I duck out of my car, the heat gripping me in its oven-like vise, I can't shake the feeling that something is wrong.

That something bad is about to happen.

Stop it, I tell myself. It's just leftover nerves from a manic summer internship. Today was my last day at a small residential builder. I wasn't crazy about it, to be honest. But for the most part, the really good internships—the ones at the big architecture firms—are reserved for rising college seniors, and I'll only be a junior this year. Luckily my dad has contacts at a few firms here in Atlanta, and he's promised to help me land a primo internship for next summer.

That kind of internship will help me stand out when I apply to grad school. So will a really solid thesis—a thesis that explores historic preservation, maybe, or sustainable development. The more esoteric and complex the subject matter, the better. Most of my peers are focusing their research on sites here in the States, but I want to focus on something much different—a site I really, really hope to find during my upcoming semester abroad in Madrid. I mean, what's cooler or more complex than a city that's close to a thousand years old?

I enter through the side door. The house is cool and quiet. Too quiet.

Holding my breath, I creep down the hall. Past the cavernous butler's pantry, the wine room, the powder room with the hand-painted French wallpaper that landed our house on the cover of *Beautiful Homes and Gardens*. I see two crystal tumblers, one empty, the other filled with a few fingers of brown liquor on the kitchen counter.

Huh.

I look up at a muffled thud from the floor above, followed by a trill of female laughter. My parents' bedroom. They must be doing—ew, ew, *ew*—only God knows what.

Apparently Dad came home for a little afternoon delight. A quick drink and a quicker you-know-what.

Seriously ew.

I hurry down the hall to the family room, plopping on the

couch and digging my phone out of my bag. I can't shove the ear buds into my ears fast enough; the laughter has devolved to muffled moaning. I was unaware my mom could make sounds like that.

I mean, I get it, it's probably a good thing my parents are still doing it. Their marriage *is* pretty perfect.

Still. The ick factor of hearing your parents go at it is a million times many more millions. So until they . . . uh, finish . . . I will be downstairs, and not in my room just down the hall from their bedroom door.

Blasting some country music, I catch up on texts, social media stuff, some emails about Madrid (I leave in less than a week!). I'm more excited than nervous, but I feel a little bit like I did the summer before I started my freshman year at Meryton University. I'm anxious to know what my new life is going to be like, and uneasy about leaving behind a pretty sweet and cushy life here.

I glance up from my phone, blinking, and see my dad making his way down the back staircase. He's tugging at the fly of his khakis.

I blink again when I see a dark-haired woman following closely behind him. She's buttoning up her shirt.

She is not my mother.

My heart kicks against my ribs, a hollow, panicked beat as the realization hits me. Someone was definitely doing it upstairs with my dad.

That someone wasn't my mom.

My dad is sleeping with a woman who is not my mother.

The saliva in my mouth thickens. Holy shit.

He draws up short when his eyes catch on mine.

"Maddie," he says.

"Oh, Christ," the woman mutters, and turns to scurry back up the stairs.

"Dad?" I say. My voice trembles. I feel like I'm getting sucked into the hole that just opened up inside me.

He hooks his belt through its monogrammed buckle as he descends the last step.

"It's not what you think," he says. "Before you misunderstand what you just saw—"

"What is there to misunderstand?" I rip the ear buds from my ears with fingers that shake. "What the fuck, Dad?"

His eyes narrow. "Don't you dare talk to me that way—"

"Who is she?" I ask. "How long? I don't understand."

I don't. Our friends call my parents Barbie and Ken. They are perfect in every way. Even their meet cute is perfect: they met at a tailgate at the University of Georgia, when Dad's fraternity and Mom's sorority set up camp beside each other in a parking lot outside the stadium. Dad proposed the day after they graduated on the fifty-yard line.

"Like something out of a fairy tale," my grandmother said.

A fairy tale I believe in. Deeply. Passionately.

A fairy tale I want for myself—the happy marriage, the pretty house, the two kids, and the dog and the white picket fence. Say all you want about true love and how it only exists in the movies, but I disagree. My parents share that kind of love.

Only they don't, I guess. Maybe they never did.

My dad is sleeping with someone who isn't my mother.

My dad levels me with his gaze from across the room. The look in his eyes makes my pulse run cold. He doesn't look repentant, or embarrassed. Actually, he doesn't show any of the emotions you would expect to see in a man just caught cheating on his wife of twenty-five years.

He looks *angry.* Disgusted even—not with himself, but with me.

He's never looked at me like this before.

"You listen to me, Madeline." His voice, like his eyes, is

cold, calm. "This is an adult matter. It has absolutely nothing to do with you. Forget what you saw. You won't speak of it again, understand? You are not to tell anyone."

I am frozen, stuck shaking on the couch. Who is this man? I don't recognize him. The man looking at me like I'm dog shit on his shoe—saying such horrible, mean things to me —he's not the man who raised me.

He's not my father.

"Are you serious?" I manage. "You really think I'm not going to tell Mom?"

Dad takes a step toward me. We're still a couple of feet apart, but that one step makes a world of difference. I feel like he's hovering over me, pinning me to the couch with his quiet, confident anger.

"If you tell your mother, you'll ruin everything she loves. Everything she's worked for—you and I both know this family is her life. You take that away from her, and she'll be left with nothing."

I bite my bottom lip to keep it from trembling. I won't cry in front of him.

I won't cry. I won't give him the satisfaction of knowing how terrified I am. How confused that he's putting me at fault for his mistake.

"Who do you think pays her bills? *Your* bills?" he continues. "Don't you forget that I'm paying for your education. You're getting the money for your semester in Spain from *me*. Don't screw all that up by opening your mouth."

He takes another step closer. "You tell your mother, and you'll destroy this family. You're a smart girl, Maddie. I know you'll do the smart thing."

Chapter One

MADDIE

November
Madrid, Spain

Tucking my chin into the collar of my jacket, I step inside Ático. A pleasant shiver arrows up my spine as the heat inside my favorite discoteca hits me. The potent smells of liquor and cologne, along with a hint of sweat, fill my head. Considering the week—the semester, really—that I've had, a drink sounds downright heavenly.

I take a deep breath. My heart feels heavy and sore. Par for the course these days. Considering I was the one who basically caused it, I can't get past my parents' divorce. Mom's depression and Dad's newfound cruelness have left me reeling. Of course I told Mom about Dad and that woman—how could I not?—and she kicked his ass to the curb that night.

I offered to stay home this semester. You know, help Mom figure everything out, be a shoulder to cry on. She is the backbone of our family. She quit her job when I was born and has done the mom thing ever since, sacrificing everything for us, and our family is all she has. *Had.* All she had.

She really fell the fuck apart when I told her about Dad. Like. *Really* fell apart. Some days it's so bad even a team of shrinks and a potent cocktail of antidepressants can't get her out of bed.

Still, she insisted I go to Spain.

"The trip is already paid for, and we may not be able to count on your father for that internship you want for next summer," she'd told me. "You'll need to fall back on your grades, and maybe your thesis, for that. And it might be good for you to get away for a while."

The whole thing sucks. But Saturday nights at Madrid's infamous discotecas make the heaviness I carry around inside me a little bit lighter.

Shrugging out of my coat before I check it with the girl at the counter, I spot the cute couple tucked in the corner of the bar right away. Sipping on their Cuba libres—rum and Cokes—they're leaning toward one another, the girl grinning as the guy murmurs Spanish nothings to her that are probably more saucy than sweet. The bar's red lights gild their profiles, catching on their eyelashes, making haloes of their hair.

It's such a pretty picture, my best friend and the guy we both fell for—the guy who's now her boyfriend—that I wish I brought my camera to capture it.

My heart clenches. Not because I'm jealous that Vivian got the guy, and nabbed such a hot foreign piece. It took a while for us to get here, for Vivian and me to forgive each other, and ourselves, for the awful, stupid things we did while embroiled in our little love triangle with handsome Spaniard Rafa Montoya. They suck with a capital S, those triangles, despite what the vampires and werewolves would have us believe. I haven't exactly been myself these days—not that that's any excuse—and watching Vivian's dreams come true while my parents crushed mine was not easy.

But now, more than a month after our friendship almost

imploded, I can honestly say I'm happy for Vivian. Genuinely, deliriously happy she found a guy as excellent and delicious as she is.

No, I'm not jealous.

My heart clenches because I miss, I *miss*, the kind of home Vivian and Rafa have obviously found in each other. Home doesn't exist for me. Not anymore. And after I found out my dad was sleeping with his secretary of eight years, I wonder if my happy, wholesome home ever did.

I've always thought your twenties were all about finding yourself.

But at almost twenty-one, I feel more lost than ever.

My one saving grace this semester is that I'm four thousand miles away from the broken place I came from. Madrid, thank Dios, is the perfect distraction, the perfect place to escape the ever-expanding universe of hurt inside me for a little while. It's all about long, lingering meals with my friends, the Madrileñas, that always include too much vino and talk of penises, an awesome library at San Pedro University that I'm using to put together some ideas for a thesis proposal, and a hedonistic club culture that encourages anonymous encounters with handsomely Eurotrash Spaniards.

Encounters I am *all* too happy to partake in. After crushing, disastrously, on Rafa, I realized a relationship wouldn't do this body good anyway. I don't need a boyfriend. I need a hookup—many hookups—where the only faith required is in a guy's ability to make me come.

And oh, are Madrileños good at that.

From her perch in the corner, Vivian glances over her shoulder and meets my eyes. She grins, the kind of grin that lights up her face, and that happy-squidgy-best-friend feeling fills me to the brim. It never gets old, does it, the happiness you feel seeing someone you know and love across the room?

"Hey lady!" she says, her grin widening to a smile as I wrap her in a quick hug. "Holy shit you're cold. We gotta warm you up with some liquor."

Rafa leans over the table, pressing the standard Spanish *kiss-kiss* into my cheeks. "Buenas noches, Maddie. How are you feeling?"

Viv and Rafa look at me, hopefully, as they wait for my answer.

Vivian has been *my* shoulder to cry on this semester. Aside from our little snafu with Rafa, she's played her BFF role with aplomb. Granted, I haven't told her everything. She knows my parents are splitting, and that it's pretty nasty. But she doesn't know about my dad cheating or blaming me for ruining the family every time we talk.

It hurts too much to talk about, especially the part about me catching my dad in the act, the part about him threatening me, telling me it would be *my* fault if our family fell apart. I haven't told her Mom takes a handful of pills every morning just to get through the day.

I don't want to think about the consequences of me telling my mom about Dad and his secretary, and I *definitely* don't want to talk about it. Even Vivian can't help me get over my secret fear that Dad treats me like shit because I *am* shit. I mean, maybe I don't deserve respect. Or love. What kind of daughter ruins her mother's life and destroys what was once a happy family?

No, I don't want to talk about these things, even with someone as cool and understanding as Viv.

I swallow, hard, and pull my lips into a smile. "I'm feeling good. A little tired, but better than last week. How about you guys? What's new and exciting?"

"I hope you don't mind," Rafa says. "But I invited my uncle Javier to join us. For one drink only, he says the weather is very good tomorrow so he wants to fly."

My eyes flick to the illuminated shelves of liquor on the far wall. "Fly? Is he, like, a pilot or something?"

Rafa nods. "He has his own plane too. Little plane, but it is still very fun. He is just back from a long trip for business, and he hasn't been able to fly for many months. I am excited for you chicas to meet him. He asked me and Vivian to fly with him, but we've got tickets to the fútbol match tomorrow." Rafa offers me that lady killer grin of his. "Maybe Maddie can go with Javier?"

"That wouldn't be awkward at all," I say, "being alone on a tiny little plane with your uncle who I've never met."

"You're going to like Javier. He is not like other uncles."

I shrug. Even if Javier has George Clooney's salt-and-pepper smexiness, mature guys aren't exactly my thing at the moment. I'm into dudes who are young, and eager to please. It's shallow and stupid, I know, but hey, they get the dirty job done. I've slept with quite a few wonderfully foreign dudes in the past month, and I have yet to be disappointed.

I order a gin and tonic from the bar. It's delicious, and it is fuerte—strong, the only way Madrileños like their liquor drinks—so strong I already feel the gin working its black magic on my sluggish brain.

My body and my mood begin to thaw.

I offer Viv a small grin. "I like this little Saturday night tradition. You guys take care of your third wheel, and I appreciate that."

She reaches across the table and flicks her thumb across my top lip, wiping away a stray chunk of lime. The gesture is so sweet, so familiar, I have to look away. "Wouldn't be Saturday night without you," she says. "We started that tradition freshman year, remember? Just because we're in Spain—"

"And just because you sleep over at your super-hot Spanish boyfriend's apartment," I say.

"Right. Just because things are a little different doesn't mean the tradition has to change."

Rafa sets his drink on the table and leans down on his elbows. "I guess I'm the third wheel, then, aren't I? I should be thanking *you*"—he looks at me—"for letting me crash *your* Saturday night with Vivian."

I'm about to make fun of Rafa for being such a relentlessly cute cheeseball when a gust of cold air hits me. Skin prickling with goose bumps, I glance toward the entrance hall.

A broad-shouldered guy strides into the club, hands tucked into the pockets of his bomber jacket. The collar is turned up against the cold and the leather is lovingly scarred, distressed in a way a machine couldn't replicate.

I can't see his face—he's looking away from us, searching the other side of the bar—but something about the way he's built, the dark scuff that covers the square lines of his jaw, catches my wandering eye.

He's built like a quarterback, deliciously thick about the shoulders and arms and chest. Not huge, just the *very* right side of athletic. But his chocolate brown hair—cropped close at the sides, a combed swoop of longer hair at the top—along with all that scruff scream hot hipster. His clothes are somewhere in between: dark fitted jeans, tidy suede boots, the hem of a button-down shirt peeking from underneath the bottom of his jacket. It's like he's part Madrileño, part rookie NFL player, part hipster country music star.

I'm intrigued.

Who are you, I wonder. *What is your story?*

And would you like to get naked with me tonight?

He turns his head and our gazes collide. I look, and he looks, and we both keep looking.

My stomach does a backflip. He is *so* handsome. Hot. He is handsome *and* hot—he walks that fine line with finesse.

12

His eyes, light brown, burn amber in the red light of the bar.

I know in the space of a single heartbeat that I am going to fuck this delectable Madrileño tonight. I am shameless in my pursuit. When I want a guy, I have him.

And I *want* this man. Badly. My blood warms as I imagine the way he'll move. The way he'll taste.

I imagine the blinding, forceful blankness of my orgasm.

Hell *yes*. He'd be my hottest conquest yet.

"Are you okay?" Viv asks me.

I don't need to answer her. She glances over her shoulder and she, too, is rendered speechless by this guy's hot-handsomeness.

My stomach flips again when señor NFL hipster hot body flashes a smile of recognition and starts walking toward us.

No way. He can't be.

No way this guy is—

"Tío!" Rafa stands and gathers his *uncle* in a hug.

I blink. *This* guy is Rafa's uncle? It doesn't make sense; they're practically the same age. From what I can tell, Javier is twenty-four, maybe twenty-five, tops.

Viv turns around and meets my eyes. She's thinking it too. *How is this Uncle Javier? And how is he so ridiculously good-looking?*

He's related to Rafa, that's how. The Montoyas must have a pretty sick gene pool to make such handsome babies.

Rafa introduces Javier to Vivian, who, like me, is still staring at him in mute adoration-slash-confusion. He smiles, a blinding, half goofy, half devastating thing that works two grooves into the stubble on either side of his mouth.

"Wow," she says at last, standing. "Just. Um, wow. I gotta be honest, Javier, you are not at all what I was expecting."

"Javier is more like a brother to me," Rafa explains. "It is a joke, yes, that I call him uncle, really, because we are almost the same age. My grandfather, he married again when he was very old to a younger woman. They had a small family. Javier is part of that family."

Viv's brows snap together. "How much younger are you than Rafa's—"

"Father?" Javier says. His voice is deep, a little gravelly. A lot sexy. "I am twenty-four now, so that is, what, Rafael, twenty-two years between me and my brother?"

"Wow," Viv says.

"*Wow*," I say, getting up.

Javier turns his gaze to me. A rush of tingly awareness moves from my head to my toes. It's powerful, his gaze, not because it makes me feel like he can see what I'm wearing underneath my clothes (a lacy bra and no underwear. I always come to Ático prepared).

It's powerful because there's something honest about it. A little playful.

Granted, I've only been ogling him for one and a half minutes, but he's got this easy, masculine confidence that makes me think Tío Javier isn't one to hide what he's feeling.

I like it, his straightforward masculinity, the virile energy simmering behind his brown eyes.

I like it a lot.

I step around the table to stand beside Viv, in front of Javier. "Javier, this is Maddie Lucas, my best friend," she says.

Before I can do the awkward American thing and offer him my hand, Uncle Javier leans forward and greets me in the Madrileño way, pressing quick kisses into either of my cheeks. The stubble of his beard brushes my skin, the scent of cinnamon mints trails in his wake as he pulls away.

I love a lot of things about studying abroad in Spain.

The double-kiss greeting, though, has to be the thing I love most.

"Maddie," he says, my name a pleasant rumble that rolls off his tongue. "Encantado."

It's the Spanish equivalent of "nice to meet you" but when Uncle Javier says it in his husky, come-hither voice, it sounds like an invitation to join the mile-high club in this plane he supposedly owns.

I am so, so game. I've never done it on a plane before. I bet it's fantastic.

I meet his gaze head-on with the sauciest smirk I can muster. "*Very* nice to meet you, Javier."

He nods at my empty glass. "Might I get you another drink, Maddie? What is that, a G and T?"

His English is better—much better—than Rafa's, and tinged with a British accent. Hearing a Spanish dude speak the Queen's English gives me a sense of cultural vertigo, but I mean that in the best way possible. Europe—the world, really —can be such a cool melting pot.

"Yes," I say. "It's a gin and tonic. Another would be great —thank you very much."

"Vale," Uncle Javier says. I love that word, so particular to Madrid, and one Madrileños use to glorious excess. It can mean everything from "okay" to "cool" to "fine by me."

Javier shrugs out of his jacket, revealing more of that physique that is *definitely* fine by me. I watch, pulse throbbing, as he rolls back his shoulders and shrugs out of his bomber jacket. He's wearing a white button-down that hugs the rounded slopes of his shoulders and arms. He cuffs his wrists in his hands, and slides the rolled sleeves up his arms, baring tan forearms ridged with sinew and vein.

I don't bother to hide my grin of appreciation.

He catches me checking him out. He holds my gaze for one beat, then another. I bite my lip. He looks away. He runs a hand down his face, trying—and failing—to hide a small, enticingly secret smile.

"C'mon, Rafa," Javier says, his eyes flicking to meet mine. "Let's grab those drinks—I do believe Maddie is quite thirsty."

Oh, yes.

A million times yes.

I am definitely going to fuck Javier tonight.

Chapter Two

MADDIE

I watch Javier's broad back disappear into the crowd. My body still rings with the memory of his lips on my skin. Just that brief touch—along with some serious eye fucking—and I am hornier than I've been in a long time.

"Do you know how often Javier's in town?" I ask, turning back to Viv.

"I don't. Not often, from what I hear."

I bite my lip. "Perfect."

She pins me with a look.

A look I've come to know and loathe.

"What?" I ask, jabbing my straw into the ice at the bottom of my glass.

"You're going to sleep with him, aren't you?"

"I hope so. He's ridiculously hot." I meet her eyes. "C'mon, Viv, I haven't fooled around with someone in more than a week! I'm practically dying over here."

She cocks an eyebrow. "Are you really?"

"I feel like you're judging me."

"I'm not," she says. "I'm all for having some fun and getting your rocks off. Now that I know how great sex is—"

"Thank God you finally swiped that V-card," I say with a grin. Maddie was a virgin until very, very recently. Until she met and fell in love with Rafa.

"Thank *God.*" She grins too. "My point is, I'm all for having wild sex with as many Eurotrash men as possible as long as it makes you happy. That's all I want for you, Mads—I wanna see you smile again. But I'm not entirely sold on the idea that sleeping with all these dudes is upping your happiness quotient."

The happy buzz in my blood dims. I look down at my empty glass and close my eyes. For a split second I see my dad's face, his gaze terrifyingly cold as he betrays me. Speaks to me like I'm a piece of garbage.

A prickly pressure builds inside my head, like someone is pressing his thumbs against the backs of my eyeballs.

My eyes fly open. I suck in a breath.

"You know I had sex—lots of sex—with guys back at Meryton before this whole divorce thing blew up in my face," I reply. "And I was happy. It made me happy, Viv."

"I know it did, and that's awesome," Vivian says. "It was fun for you. It made you feel good."

"It still makes me feel good."

Viv gives me that look again. "You can't tell me the divorce isn't screwing with your head. Are you sure your reasons for going after the sexy-times haven't changed? I don't know. Maybe you're having sex because it helps you forget. Or maybe you have these one-night stands and keep guys at arm's length so they won't hurt you the way your parents have?"

I roll my eyes, even as my chest contracts. "I really hate it when you go all Dr. Phil on me, Viv. And I kinda resent the implication that I'm this raging slut bag who only has sex because I'm, like, damaged inside or something. I like sex. I have a lot of it. That doesn't make me a basket case, and it certainly doesn't make me a skank."

"That's not what I'm saying," Viv replies. Her face is red with hurt. "I hate those words, by the way. I'm just looking out for you is all. Trying to be a good friend."

"I hate those words too." I sigh. "I know it hasn't been easy being my friend this semester. I'm sorry. I honestly haven't given much thought to my hookup situation. Maybe my reasons have changed—I don't know. I *do* know I can't forgive right now. Not my dad." *Not myself*, I want to add, but don't. "So yeah, it's possible I'm settling for the forgetting part. And the orgasms. I mean, they help too. An orgasm is never a bad thing."

"No, it's not." Viv offers me a smile of sympathy. "But promise me you'll rethink your strategy if it stops being fun."

I nudge her shoulder with my own. "I promise."

Javier

Waiting at the bar for our drinks, I glance over my shoulder at Maddie. Christ but the girl is gorgeous. Flaming blue eyes, full lips, legs that go on for days and days and days. An ass that makes my heart skip a beat every time I look at it.

I keep looking at it. The tiny dress she's wearing barely covers the tops of her thighs. Raise it an inch or two and I have no doubt I would very much like what I'd see.

She runs a hand through her long, dark hair, mussing the strands at the crown of her head. She arches her back as she does it, the hem of her dress creeping up, up, revealing more leg, more skin. I'm staring now. Everything about Maddie is sexy. Her body. The challenge in her eyes. Even the way she moves makes me think naked thoughts.

I blink. *Stop.* I have to stop looking. I didn't come all the way back to Madrid to hook up with another girl at another club. I know what I want now, and that isn't another meaningless encounter. After being on the road for so long, I've had enough of those to last a lifetime.

But one more look can't hurt. It's such a lovely backside. Just one more—

My heart skips a beat, but this time it has nothing to do with her ass.

It skips because she catches me looking.

And then she grins. A devilish, lively grin that makes her eyes glitter. Eyes that flick down the length of my body to rest on *my* ass. Her grin twitches, lips pursed in what appears to be appreciation.

It's an entirely shameless perusal, and I'd be lying if I said I didn't like it. It's an eye for an eye—in this case, it's an ass for an ass—although I do believe I got the better end of the bargain, as her behind is far, *far* superior to my own.

I wonder if she knows where I've been for the past year. *Who* I've been. If she was one of the hundreds of thousands of people who came out to see me playing with Juan Ramos at stadiums across the world.

I wonder if she knows I'm that guy. The so-called rock star.

I really hope she doesn't.

As much as I enjoyed being the star—let's not kid ourselves, I enjoyed it a *lot*—it got tiresome toward the end. Being surrounded by women who loved the celebrity but couldn't care less about the man left me feeling empty, and more than a little lonely. It got me into some trouble too.

I've missed the normalcy and the comfort of real life, of *home*. I've missed my family, being around people who love me for me.

But I've really missed one person in particular.

Rafa and I gather our drinks in our hands. Condensation runs down my forearms as we make our way back to the table.

"Thank you very much," Maddie says when I hand her a gin and tonic. She leans in. "I appreciate it. Almost as much as you appreciated my ass."

I run my tongue along my bottom lip, grinning. I shouldn't flirt back. I've been burned by this kind of thing before.

But I can't help it. She's too fun, and too sexy, to leave hanging.

"Might I ask what you thought of mine?" I ask.

"Delicious." She sips her drink. "Absolutely delicious."

Rafa clears his throat. He's looking at Maddie and me, a knowing gleam in his eye. Are we really that obvious?

"Vivian and I are going to dance," Rafa says, pointing his thumb in the direction of the dance floor. "Is it okay if we leave you two here together?"

"More than okay. You guys go have fun." Maddie hooks her arm through mine. She's standing close now, so close I can smell her coconut shampoo. My pulse spikes. She smells lovely, like a tropical drink you'd sip in the nude while lying on a beach in the Caribbean. "I'll take good care of Javier."

Viv gives Maddie a long, hard look.

"You sure?" Viv asks.

Maddie lets out a breath, an impatient sound. "I'm sure. See you guys later."

And just like that, Maddie and I are alone.

The music starts pumping, the floor bouncing in time to the bass. It's crowded now, and loud. I scoot a bit closer to Maddie, my leg brushing hers.

"So, you and Vivian—you're in the same program here in Madrid?" I ask.

"Yes—Meryton in Madrid, basically a semester in Spain

for juniors. I don't know if you've ever heard of Meryton University. It's a liberal arts college in North Carolina, on the East Coast."

I nod. "I know it. Famous for basketball, right?"

"Right," she replies. "Are you a basketball fan?"

"A little bit. I went to university in the U.K., so I'm a bit more into rugby, to be honest. And then of course football—soccer—I love that too."

"I went to my first match last week," she says proudly.

"And?" I arch a brow. "What did you think?"

"It was *so* much fun. And so freaking loud. My ears were ringing for three days afterward. A pretty epic hangover didn't help. Madrid won, and we had about thirty-seven cele-bratory drinks too many."

"You did it right then. I'm excited to finally be able to go to a match myself now that I'm home."

"That's right," she says. "Rafa was telling us you've been traveling for business. What do you do, if you don't mind me asking?"

My pulse leaps. I bite the inside of my lip to keep from smiling. So Maddie doesn't know who I am—who I *was* over the past year.

She's just a cute girl trying to get some action from a dude at a bar on a Saturday night.

The relief I feel, mingled with a hint of excitement, makes me almost giddy. She appreciates my ass not because it belongs to a (slightly) famous guitarist, but because it's appar-ently delicious. This is the first time I've talked to a girl who wasn't out to bang a rock star, any rock star, in forever.

Not that there will be any banging involved. Maddie is sexy as hell, yeah, but I'm not into that sort of thing anymore. I'm ready to settle down, make a home with a novia—girl-friend—here in Madrid. A girlfriend I did not meet, drunk, at a discoteca.

"I'm in the music industry," I say.

"That's cool," she says. She holds up her nearly empty glass and arches a brow. "Want another? This round's my treat."

I look down at my gin and tonic. I promised myself I'd only have one—I'm hoping to fly tomorrow—but suddenly I feel as thirsty as Maddie looks.

"I'll have another," I say, "but only if I'm buying. You're in my city, guapa. My treat."

"Guapa." She looks at me. "Pretty?"

"It means beautiful girl."

She smirks. "That's laying it on a little thick, don't you think?"

"What would you prefer I call you?"

She's standing in front of me now, her bottom lip stuck distractingly between her teeth. I step toward her. She mirrors my move, angling her neck to look up at me. That *neck*. I resist the urge lean in, put my mouth on the place where the soft shell of her ear curves into the sinews of her throat.

I wince at the tight warmth that pulses between my legs. *Stop*. Seriously stop.

"You okay?" Maddie asks, furrowing her brow.

"Yes. Yeah." I put my hand on the small of her back, nudging her toward the bar. "Let's go get those drinks."

"Oh? And Javier?" she says over her shoulder, eyes flashing. "You can call me whatever you like."

I grin down at her. "Now isn't *that* laying it on a little thick?"

She shrugs. She's biting her lip again.

Stop.

It would be easier to stop if Maddie wasn't so damn sexy.

A few hours and many more drinks later, Maddie and I collapse in a sweaty heap on a white pleather sofa by the bar.

"For someone old enough to be an uncle," she pants, "you're one hell of a dirty dancer, Javier."

"Thank you," I reply, smiling. "You're not so bad yourself."

"Oh, God, you and I both know I'm a horrible dancer. Like, horrible. But it's sweet of you to pretend I'm not."

My smile widens. Maddie can be charming when she isn't trying so hard to be sexy.

"You're not *that* bad," I say.

She pins me with a look. "I am too *that* bad. I'm even worse. Vivian says I dance like a mom who gets drunk at her niece's wedding and thinks she got her groove back."

"Wow," I say. "That's very . . . specific."

"And very true."

"No-o it's not?" I try.

Vivian looks at me again. We both burst into laughter.

"You're cute," she says.

"You're funny," I say.

She sidles up next to me on the sofa to make room for another couple. Before I can think better of it, I move my arm to rest on the back of the sofa behind her, inviting Maddie to curl even closer against me. She does.

I shift my hips, crossing one leg over the other. I've had a raging hard-on from the moment we stepped onto the dance floor, and the way she smells isn't helping. Drunk-mom dancing or not, I saw stars when Maddie pressed her ass into my groin and shimmied her hips.

An ass that felt even better than it looked.

All night I've tried to be a gentleman. Tried to stop myself when I wanted to put my hands on her, when I wanted to slide my fingers between her legs to see if she is as hot and bothered as I am. I'm not that guy anymore. I'm so done with that shit. I don't want to wake up tomorrow with a raging hangover and a stranger in my bed. A stranger I don't care to know, one who doesn't care to know me.

I want *her*. The woman I've been dreaming about for months now. The woman I came back to Madrid for. Even if that woman isn't exactly available at the moment.

But when Maddie looks at me the way she's looking at me now—blue eyes sultry with interest, with arousal and intelligence—I am filled with a decidedly ungentlemanly urge to grab her hand and take her home and finally tear off that dress.

I look down at her crossed legs. The muscles in her thighs stand in relief against her smooth skin. I wonder if she's an athlete, a runner. I wonder what it would feel like to be cradled between those lithe legs. She'd be all sinews and softness, her skin hot to the touch—

I almost jump when Maddie's hand lands on *my* leg. My cock pulses, hard, when she gives my knee a small squeeze. She leans in, presses her body against mine. Her breast nudges my arm, and her hair falls across my shoulder. Our faces are inches apart. I need only duck my head to take her mouth in mine, to start the thing we both really, really want to do.

I look up to meet her eyes. She's looking at me like *that*. Like she knows exactly what I'm thinking, and she's thinking it too.

Let's get the hell out of here.

She doesn't say a word, just waits for me to respond to her unspoken proposition, her slate blue eyes intent, intense.

I clear my throat. Why does she have to be so fucking sexy? It'd be so much easier to stick to my guns if I wasn't wildly attracted to her. She just . . . she smells so good and looks so good, and the way she moves makes my dick pulse in agony.

God *damn* it. I shift my legs again.

"Listen, Maddie. You're a gorgeous girl. And I'm having a really wonderful time with you." I wince at the sound of my own bullshit. Best to go with the truth, I suppose. "But, um. I'm not really looking for something quite so . . . um. You know. Sudden. Fleeting."

"Ah." She smiles. "You're a relationship guy."

I nod. "Trying to be, now that I'm back home. And I'm buzzed enough to tell you that I'm looking for el amor. Love."

"Do you have a girl in mind?"

"I do." I glance down at her hand. It's still on my knee. "Unfortunately she has a boyfriend at the moment."

That girl is María Carmen Burgos. We fell for each other, hard, when we were just eighteen. Funny, but that seems so young now. After breaking up a few years ago, we've recently gotten back in touch. I'd love nothing more than to fall for her again—she's just the kind of forever girl I'm looking for. Smart, established here in Madrid, ready to settle down.

I don't have feelings for her. Not yet. And she is in a relationship with some guy who works in finance. But I'm secretly hoping the spark between us is still there after all these years. I guess we'll see.

Maddie slides that hand up my leg, a slow, lazy movement that drives me insane. Her touch is patient, intentional, confident. It drives me wild, knowing she's into me for *me*. It's all I can do not to leap off the couch and make like hell for my flat with Maddie slung over my shoulder, horny ninja-style.

"This works out perfectly, then," she murmurs in my ear. "One last lay before you go off and steal your lady love from the other guy."

I blink. "A lay?"

"Listen, hombre, not all of us are in the market for a happily ever after."

Her hand is at the top of my thigh, each fingertip sending spikes of fire through my entire body. Her bottom lip grazes my earlobe. The fleshy curve of her hip presses against my leg.

"I shouldn't," I manage. "This isn't what I'm looking for right now."

She pulls back. "So you don't want to leave with me then."

I look at her. A beat passes. Then another. Inside my skin my blood, hot, traitorous, riots; inside my jeans my dick is dying to be let out to play.

I settle my eyes on her mouth. Her lips are parted, the remnants of lip gloss making them appear slickly pink. Swollen.

I bet she's just as swollen and slick between her legs.

"I didn't say that," I reply.

And then I look in her in the eye and reach down and slide my hand between her thighs. Her eyes darken when I discover she's not wearing panties.

Jesus Christ, this girl is trying to kill me.

I press the pad of my middle finger between the lips of her cunt and they part. They let me in.

She is. Oh, she *is*. Slick and hot and tight and so wet my hand is already sticky with it. With her arousal.

I find the swollen nub of her clit and give it a stroke. Maddie inhales and bites her lip, eyes fluttering shut.

I swallow, hard.

"Let's go," I growl. "Now."

Chapter Three

JAVIER

One side of Maddie's mouth kicks up as I take her hand and pull her to her feet. A saucy, knowing smirk, confident and full of promise. I want to kiss that smirk off her face, ravage her mouth with mine.

I want her. *Now*.

I hold her close behind me as I stalk toward Ático's back entrance. I know a few of the bouncers here, and they let me in on this well-kept secret—on nights like this, when a swift exit is necessary, the back door is a godsend.

Just outside the bar, we pass the table where Maddie and I met. I narrow my eyes at a rumpled leather jacket that's shoved onto a nearby ledge. I never forget my bomber—I've had that thing since I was eighteen, for God's sake, a gradua-tion present from my parents—but I guess I was distracted by Maddie's eyes, or maybe it was her legs, or her ass, or her fearless interest in *my* ass.

This girl is fearless. And I fucking love her for it.

I grab the jacket, but I don't put it on.

I tug Maddie closer to me, the front of her body plastered against the back of mine. I feel the rounded softness of her breasts pressing into my shoulder blades, her long, lean thighs plastered against my backside.

Desire, dark and impatient, coils at the base of my skull, between my legs. I walk faster, holding Maddie's hand firmly in my own. She doesn't ask me to slow down, she doesn't stumble. She keeps pace with me, her breaths coming fast and hot against the nape of my neck.

I grit my teeth, praying there's no traffic on the way to my flat. I'm going to explode if I don't get Maddie in my bed, naked, in the next five minutes.

I can't wait to see her—all of her—naked. I imagine the way her tan legs would slope into hips and soft belly. The fullness of her breasts, the hardened points of her nipples.

And that pussy. I can't wait to see it, feel it, taste it.

You'd think I hadn't been laid in a decade for how badly I want it.

I burst through the door. I feel like I'm about to burst out of my jeans too.

It's freezing outside, but I hardly notice. The alley is dark and quiet, and my ears still ring from hours spent dancing too close to the DJ booth. In the sliver of sky visible between two buildings, stars pulse silver against a black velvet sky. I inhale the faint smell of churros, fresh from the fryer. A nearby streetlamp provides the only light—dim, soft.

Madrid after midnight. I've really missed this place.

I'm about to make for the street—*please, please let there be a taxi*—when Maddie gives my hand a solid tug, pulling me around to face her.

Her eyes gleam in the darkness, a dirty little smile playing at the corners of her mouth. She takes a step back, pulling me after her, then she takes another, and another, slowly, her hips swaying, heels sounding a decisive beat against the pavement.

We're three steps from a brick wall when it dawns on me.

She wants to fuck here. Now.

She wants to fuck against this wall.

My pulse leaps.

"Maddie," I say, squeezing her hand. "I have a bed. A really nice bed. A *warm* bed."

She takes another step back, our hands still intertwined between us.

"What if I'm bored with bed?" she asks. "I've been in lots of beds."

I pull her to me, curling my body around hers as I attempt to move her away from the wall. My mouth hovers over her mouth. As I talk my lips brush against hers.

"But you haven't been in my bed." I glide my tongue along her bottom lip. She tastes like lime, lime and sugar and heat. "I'll do things to you those others guys haven't done, I promise you."

"You know what those guys haven't done?" She stands on her tiptoes, pressing her lips to my ear. She curls a hand around my neck and glides her fingers through my hair. "Me, against this wall."

I don't need to ask her if she's sure, if this is what she really wants. She knows what she wants and isn't afraid to go after it. And now it's what I want too, more than I've wanted anything in a long time.

Using the bulk of my body, I turn her so that her back is once again to the wall. She lets out a small hum of approval as her mouth moves from my ear to my jaw, nicking the stubble there with her teeth. We begin to move backward, small, slow steps.

I clutch my jacket in both hands and pull it over her shoulders, tugging the leather into place. She's a tall girl—definitely not petite—but still my jacket swallows her from her shoulders to the tops of her legs.

Good.

"Wait," she says. "Wait. Why are you putting clothes on me? Aren't you supposed to be taking them off?"

"Because." I take her chin in my hand and thumb her lip. "I don't want you to get hurt. The bricks will tear the skin off your back if . . . if it gets a little rough."

Maddie bites down on the pad of my thumb. "Is it going to get rough?"

I grin. "Only if you want it to."

"Show me what you got, hombre."

I don't hesitate.

I lean forward, pressing my hips to hers, pushing her backward with one large, forceful step. She draws a sharp breath when her back meets with the wall, eyes flashing with wicked, searing heat. She rolls her hips against mine, her hands trailing ribbons of tingly heat as they move up my torso.

"Show me," she breathes. "Show me everything."

I pull my thumb across her lips, a possessive, almost lewd caress, erasing the last traces of her lip gloss. The soft slickness of her mouth against the calloused pad of my thumb is incredibly, frustratingly erotic. She's so hot, so soft. So feminine.

I slide my hand onto her face, burying the tips of my fingers in her hair, and pull her to me. Her skin is silken, and so are her lips.

There is no preamble, no tentative exploration. I duck my head and kiss her hard. I kiss her hungrily. I kiss her deeply, and she kisses me back like she means it. Like she wants more, more, always more. Our bodies move against one another, into one another. She is so goddamn sexy.

I glide my other hand up the length of her leg. Goose bumps break out on her skin, and I curse—it comes out in Spanish—against the insistent press of Maddie's lips, her tongue.

"What?" she pants.

"You're cold."

She curls her fingers into the front waistband of my jeans, her first finger toying with the button.

"Then warm me up."

"I'm trying. You sure you don't want to go back to my place? It'd be a hell of a lot more comfortable." I curse again when, through the thick denim, her curious finger finds the hypersensitive tip of my dick. "Maddie. Maddie, I also don't have a condom with me."

She reaches down into her bag—it's a tiny thing, the strap slung across her chest—and holds up a foil packet between her first two fingers.

Carefully, her eyes never leaving mine, she tears open the condom with her teeth.

I bite the inside of my bottom lip, tucking her thick hair behind her ears as I stare down at her like a man possessed. I watch as her tongue works at the crinkled seam of the foil packet.

She's done this before—the tease. The instigation. And she is painfully good at it.

I am *this close* to losing my shit.

I grab the packet from her mouth.

"You're fucking ridiculous, you know that?" I say hoarsely, reaching for the fly of my jeans.

Maddie beats me to it. Digging her teeth into her bottom lip, she pops open the button and slowly—*fuck, fuck me*—slowly tugs down the zipper.

A flick of her wrist and she's reaching inside my boxers. The head of my dick meets with her palm, and then she wraps her fingers around me, tight, so tightly, and gives me a slow, hard tug.

For a minute I think I've gone blind.

"So are you," she murmurs. "More than a handful, Javier. I'm impressed."

Grunting, I pull the condom out of its foil packet. I wrap my hand around Maddie's, and guiding our fingers down, down, I roll the condom onto my dick with brisk, almost violent strokes.

And then I'm pressing her against the wall and grabbing the back of her thigh and hitching her leg around my hip. I settle myself between her parted thighs and all the while she's panting, hot, hurried intakes of breath, her chest rising and falling against my own, my dick throbbing between us as she fists the front of my shirt in her hands. I revel in the feel of her body, all lush curves, all coconut-scented softness, pressed against mine. I crush my mouth against hers, opening her lips with my tongue as I reach down and shove up her teeny tiny dress and open her pussy with my fingers.

I don't know how, but she's wetter than she was before. Hotter. My fingers sink easily into her folds. She is so small and so sweet and so perfect I want to scream.

"You have never," I pant, stroking her clit, "been fucked as well or as hard as I'm about to fuck you, guapa."

"Now who's being ridiculous?" she murmurs, smiling against my lips as she rolls her hips, begging, pleading for more.

"I'll show you," I reply. "You asked me to show you, and I will, guapa, I'll show you things you never knew you wanted."

Holding her leg in one hand, I take my dick in the other. I don't know if I've ever been so swollen, so huge with anticipation. I hope, I *hope*, I can hang on for another minute or two. I am determined to be a gentleman in this, if nothing else.

I guide myself into her folds. She moans when I press the tip of my dick against her clitoris. She cries out when I press harder, circling it against her. Her arms fall from my neck, and the next thing I know she's reaching inside the front of her dress, sliding her fingers inside her bra, touching herself.

I close my eyes, swallow. She's close, I can tell from the way her body winds tighter and tighter against me, from the way her hips buck against me. It's an agony, not being inside her, but I hold on for dear life and keep pressing against her clit, harder and faster.

Maddie lets out a cry that I muffle with my mouth—"Oh, oh, God, Javier"—and then she's coming. Without a second thought I slide my dick down her pulsing flesh and enter her and buck my hips and in a single, hard thrust, I'm inside her. She's still coming, crying out against my mouth, her pussy clenching around me as I begin to pound into her, again and again, swiveling my hips at the beginning of each thrust, swiveling them again when I'm inside her.

I press my body against hers, harder, closer.

"Hold on to me," I say. "Let me hold you."

"No," she pants. "No. Just keep going, Javier, please."

I press against her again. "Fucking hold on to me," I growl, spearing her with one hard, vicious thrust.

With a trembling moan, Maddie snakes her arms around my neck, and I move into her, and she moves into me, our movements ardent and manic and so in synch I have to hold back to keep from coming. It's hell, not surrendering to the release. I feel sweat break out along my scalp. My legs feel like they're about to give out.

I reach for her other leg with my free hand. With a grunt I wrap it around my waist, my hands moving to cup her ass.

"Javier, Javier—no, I'm going to fall—"

"I've got you," I reply. "Trust me, Maddie, you're not going anywhere."

After a beat of hesitation, she relaxes into my grip. She surrounds me, her body warm and eager, her mouth greedy, sweet. She's good at this.

Almost as good as I am.

That's it, I whisper in her ear in Spanish. *That's it, guapa, come again, come with me.*

With each thrust, the monumental weight of my impending orgasm gets that much heavier, that much closer. I close my eyes and lose myself in Maddie's taste. Her tongue glides inside my mouth, and the small sounds she makes drive me insane in the best way. They're little pants, little moans, so her, so honest and unguarded. I could come on those sounds alone.

My hips work double time, but Maddie keeps pace with me. I can feel the frantic beating of her heart against my own. She's tightening around me again, and all I need to do is move my hand and stroke her swollen clit with my thumb once, twice, and she comes, Dios mío, and I come.

Holy shit do I come.

Great, gasping pulses that leave me boneless. I squeeze Maddie's ass and she cries out, louder this time, pulling the hair at the nape of my neck. The smell of sex hangs heavy between us as the warm stickiness of my cum fills the condom.

The pulses fade, slowly, and the world materializes around us. I pull back, my pulse hammering. Maddie is looking at me. I grin. She looks dazed. Stunned.

Satisfied.

I wince when I slide out of her. Fucking Maddie was supposed to douse my thirst for her.

Turns out it only made me thirstier. So much thirstier. I'm wide awake and I want more. I want whatever this girl is willing to give me tonight.

I set her on her feet. She weaves and I catch her, holding her by the hips until she's steady enough to stand on her own.

Maddie wipes back the hair that sticks to her forehead. "Wow. You weren't kidding, Javier. That was . . . perfect."

I pull her dress down, tucking my jacket around her. "Guys don't usually make you come twice in two minutes?"

"No." She's biting her lip again, grinning up at me. "That was a first. Thank you, hombre."

"Don't you have another name for me? 'Man' seems kind of generic."

"I don't," she replies, adjusting her bra. My eyes flick to her breasts. I resist the urge to fondle them. "Do you have any suggestions?"

"Tío bueno."

"Good uncle?" She scrunches her nose. "That's kind of lame, even though you *are* an uncle."

"No no no. In España, it means something more . . . explicit. Like, *hello sexy*. Except filthier than that."

"It's filthy?" Maddie nods her approval. "All right. I approve, tío bueno."

We look up at the sound of voices coming from the street ahead. People are starting to leave the discotecas, stumbling across the sidewalk in search of churros and street food. It must be two, three in the morning.

So much for flying tomorrow. Not that I regret my night with Maddie. I definitely don't regret the screwing-against-the-wall bit.

As a matter of fact, I'd really like to screw her again.

"Well." Maddie ducks out of my grasp. She starts to take off my jacket, revealing a milky white shoulder. My dick jumps. "It's been fun, Javier, but I gotta get going—"

I grab her hand.

The dark look she gives me—I can't tell what she's feeling. Impatience? Fear? Arousal?

I hope it's arousal, because I'm already hard again. This is crazy—this girl is making me forget myself, forget everything except her taste and her touch—but I don't care.

I've never had grittier, more fun sex, and I want more of it.

"Wait." I lower my head and press my lips to her ear, the stubble along my jaw scraping her cheek. "I'm not done fucking you yet, guapa."

Chapter Four

MADDIE

The Next Morning

Heat spikes through me. Hungry, throbbing heat, growing hotter and hotter between my legs. The tightness—the need —it's unbearable. I try to move away from it, but it keeps coming at me, relentless. I hear a gasp, a plea. A not entirely unpleasant moan.

Only when my eyes fly open, the room around me hazy with grey morning light, do I realize that *I'm* the one making these mewling baby cow sounds. I should stop—I need to be quiet, what if Viv hears me, or our señora—

I gasp again when the heat, velvety and wet, presses against my pussy.

I look down to see a very handsome—and very scruffy— head ducking between my thighs.

Ohmigod.

Javier.

I am in Javier's "flat" as he so charmingly called it last night in his adorable British-Spanish accent.

I am in his flat, and he is *eating* me *out*.

Ohmigod—

I grab the sheets when his tongue finds my clit. I'm wet. How am I already wet? I'm also completely naked.

Last night comes back in a rush. The epic against-the-wall fuck. The back to back orgasms. The very—er—*athletic* sex we had when we got to his apartment. I feel the way I did after I ran (limped, honestly) a 10k race: sore legs, sore in small, strange places I didn't know even existed.

I also remember him asking me as we fell asleep if it's okay to wake me with an orgasm. I remember smiling and saying hell *yes*.

His tongue circles me. Laps at me. My body sinks into the downy softness of his bed. My tiny little trundle at my señora's house is hard as a rock and hugely uncomfortable in comparison.

This—this is heavenly.

His teeth nick me and I gasp, louder this time. He looks up, his light brown eyes warm like honey, and grins, a lazy, self-satisfied thing.

"Buenos días, guapa," he says. *Good morning, beautiful.*

My pussy clenches as a shiver arrows up my spine. I love it when Madrileños speak Spanish with me. There's something so . . . sexy about it. So thrillingly foreign.

"Hola tío bueno," I reply.

His grin widens. "You remembered."

"Of course I did. The tío bit is way too awesome of a coincidence to forget."

He kisses my clit, pressing his palms to the inside of my thighs to spread my legs wider. "And how are you feeling this morning?"

"Good," I manage, my eyes fluttering shut when he puts his mouth on me again. "Really good."

"This still okay?"

I bite my lip and nod my head. "Yes. More than okay. This is . . . oh, this is everything, Javier."

He laughs, a deep, masculine rumble, and I find myself smiling even as the pressing tightness in my body becomes acute. He reaches up, cupping my breast. His thumb finds my nipple and I arch into his touch, digging my fingers into his hipster swoop of hair.

"What," I pant, "is up with this haircut?"

"You don't like it?"

"I like it"—another gasp—"a lot. It's just different."

"I"—lick—"told"—nip—"you"—slow, lingering lick, holy mother—"I was different from the other guys you've been with."

My hips begin to roll against his mouth. He's—good Lord, he's *really* good at this oral sex thing.

"And I told you," I say, giving his hair a tug. "Show me. Show me how you're different, Javier."

He grins, revealing the deep groves of his dimples inside his heavy scruff. I want to reach out, press my thumb into each dimple. Along with those molten eyes of his, they're nothing short of killer. He is killer. He is so, *so* hot I can hardly breathe looking at him.

Working my nipple with the fingers of one hand, he moves the other to my pussy, opening me to him. He sucks my clit, hard, and I cry out when he slips a finger inside me, pulling it in and out, in and out, slowly, so slowly.

"Did they do this?" he murmurs.

I almost combust when the low growl of his voice vibrates through my folds.

"No. No, they—oh—they didn't."

"What about this?" His tongue and finger switch places. Now he's thrusting inside me with his tongue, warm and pliant, while his finger traces slippery circles around my clit.

"No," I breathe. "Not that. Javier, I'm going to come—"

"Not yet. You'll come harder if I'm fucking you."

I'm practically writhing with need, hanging on by a

thread. The beat between my legs is so strong, so forceful, it hurts. "I don't—I don't know if I can wait."

"Wait."

His hand leaves my breast. A beat later I hear a familiar tear. Another beat and Javier's mouth is on mine, plying my lips with the taste of my own arousal. It's lewd. It's dirty.

It. Is. *Awesome.*

He sucks on my bottom lip as the weight of his body shifts over mine, settling between my legs. I love that delicious weight, love the feel of him pressing me into the mattress, surrounding me, holding me captive. I can't move; I can hardly breathe.

The tip of his dick finds my entrance. I open my eyes and look down and watch him cant his hips, a solid, swift movement, and then he surges inside me, huge and hot and impossibly perfect.

He trails his mouth down my neck. I wait for the manic thrusting to begin, but he keeps a slow, steady pace, each stroke deep, devastating in its thoroughness, its gentleness. I'm glad we're taking our time since my junk is as sore as my legs, and going hard wouldn't exactly be pleasant right now.

He takes my arms from around his neck and coaxes them above my head. His hand finds my wrists, moving up, up, and he begins to tangle his fingers with mine, meeting my eyes.

"No hand holding, tío," I manage, tearing my mouth from his.

A lock of dark hair falls across his forehead as he moves over me. His eyes are still on mine, steady with slow-burning heat. I fight the urge to close my own eyes, to look away, and for a minute allow myself to fall into that heat. It surrounds me, fills me, makes me feel like I'm soaring. The beat between my legs grows louder. Sweeter.

"We held hands last night at Ático," he says. He's a little breathless. "How is this any different?"

"It's very diff—"

Javier swivels his hips, eyes flashing darkly, and hits me *right there*.

The orgasm crashes into me so hard I forget how to speak, I forget where I am, I forget everything except the painfully sweet convulsion of my pussy. Tears prick my eyes—this hurts, this *hurts*, this feels so fucking good—and Javier swallows my whimper in his mouth.

This must be my fourth—fifth?—orgasm with Javier, and it's the best one yet.

How the *hell* does this man do it?

As my orgasm fades, his comes. He releases my hands and I run them over the muscles in his shoulders and back. Muscles that tighten and bunch as he gets closer. This body of his—holy hell. It is big-screen-sex-scene worthy. Thick in all the right places. Ripped and built just where he should be. And warm. His skin is very warm, and covered in a fine sheen of sweat.

I smile when he grunts into my mouth, slowing to a stop. He tilts his head and, seeing my smile, gives me one of his own.

"Was I right?" he asks. He ducks down and takes my nipple in his teeth.

The breath stalls in my throat. "Right? Right about what?"

"Your orgasm was better while I was inside you, wasn't it?"

"Oh. Oh, hell yes. Although all the orgasms you've given me were pretty . . ." I give him the *okay* sign.

Gently he guides himself out of me. "I could feel it. You came *hard*."

"Now you're just bragging."

"I am. I work hard to make that pussy happy." He pecks my lips. "And now I'm starving. Any chance I could convince you to stay for breakfast? I make a pretty solid tortilla, and even better coffee."

I turn my head on the pillow and look away, focusing my gaze on the enormous windows at the other side of the room. I'm hungry too—sex with Javier is a workout—and a tortilla, Spain's version of an omelet with potatoes and veggies, sounds seriously yum. So does a giant cup of café.

But when I look at Javier from the corner of my eye, meeting his kind, sated gaze, panic flutters inside my chest. I don't like this intimacy. I don't want this. I don't like the way it makes me feel.

Suddenly I can't breathe, and it has nothing to do with orgasms or the delectable bulk of Javier's body.

I gotta get out of here.

"I don't do breakfast," I say, untangling my legs from the sheets.

"You should," he says. "It's the most important meal of the day, right? Might soak up a bit of that gin we drank too."

"Ugh. Just hearing you say that word makes my stomach hurt. I'm good, thanks."

He props himself up on his elbow and grins down at me. "What about a shower, then? I've got a lovely shower. Big enough for two."

My eyes trail over the bulge of his bicep, the long, lean muscles in his chest and stomach. I'm tempted. Oh, am I tempted. It could be a repeat of last night. Only this time we'd be doing it up against the wall of his shower, hot water and steam and soap everywh—

We both jump at the sound of my phone. My ringtone blares, filling the quiet, intimate space between us with a garbled country song.

A familiar knot of dread tightens in my belly. That is Dad's ringtone I set after a concert we went to together last year. It's early here, a little before noon if I had to guess, which means it's *really* early—like five A.M. early—back in Atlanta.

Dad's called me at this time before. He was a fucking disaster then, and I have no doubt he's just as messed up this time around.

Shit.

"Sorry," I say, attempting to reach over Javier. "I gotta get that."

Javier extends one of his well-muscled arms and grabs the squalling phone from the nightstand, knocking a handful of opened foil packets to the floor.

He hands me the phone and presses a kiss into the hollow just beneath my ear. "You stay. I'll go start the shower."

For a minute I stare at the screen of my phone. My heart hammers in my ears; a lump forms in my throat. *Don't cry, don't cry, don't cry.*

Javier climbs out of bed. I slide my thumb across the bottom of the screen, willing my voice to remain steady. It doesn't.

"Hey, Dad," I say. I'm aware, vaguely, of the spurt of water as Javier turns on the shower.

"Where the hell have you been?" Somehow Dad manages to spit and slur his words all at once. He sounds violently accusatory.

The lump in my throat swells.

"Dad, I've been sleeping."

"I called your phone ten times, Maddie. I'm paying for the goddamned thing. When I call you, I want you to answer. Immediately."

I sit up, pulling the phone away from my ear.

No missed calls. Anger rises in my chest. Anger and a potent, sharp sadness.

"You're drunk," I say.

About a month ago, my dad went crawling back to my

mother, apologizing, telling her that he was an alcoholic and needed help. I knew he was a drinker—he was religious about having his two or three bourbon cocktails after work every night—but being away at college for the past few years, I had no idea how out of hand his habit had gotten. He went to his first AA meeting a few weeks back. According to Mom, he's been doing very well.

Until now, I guess.

I remember, with sudden, heartbreaking clarity, the cocktails I saw on the kitchen counter that day I walked in on my dad with that woman. One was half-full, the other empty, finished.

Dad's had to be the empty one.

"I called your señora," he says. "She told me you were out with a friend."

"Yeah," I say. "I was with Vivian."

"You're not with some piece of trash Spaniard, are you?"

My anger flares to new heights. "You know what, Dad, that's none—"

"Hey, Maddie!" Javier calls from the shower, his deep, rumbling voice filling the room. "I hung a clean towel for you on the door. Hurry up!"

My insides turn to ice. Dad would have to be deaf not to hear Javier. Oh God. Oh God, oh God, oh God.

"Ah," Dad says, smacking his lips. "So I got it wrong. *You're* the trash. You're trash, and you're a slut. I knew sending you to Spain was a bad idea."

I blink back the tears. They're angry tears, hot and thick, choking me.

Slut. To say I hate that word is an understatement. I know Dad is blitzed out of his mind, but in my book, it is never, *ever* okay to call someone a slut. Especially when that someone is your daughter. My sex life is and always has been none of his business.

And really, who the hell is he to call me out for sleeping around? He's a hypocritical son of a bitch, and I don't know if I've ever been angrier with someone, more upset, in my life.

I swallow, hard, and lower my voice so Javier won't hear me.

"That's rich, coming from you," I bite out. "Screw you, Dad. Seriously screw you. You can't say shit like that to anyone, least of all me. Don't call me again when you're like this, or so help me I'll record everything and give it to Mom's lawyers." I swallow, hard. "What is *wrong* with you?"

And what is wrong with me *that'd make you treat me like this?*

"If you hadn't gone and ratted me out to your mother," he says, "this divorce would've never happened, Madeline. Our family would still be a family."

I wish I could keep it together, but I'm really crying now, my voice wobbly, unsteady.

"I hate you, you know that?" I say. "I really fucking hate you right now."

Javier

I clamp the doorknob in my hand, brow furrowed as I listen to Maddie cry through the crack in the door.

The water in my massive—and massively sexy, it must be said—shower has finally gotten hot, and, wild from imagining her body swollen and slick under the showerhead, I'd been about to scoop Maddie out of bed when I heard her voice. A voice that wobbled and broke.

A voice that couldn't be more different from the sexy purr I'd had the pleasure to witness a few minutes ago.

It's a struggle for her to get the words out. "It's unfair— it's so unfair of you to take it out on me," she says.

46

My grip on the knob tightens. The bathroom has begun to cloud with steam. The half chub I've been sporting in anticipation of my aquatic adventure with Maddie disappears.

I hate to assume—obviously there's quite a bit going on here—but Maddie's father sounds like a dick. What in the world is he saying to her to make her upset like this? What happened between them?

I don't understand. This Maddie, this broken girl pleading with her father on the phone, can't possibly be the same girl who so suavely picked me up last night and blew my mind with some of the best, most carelessly fun sex I've had in a while.

This girl cares. She cares enough to fight back instead of just hanging up. She cares deeply enough to be hurt by whatever is going on with her father.

Maybe she cares too much.

This girl is vulnerable in a way the Maddie I spent last night with wasn't.

There's a pause in her end of the conversation. I lean forward, straining to hear. She sniffs, sighs.

"Stop," she says at last. "Go to bed, Dad. And please, *please* don't call me again when you're like this. I don't have the time—I just. I gotta go."

I hear the *click* of her phone as she blanks her screen, hanging up. I haven't a clue about the situation, I know, but still, I have to squash the desire to go to her and grab her phone and call her father myself so I can give him a piece of my mind. Nothing she could've done merited the way he's made her feel.

Nothing.

Peeking through the crack, I see Maddie wipe her face with the pads of her fingers and reach for her clothes, which are in a pile on a nearby chair.

Behind me, the shower is still on.

Damn it.

Quickly wrapping a towel around my waist, I duck into the bedroom.

"Hey," I say, softly. "Everything all right?"

Maddie looks up, startled, her eyes full of hurt. My heart turns over in my chest.

"Maddie—"

She turns away from me, guiding her dress over her head.

"What did you hear?" she asks. Her voice is flat, dead almost.

"A few things." I venture a step closer. "Are you okay?"

She grabs her phone and stuffs it in her purse, jamming her feet into her high-heeled shoes.

"I'm fine," she says, moving toward the door. She doesn't look at me. "Thanks for last night, Javier. I had fun. See you later."

For a second I just stand there, dumbfounded, as Maddie exits my room and clomps down the stairs. The 180 she just pulled is making my head spin—she went from hot and soft to cold as ice in the space of five minutes.

I don't know what to do.

"That's all you have to say after—after last night? After what I just heard?" I follow her, blinking at the onslaught of late morning light as I descend the staircase and hurry into my kitchen. "Maddie, you're not all right."

She doesn't respond, she just keeps moving through the kitchen into the tiny foyer.

"Maddie," I say as I catch up to her, grabbing her arm. "Wait, please. At least let me give you a jacket—"

"You and your damn jackets," she mutters and twists out of my grasp. "Really, I'll be okay."

"No, you won't." I tug open the coat closet beside the front door. "It's twenty degrees outside and your dress is . . . hardly a dress. Here, take this—"

But she's already out the door, disappearing into a stairwell before I can so much as blink.

"Maddie!" I call after her, but I know she's already gone.

What the *fuck*?

Chasing her would be a waste of time—it'd just make her angrier, more upset, and that's the last thing I want to do—but still, it's hard to close the door on her.

Tugging a hand through my hair—yikes, I've got some serious bed head going on—I close the door, slide the lock into the bolt, and hang my bomber back in the closet.

My hangover hits me all at once. My head throbs and my dick hurts. Maddie and I fucked too much, if that's even possible, and now I'm tired and hungry and confused as hell.

The shower is still on.

I can't stop thinking about her as I pad upstairs to my bedroom. What is her story? What tore her family apart? Why does her father blame her for what happened?

And how can someone so confident, so sexy and fearless, be so *vulnerable* at the same time?

I pull the charger from my phone and scroll through my contacts.

Rafa picks up on the third ring.

Hello Javi, he says in Spanish. His voice is thick with sleep. Shit, I hope I didn't wake him up. But this can't wait. *Everything okay? It's kind of early.*

"Tell me about Maddie," I say.

Chapter Five

JAVIER

One Week Later

A bell jangles above my head as I step inside the café. My stomach rumbles at the homey smells of steamed milk and freshly baked pastry. You couldn't have paid me to go out to the discotecas last night—if I wasn't into clubbing before the whole Maddie thing happened, I'm definitely not into it now —but you'd think I was a maniac on the dance floor for how hungry I am this morning.

Rafa waves to me from the counter. I smile. I love this, meeting some family for coffee on a Saturday morning. It's amazing how much better you feel when you're surrounded by familiar faces. Faces that belong to people who have known you for your whole life.

We order espresso and croissants, and Rafa leads me to a big table near the windows that overlook the street. It's only November, but already the sidewalks bustle with holiday shoppers. This is my favorite time of year—the anticipation, the excitement, the way Madrid looks all decked out for Christmas. Really gets me in the spirit, I guess.

I'm so glad to be home.

"Any big plans for today?" Rafa sets his cup down on its saucer with a small *clink*.

"As a matter of fact, yes," I say. "I've started a new band with some of the guys from way back—you know, Leo Gomez, Sergio, a few others. A bit of a pet project—I'm craving something different after playing Juan's stuff for so long. I haven't written very much so far. I guess I have a bit of writer's block. But I'm hoping to have more luck now that I'm home."

"That's awesome," Rafa replies. He still has a pretty heavy accent, but his English has gotten much better now that he's with Vivian. I'm proud of him. "Where are you practicing? Not your flat, right?"

I spoon a little more sugar into my espresso and give it a slow stir. "God, no. You know how Leo plays—I'd get evicted. I actually got back in touch with María Carmen. Did you know she works at El Monasterio de los Humildes Reales now? She finagled a bit of practice time for us there. It's really a lovely venue."

"María Carmen." Rafa tilts his head, spearing me with a look. "I didn't know she was back in the picture."

Heat creeps up my neck.

"She's not," I say. "I guess she's dating some hot-shot bond trader or something, so . . . yeah. She's taken."

"You seem disappointed."

I shrug. "I'd be lying if I said I wasn't a little bummed. I've been thinking about her a lot lately."

The look of censure in Rafa's eyes bores two holes into my head.

"You guys broke up, what, five years ago?"

"Three and a half," I reply, more defensively than I mean to.

"You know, Javi," he says. "I've always believed it's better to look forward than to look back. Things—people, places, relationships—in your past should stay there, and for good reason. I've found better things, better people, usually lie ahead. You've changed. Carmen's changed."

I tear at my croissant, flaky bits of pastry falling onto my lap. "Maybe. But one thing that hasn't changed is the fact that she knew me before I was famous."

"You're not *that* famous." Rafa smiles. "You're D list at best. Maaaybe."

"I'm a solid C list celebrity, thank you very much. But my point is, Carmen fell in love with me when I had nothing to offer except my good looks and keen sense of humor."

"Again, you're not that funny. Or very good looking, now that I think about it."

I roll my eyes, grinning. "She loved me when I was nobody. She loved me for me. Rafa, that's what I've been missing. That, to me, is happiness. What I had with Carmen made me happy."

"And you don't think you can find that kind of happiness with someone else? Someone new?"

"Who?" I scoff. "Someone like Maddie Lucas? She ran out of my flat like it was on fire."

"I know you're annoyed with her for what she did. But I told you her parents are going through a very bad divorce. The call with her dad was probably about that."

"I know. Still. Don't you think she owes me an explanation?"

Rafa's eyes flick to a spot over my shoulder. "Maybe you'll get one right now."

My hands go still on my plate. I look pointedly at Rafa.

"What did you do?" I ask.

It's his turn to shrug. "No big deal. I invited the girls to breakfast."

"The girls?" I ask. "Meaning Vivian and Maddie?"

Rafa's about to answer when his face breaks into that

love-struck smile he wears whenever Viv is around. I would think it was cute if I didn't want to wring his neck.

I close my eyes and let out a long, low sigh.

The way Maddie left me last weekend was definitely not cool. I know the call with her dad upset her, but she can't run out on me like that. It makes me think that I did something wrong—that I offended her, or hurt her. Maybe I have, maybe I haven't, but I wouldn't know because Maddie didn't stay to explain herself.

"Buenos días, Rafa," I hear Vivian say.

Sitting back in my chair, I glance over my shoulder.

My gaze collides with Maddie's. Cappuccino in hand, she draws up short. Her blue eyes widen in naked surprise. For half a heartbeat, something—something like fear, or embarrassment—flashes across those wide, intelligent eyes.

For half a heartbeat, she's the vulnerable girl who left my flat in tears.

But then she blinks and that girl is gone. She meets my gaze head on, a suggestive smirk playing at the corners of her pretty little mouth. This—*this* is the girl who picked me up and took me home and fucked my brains out.

I stare at her. It's obvious that something is going on with Maddie. Her bravado, the sex, her hurt—it doesn't add up. It goes much deeper, that hurt, that vulnerability, than I thought.

She's covering up something very painful by pretending like this.

Not that I'm ever going to know what that something is beyond the things Rafa told me about her parents. Maddie made it clear she wanted nothing more than a hookup. No strings attached, no expectations. No follow-up, and no friendship. Even if I am curious—even if I do hate the thought of her hurting—there's no way she'll allow me to get close enough to help.

Besides, I finally get to see María Carmen today. I've been thinking about our meeting for a while now. We've caught up on a few phone calls over the past few months, but it's been years since I last saw her. I have no doubt she's just as beautiful, as lovely as she was back then, when we were eighteen and in love.

She's the girl I want. Not the messy, maddening girl standing behind me.

"Why he*llo*, Javier," Maddie says. I take the plate of churros she's holding and place it on the table.

Then I stand and press a kiss into each of her cheeks. Her skin is smooth and soft. It's my turn to pretend, pretend that my pulse doesn't leap at her feminine warmth.

"Como estás, Maddie?" I ask her the more formal version of *how are you*—I usually use 'qué tal' with my friends—and wonder if she'll pick up on the fact that I'm a bit ticked off.

She doesn't, or at least pretends not to. She glides past me, her arm brushing mine, and slides into the booth opposite my chair.

"I'll be all right after I pound this coffee," she replies. "The espresso in Spain was pretty intense at first, but now that I'm used to it, I'm addicted."

Maddie sips carefully at her cappuccino. I sit down. A beat of awkward silence settles between us as Viv and Rafa embrace and suck each other's faces for a few excruciating seconds.

"So I never got to thank you for last weekend," Maddie says. Her purring voice is pitched low, low enough so that I have to lean forward in my chair to hear it. "I had a good time."

A good time? I want to shout. *You call running out on me in tears with no apology or explanation after a night of seriously awesome sex a* good time?

I just look at her. I don't even try to come up with something polite to say back. This is exactly why I am so ready to settle down. I'm done with these games, these half-truths. Navigating them is exhausting.

"Everything all right here?" Vivian asks when she and Rafa finally come up for air.

"Yeah." Maddie's eyes don't leave mine. "Everything's perfect."

I look away from her and run a hand down my face, giving my growing stubble a good scrape.

"So Vivian," I say. I pick up the plate of churros, offering Viv and then Maddie one—she takes me up on it—before I dig in myself. "I hear you're enjoying the museums here in Madrid. You're an art major, correct?"

"Art history," Viv says around a mouthful of churro. "Maddie's the real artist though. You should see her drawings."

I arch a brow, venturing a glance at Maddie. "Are you an art history major as well?"

Her brown hair curls over her shoulder as she shakes her head, swallowing the last of her churro. "Architecture. History has always been my favorite subject, though, so I'd like to one day do something in historical preservation. I used to think I'd work in Charleston, close to home—they have these great antebellum mansions and plantations that are just so cool—but now I'm kinda thinking the opposite."

"Meaning you *don't* want to work close to home?"

It's subtle, her movement, and if I wasn't paying attention I would've missed it. But her whole body tenses, shoulders screwing up to her ears as she takes a long breath, lets it out. A shadow passes across her face.

"No," she says. "I don't. The farther away the better, actually. Which is why this study abroad thing couldn't have come at a better time. Considering how old this city is, I've been hoping to find some inspiration for my thesis. You know, a preservation project I could study, or a palace that needs some work. It'd be cool to come back here for grad school and continue something I started. But so far, no dice."

"Really?" I pull back. "That surprises me. Spain's the perfect place for that sort of thing. We've literally got layers upon layers of history here. First the Romans, then the Moors and the Jews. The Catholic monarchs, and Napoleon. Our cities are ancient. I'm surprised you can't find something to work on, something that inspires you."

Maddie shrugs, her shoulders falling back to where they should be. "It's not the inspiration that's the problem. Madrid is endlessly fascinating—I've maxed out my laptop's memory with all the pictures I've taken—but it's the access I'm struggling with. I'll find this cool medieval alley, or a little church tucked away on a side street. But when I ask for permission to study the structures, I'm ignored, or flat out denied. It happens every time. Apparently you need to know someone who knows someone. And I don't know anyone in Madrid, aside from my American classmates at San Pedro."

"You know me," Rafa says. "And now you know Javier."

I look down at my empty plate. Maddie knows me in the Biblical sense, yeah.

But beyond that? Not really.

"No offense," Maddie says. "But unless either of you have a contact at a palace or castle I don't know about, I don't think you'll be of much help. But it's sweet of you to offer, Rafa. Thank you."

Rafa looks at me, lips pursed thoughtfully.

Oh.

Oh no.

He wouldn't—

"As a matter of fact," he says, "Javier does have a hookup. And at a castle too—very old. It was a monastery for a while, but now it's a place for concerts and a museum. Very cool building with lots of history."

Maddie's narrowed eyes dart to me. "A castle-turned-monastery-turned music hall? That sounds, like, way too good to me true."

"It's not very glamorous, this place," Rafa says. "It is a bit . . . how do you say? A bit hidden, not very many tourists go there. But it might be the perfect place for your thesis, because Javier knows a girl who works at the monastery. And his band, it will play there too."

"Holy shit," Maddie says, setting down her empty cup. "That'd be amazing. Honestly, the farther off the beaten path, the better. A unique spot like that could really make my thesis stand out."

"Javier is going there today," Rafa says. "He could take you, make some introductions. Maybe you could explore the architecture too."

"Really?" Maddie says. "You'd really take me with you?"

I feel Maddie's eyes on me, but I focus my glare on Rafa. He's killing me today. "Sure," I grind out. "No problem."

It's a big fucking problem, actually, but what the hell am I supposed to say? I don't want to be rude.

I also don't want to ruin my meeting with Carmen. It's really important I'm on point today. And with Maddie in tow, chances are I'll be more than a little distracted.

All I wanted today was some quality time with my band and a flirty one-on-one with Carmen. But the flirting isn't going to happen if Maddie is there. She's too . . . distracting.

"Are you sure?" Maddie asks.

"Yeah." I tug a hand through my hair and offer her a tight smile. "Yeah, I'm sure. The monastery's a pretty special place."

"I can't wait to see it. Seriously, I haven't been this pumped in a long time." Her features soften in genuine gratitude. She really is a pretty girl. "Thank you, Javier, for offering to take me. I appreciate it. A lot."

"Sure," I say, wondering if she noticed that I didn't offer. Not at all.

"How great is this, Viv? All these months of research and I finally have a lead." Maddie claps her hands. "But first, I need more caffeine."

"More?" I ask. "That latte would bring the dead back to life. They make them strong here."

Maddie looks away as she digs her wallet out of her purse. "I'm so sleep deprived I could drink, like, a bathtub of coffee and still feel sluggish. Should I get it to go? Do they even *have* coffee to go here?"

Taking your coffee to go is a relatively new concept in Spain. We're big believers in sitting down to enjoy a meal, whether it's a quick espresso and croissant in the morning or ten rounds of tapas and vino de la casa—the house wine—at a restaurant at night. Meals are never rushed, and they are usually shared with people you love—friends, family, significant others. It's one of the things I missed most while I was on the road. Who wants to slurp a lukewarm latte from a paper cup while running off to work in the morning? Call me old school, but I find that idea a bit depressing.

"As much as I hate to say it, it's probably a good idea to get it to go," I reply. "I'm supposed to be at the monastery at one."

Maddie and Viv slide out of the booth and head for the espresso bar.

Once they're out of earshot, I lean across the table and pin Rafa with the nastiest glare I can muster. "Listen, mate, what the hell do you think you're doing? You know I'm supposed to meet María Carmen at the monastery."

He shrugs, like it's no big deal he just ruined the day I've been looking forward to for months. "Carmen has a boyfriend, yes?"

"Yes, but—"

"And Maddie, she is hurting, Javi. She drinks all these cappuccinos because she can't sleep. She is too sad over her parents. You don't like it when people are hurting—"

I scoff, so loudly the couple at the table next to us look up from their mugs.

Rafa looks at me. "You know what I mean. You hated seeing your mother hurting after your father passed away. I know you hate seeing Maddie hurting, too, even if she did not treat you very well last weekend. You're the only one who can help her right now, Javi. Please."

"I can't *help her* help her," I say. "I have no idea what's going on in her head. Yeah, I can help with her thesis. But isn't that a superficial sort of help? Her pain seems . . . it goes really deep, Rafa."

He shrugs again. I swear to God, if he shrugs one more time I'm going to launch out of my seat and tackle him. "Maybe. But you must begin somewhere. Her thesis is very important to her."

"I'd really prefer not to get involved," I say.

"You should prefer not to be involved with Carmen. She is your past. Time to look for your future."

I've got a few choice words for my tit of a nephew about my future foot in his future ass, but then the girls are back at the table, and Rafa is saying something about having to go get tickets for the football match from his friend.

I look at Maddie.

Maddie looks at me, her lovely eyes hopeful, almost translucent in the bright morning light.

God*damn* it.

Chapter Six

MADDIE

Javier looks down at his watch, the embossed leather strap shining dully in the light of the windows. It's a simple watch with a large round face, the color of the clock itself slightly muted, like an old newspaper. The dial is marked in three different colors, two smaller circles set into the larger one. A vintage aviator's watch from what I can tell, a watch that's ridiculously cool without even trying.

"We should get going too," he says a little gruffly, standing. "I told the guys I'd meet them at one." He looks at me. "Are you ready?"

"Yes," I say. "Ready. They didn't have coffee to go, so one cup'll have to do."

I turn around in my chair to grab my puffer jacket, but it's gone. I look up to see Javier holding it open for me, the faux fur of the hood poking up between his enormous, blunt-edged fingers.

Of course. I should've known Javier would help me with my coat.

"You Montoya men," I say. "I don't know if I've met two more polite dudes in my life."

Although there was definitely nothing polite about Javier's deliciously dirty talk in bed last weekend.

"My uncle, he takes after me," Rafa says with a smile as he helps Viv into her coat.

"Thanks, *Uncle* Javier." I turn around and awkwardly work with him to put it on. Guys in college don't help you with your outerwear—underwear, yes, but outerwear? no way—and I'm not quite sure what to do with myself.

"Just Javier," he says. His fingers brush the nape of my neck and a pulse of heat moves through me. "The uncle part is a bit creepy, don't you think?"

Tugging up my zipper, I look over my shoulder and grin. "Depends what you're into."

"I'm into a lot of things." He steps through the door and holds it open for me. "Vamos. I'm parked just up the lane."

I struggle not to dwell on what, exactly, Javier means by *I'm into a lot of things* as we say our goodbyes to Vivian and Rafa. Hands tucked into our pockets, we make our way down the sidewalk. Javier makes no attempt to talk, and awkward silence stretches between us.

I feel like a dick, frankly, for running out of his apartment the way I did on Sunday morning. Definitely not cool of me. But I was a teary, hungover mess, for one thing, and Javier's kindness only made me want to cry harder. For another, I thought I'd never really see him again, so an explanation would be a waste of time anyway. Viv did say he isn't in town that often. Why would he care why I ran?

But here we are, Javier and I, together again. I don't think he wants to spend the day with me any more than I want to spend the day with him. I don't care to revisit the whole crying-in-his-bed-while-I-yelled-at-my-dad bit, and I certainly don't want to revisit my frankly childish escape from his apartment. The impulse to tuck tail and run is strong for me today too, but Javier has the connection that just might make my thesis work. Enduring the awkwardness between us is worth it if it means acing the most important assignment of my college career.

I fight a very pressing sense of "who the fuck am I" as I climb into Javier's truck. It's a black Range Rover Defender, the kind I imagine the Queen drives while hunting prize pheasant or whatever on her Scottish estate. Like Javier's watch, the Defender is beautifully vintage, the dings and scratches only enhancing its rugged appeal.

He closes the door behind me and makes his way to the driver's seat. In true British fashion, it's on the right hand side of the truck. I watch him move from behind the safety of my opaque sunglass lenses. There are no two ways about it: he is cute as hell. His stride is long, unhurried. Restrained, even, like he's holding back his strength that ripples just beneath the surface.

Stop it, I tell myself. Javier was a one-time hookup. I haven't gone back for seconds this semester with anyone, and I don't plan to start anytime soon.

Who in their right mind would want to take me on for more than a one-night stand, anyway? I don't think it's any secret that I'm a fucking mess. A high functioning mess, sure, but still a mess. I mean, I'm no therapist, but I'd have to be an idiot not to know that feeling this way has a lot to do with my dad's betrayal. He betrayed my mother. He betrayed me by making me feel like I was the one who blew up our family, and he betrayed my sense of security, my trust in who he was and how he felt about me.

I loved my dad. I still do, as much as I hate to admit it. I thought he loved me too. But you don't treat someone you love the way he's been treating me lately.

I feel like shit about it. I feel like shit all the time, actually. About my family. About myself. Nursing a painfully unrequited crush on Rafa—then again, what unrequited crushes aren't painful—certainly didn't help. But the sex does sometimes. It may be a quick, stupid fix, but it's a nice distraction from a pretty depressing reality.

Sometimes, when it's late and I can't sleep, I start to think that maybe I don't deserve anything better than a hookup. If my own father treats me so badly, what does that say about me as a person? Am I not worthy of love, of respect?

I take a long breath through my nose, let it out in a puff of white cloud. I've started taking yoga classes to help me cope with—well, everything that's gone wrong this semester. The deep "warrior breath" that I learned seems to calm my pulse a bit when nothing else does.

Inside the truck it smells like guy, a mix of shampoo and leather, a hint of cinnamon gum.

Needless to say, my calming yoga breath has the opposite of its intended effect. I shiver just as Javier opens his door and climbs in.

"Give the heat a moment—it doesn't take long to warm up," he says, turning the key in the ignition. The engine blares to life. "Christ, but it's cold enough to freeze the balls off a brass monkey."

"Ha!" I let out a bark of laughter. "I've never heard that before."

"It's a good one, isn't it? One of my favorites I picked up from my time in England."

"Is it always this cold in the winter here?"

Javier shakes his head. "This is quite cold for us—unusually cold."

He reaches up and pulls down the sun visor, revealing a pair of gold-framed aviators he slides onto his head.

He shifts the truck into gear. Oh, dear Lord, it's a manual.

Is there anything sexier than a guy in aviators who drives stick?

No. No, I don't think there is.

I look away, focusing my gaze on the road ahead.

Javier glances over his shoulder and nudges the Range Rover into traffic. I feel his eyes on me. "You all right?"

I'm not sure what it is—the rumble of his voice, maybe, or the sweetness of his concern—but I shiver again.

Javier holds his palm up to a vent. "It's getting there."

"Thanks." I tuck my chin into the collar of my jacket. "Yeah. Yes. I'm all right. You don't have to be so polite with me all the time, you know."

He doesn't answer.

I look out the window. We're crawling toward a big intersection, the buildings around us crowding out the sun. "So who's this contact Rafa said you have? The one who works at the monastery?"

"An old friend."

"An old friend?" I ask, glancing at him with a smile. "That sounds interesting."

"It's not." He changes gears. "She's an acquaintance— someone I've known for a very long time."

I cock a brow. "*She?* Wait, wait. This is the girl you were telling me about last weekend at Ático, isn't it? The one you want but can't have because she has a boyfriend."

He shifts gears again, an authoritative thrust. The muscle along his jaw twitches. "Maybe," he says at last.

"Oh, for God's sake, Javier, relax." I tuck my hands between my legs. "I won't burst your little love bubble. If you want this chick, by all means, go after her. I'll even help you. Maybe distract the boyfriend while you work your suave Spaniard thing—"

"No," he clips. "I can handle this on my own, thanks."

"Have it your way," I say. I look out the window again. The sound of the engine accelerating fills the space between us. "I really meant it when I said I appreciate your help. My thesis—it's going nowhere. I've lost a lot of sleep over it."

Javier glances at me. "Don't you ever sleep?"

"Not really. I'll be the first to admit I don't handle stress very well, especially when it comes to my grades. So much of my future depends on my thesis. It's hard not to worry about it when I've been stonewalled again and again by every palace and museum I reach out to. And I really do want to come back to Madrid for graduate school. It'd be so much easier to do that if I already have a solid foundation of research done —research I hope to do this semester."

Rafa nods his head. "For a big city, Madrid can be a very small place. Sometimes it's a good thing. We are protective of our history, if not always proud of it. But other times? Not so much. I'm sorry you haven't made much headway. Perhaps today we might change that—in the end, Madrid rarely disappoints."

I look at him, my gaze tracing the slopes and angles of his profile. Sharp nose, square jaw, shapely, full lips. "You really love it here, don't you?"

"I do," he replies. "It's home. I was on the road for close to a year. I missed my city. I really missed my bed."

"Yeah," I say, the words coming before I can stop them. "I miss my bed too. A lot."

"Nothing like your own bed, that's for sure," he says. He looks at me. "Are you homesick?"

I look down at my hands, my chest tightening with a familiar ache. "Yes and no. Some days . . . some days, I guess, are better than others. I really love Madrid, and so far it's been an awesome experience. It's nice to get away for a while, you know, a change of scenery. But yeah, I definitely miss some things."

Like my family. Not the family I have now—broken, angry, sad. I miss the family we *were*. Things were always good with us. Better than that. I used to think they were perfect. But now I know that perfect doesn't exist.

"Where is home for you?" he asks.

"Atlanta," I say.

"Georgia," he says. "I've play—I've been there. I remember going to a concert at the arena where the basketball team plays."

"Philips Arena. I know it well."

Very well. Mom, Dad, and I used to go to concerts there together all the time. The memory of us together, singing along to our favorite country star at the top of our lungs as Mom snuck me sips of her beer, makes my chest hurt.

"It's a cool spot," I say.

Silence settles between us again. I twist my hands in my lap.

"Speaking of your home," he says at last. "Are you going to tell me what happened last weekend?"

A knot tightens in my belly. I really, *really* don't want to talk about this right now. But really, it's awesome of him to help me out like this, so the least I can do in return is explain why I ran out of his apartment like a lunatic.

I take a warrior breath.

"I'm sorry," I say, letting it out, "for the way I behaved. You have every right to be mad."

"I'm not mad." He looks away. "Well. Perhaps a bit put off. I've never had someone run out on me like that."

"I'm sorry," I repeat.

"I was concerned," he says. "Maddie, you were crying. *In my bed*. And then you just took off. I called Rafa and had him call Vivian to make sure you got home okay. I understand you may not want to talk about it, but you can't disappear on me like that. It's rude, for one thing, and worrisome for another."

I swallow. "I'm really sorry. I acted like such a shit last weekend, and you—you're being so cool, letting me tag along like this today. I'm sorry, Javier, I am. But I can't—I really can't talk about it right now. The *why*, I mean—why I was crying. And even if I could, you wouldn't want to hear it. So much bullshit . . ." I shake my head. "I'm sorry. I shouldn't have left like that."

"It's all right," he says, gruffly. "I just want to make sure you're okay."

I'm not. I'm so not okay. And I think he knows that.

But I'm not about to spill my guts to Javier on the way to a super cool monastery that may save my thesis.

"Thank you," I say. "I mean that, Javier."

Javier shifts again, weaving our way toward city center. I keep the focus on him as the streets get narrower, a zigzag of what were once ancient footpaths and medieval alleys. He navigates his truck through them with knowledgeable ease.

Where did you study, I ask. Oxford, he says, Music Theory and Political Science (how cool is that?). He tells me he plays guitar in his band. Who taught you to play it? I taught myself, he replies, until I was a bit older, and my parents paid for lessons.

Around us the city is close and beautiful, bathed in strident afternoon light. We pass Puerta del Sol, one of my favorite squares in the city, its picturesque inner courtyard teeming with well-dressed Madrileños out for a Saturday stroll. Its famous bell tower presides over the pretty buildings that line the square, each one painted a warm Mediterranean shade of dusty red, taupe, yellow, or white. The tiled roofs— terra cotta, total Spanish perfection—burn orange beneath a wide-open winter sky.

Back home in Atlanta, I'd drive past ugly strip malls, big-box stories, and gas stations on my regular routes through the city. Not all of America is a suburban wasteland, of course, but very rarely do you get to pass a place as lovely or inspiring as Puerta del Sol while you're out and about on a Saturday afternoon.

"We're passing into the old city now," Javier says, making a turn. "'Puerta del Sol' translates into the 'door of the sun.' It used to be the old city gate."

"So cool," I say. "I did a little research on it myself when I first got to Madrid. I haven't explored much of the old city, though, to be honest. I'm glad we're heading that way."

I ask more questions, Javier gives me more answers. He's so easy to talk to, the flow of our conversation natural, unhurried. For the first time in forever, I don't think about my parents, their heartache, my own. It's like a breath of fresh air after spending months underwater.

It doesn't hurt that he's freaking *adorable*. He loves olives, his mom, and *Pirates of the Caribbean*. The only type of music he doesn't like is country.

"Whoa," I say. "Wait a minute. Wait a *minute*. You don't like country music?"

"I can appreciate it as . . . um. As someone who's into music," he replies, guiding the truck down a street so narrow the side mirrors nearly touch buildings we pass. "But listening to it? I'd rather not. Why? Are you a country fan?"

"Big time. In high school, it was all I'd listen to. I may or may not have gone through a phase where I'd only date guys who drove pickup trucks. Seriously, Javier, you're missing out."

"We're going to have to agree to disagree on that one," he says, glancing at me. "How'd you end up liking that twangy cack so much?"

"I don't know what cack is, but I'm assuming it's not a compliment?"

"Definitely not. Como se dice en los Estados Unidos . . ."

Hearing him talk in easy, languid Spanish—*how would you say it in the United States*—makes my pulse hiccup.

"Crap, maybe?"

"Vale, that would probably work. That twangy *crap*."

"I happen to like that twangy crap, thank you very much, and I bet I could get you to like it too."

"You want to bet?" he asks, grinning.

"I do. I have, like, twenty euro in my bank account right now, but I'm willing to part with it in the name of Kenny Chesney."

Javier laughs, a rumbling, masculine sound that makes me want to laugh too.

"I won't take your money," he says. "But perhaps we can think of something else to wager."

I know he's not trying to be suggestive, but when you're Javier—scruffy, sexy, hipster-athlete-with-a-deep-voice Madrileño Javier—it's hard not to be.

His voice has me thinking of all those saucy Spanish nothings he whispered in my ear last weekend. God, he was good at the dirty talk. He was good at other things too. He was good at *all* the things, actually. All the things a guy can do to a girl in bed.

I'm just beginning to fantasize about how fun it would be to turn this bet into a sort of strip-poker situation when Javier guides the Range Rover into the tiniest alley ever and pulls up the parking brake.

"We're here," he says, pointing out the windshield.

I duck my head to get a better look, sliding my sunglasses into my hair.

Immediately to our right, a hulking brick and stone square of a building rises into the clear blue sky. I've never seen it before. It looks old—really old—its façade a disjointed collage of Romanesque and baroque and even renaissance styles. Its square windows, poked through stone walls three feet thick, dot the façade at uneven intervals. On the ground floor, several pairs of massive doors stand attention, the weathered wood dotted with iron bolts. It could be a castle, or a convent, or a small museum. Tough to tell.

I'm intrigued. You only see this kind of thing in the old world: hundreds of years of history writ right before your eyes. I'm already impatient to get a better look up close, to suss out details that tell stories from generations ago. A fading coat of arms, perhaps, or medieval fingerprints left in plaster. There's brickwork and stonework and even some sculptural elements tucked into eaves, set on spires on the roof.

Forget strip poker. This is way cooler. My inner architecture nerd is going apeshit.

"El Monasterio de las Humildes Reales," Javier says, the words rolling off his tongue.

"The Monastery of the Humble Royals," I say. "Am I translating it right?"

"Sí."

"Doesn't look too humble to me."

Javier scoffs. "It was built as a palace for the Spanish royals. Sometime around the Renaissance, I believe. When the king's daughter decided she'd rather become a nun than marry her cousin, he gave her the palace as a gift to found her monastery. She built a church—just over there, in the southwest corner—that was famous for its lovely acoustics. Eventually, when the nuns ran out of money, someone had the bright idea to turn it into theater."

I stare at him, disbelievingly. "And that's the theater you and your band practice in?"

"Brilliant, isn't it?" He leans toward me, taking off his sunglasses. "C'mon, I'll show you around."

His eyes are even lovelier up close; the color is startlingly vibrant, like a light shining through a brown glass bottle. His eyelashes are thick and very dark, boyish.

Even though there's a hint of playfulness in those eyes, I see something else there, something I hadn't seen before.

Kindness.

I look away, my heart fluttering inside my chest. His person, his ridiculous shoulders and scruff and leather jacket —none of that has made my pulse race any faster today.

But that look in his eyes—the softness—that did.

And I don't know how I feel about that.

Javier grabs a guitar case from "the boot" as he calls it, and together we cross the street and walk alongside the monastery's front façade. Now that we're close, I can appreciate the building's enormous scale. The whitewashed corner-stones are as long and wide as a person. The doors must be twelve to fifteen feet high, and so heavy it probably takes several people to open them.

"It's not the prettiest building in Madrid," Javier says, "but I'd like to think it's one of the more interesting ones. It's more of a local spot—like Rafa said, we don't get many tourists coming to visit."

"I can only imagine what sort of shenanigans those humble royal nuns got up to at a place like this." I crane my neck to get a better look at the series of three crosses that dot the roofline of the main entrance façade. "Do we know when it was first built?"

"I'm not sure, actually," Javier replies. "But there is someone who might be able to answer that for you."

"Your special someone?" I ask, grinning.

He rolls his eyes. "This way, please."

Chapter Seven

MADDIE

Javier leads me around the corner and taps the knuckle of his first finger on a (much) smaller side door. I trail my eyes over a maze of medieval brickwork while we wait, the bricks washed in a sooty, dripping ash leftover from centuries of rain, humidity, and pollution. It forms a sort of ancient tie-dye, tinged at the edges with green moss. This place is *old*. On my family's beach trip to Charleston last year, I remember marveling at a pink row house that was built in 1723.

The monastery came into being hundreds and hundreds of years before that, during a time when the plague was a real thing and architects were mathematical badasses, working to rediscover the theorems and equations of the Ancient Romans, the Ancient Greeks. I wonder how many architects and artisans worked on the place. Every brick, every stone and cross and column was designed and made by hand, constructed using methods unchanged since the middle ages.

The door swings open, revealing a woman who greets us with a dazzling smile. She's the kind of gorgeous that stops traffic. Tall, tan, with rambunctious, caramel-colored curls, she's got a wide mouth and big eyes.

So this is the girl, I think. Javier's girl.

He's got good taste. Expensive taste—I look down to see a Cartier Tank watch on her wrist—but good taste nonetheless.

Like most Madrileñas, she is dressed to the nines: dark jeans, flowy silk top, a pair of sassy heeled boots. I've always wondered where Spanish women find the time to always look so damn good. Being a college student, I practically live in yoga pants. I bet Javier's girl would rather shave her head than wear yoga pants, even while doing yoga.

"María Carmen." Javier steps through the door, offering her a quick, awkward kiss on each cheek. He's jumpy all of the sudden, nervous. It's kinda cute. "Como estás?" *How are you?*

Javier, she says. I notice she keeps her hand on his shoulder. *It's been a while! I am glad to see you. How was the tour?*

I blink. Tour?

It was great. But long. He smiles, shyly. *You look beautiful, Carmen.*

She offers him a blinding smile in return. *Thanks. You look well too.*

He looks at her for a minute, still smiling, then turns to me. "Carmen, I'd like you to meet Maddie. She is a friend of Rafa's, studying at San Pedro for the semester."

I hold out my hand. "Mucho gusto, Carmen."

"It is lovely to meet you too, Maddie," she replies in stilted, formal English. Her eyes sweep over me, so quickly I almost don't see it.

"Maddie is putting together a thesis in historical preservation," Javier continues, waving me inside. "I thought she might enjoy seeing the monastery, and perhaps talk to you about the foundation's work? Carmen is one of the curators here. She specializes in Renaissance art."

"Really?" I say. "That's so cool!"

Carmen's smile broadens. "Welcome, Maddie, I have no doubt you will love what you see. Please, come in, some of Javier's band mates have already arrived."

"Have they introduced themselves, I hope?" Javier asks.

"Oh, yes," Carmen says. "I already knew Leo, of course—"

"Sorry about that." Javier smiles.

"But the others said hello. Very friendly band mates you have."

A familiar, musty smell—*old*—hits me the second I step inside the door. The floorboards creak beneath my feet as I follow Javier and Carmen through the tiny entrance hall.

It's all I can do not to gasp, or jump up and down like the crazy person that I am, when we come out on a wide gallery. Ardent afternoon light streams through the wavy, hand-blown glass of the windows, turning the terra cotta floor tiles into a shining pool of red. Every inch of wall space is covered in ornate frescoes, flowers and animals and a *lot* of Jesus, drawing the eye upward to a ceiling of dark wooden beams. At the end of the galley, there's another entrance hall, this one huge and ornate, with ceilings covered in angels that soar three, even four stories high. There is so much to look at, it's making me dizzy.

"Wow," I breathe. "Just—wow. This place is amazing."

Javier grins at me over his shoulder as we climb the stairs. "Wait 'til you see the church. It's one of the most beautiful places in all of Madrid."

His voices echoes off the walls, a deep, masculine rumble. I look up to see him and Carmen taking the steps in time, their movements so in synch, so naturally complementary to each other, I wonder if the two of them were ever together. First loves, maybe? It wouldn't surprise me; they make pretty hot pair. I get it. If I was a guy who looked like Javier, I'd want to date a girl who looked like Carmen.

If, of course, I was into dating. Which I'm not. Definitely, definitely not.

"When was the last time I saw you?" Carmen turns her head and offers Javier a red-lipped smile. "It has to be almost three years?"

He digs a hand into his hipster wave, mussing it into a tidy spike. "More than that, I think. Too long. I'm really excited to be back home."

"And your band—it is new?"

"Yes." Javier nods. "An entirely new project. I've missed the classical stuff—the stuff I started with."

I've missed the classical stuff. That's interesting. What has he been doing that's kept him from the music he loves?

"Going back to your roots," Carmen says.

"Exactly. I got a few of the boys together, and we decided we'd give it a go. I don't have plans for us, not yet. But it could be fun."

"Classical stuff?" I ask. "Like Bach and Handel and violins?"

"Sort of," he replies. "I was trained as a classical guitarist. Flamenco was always my favorite, so that's what I wanted to study. Now it's what I want to play."

"I can't wait to hear you play again," Carmen says. She glances at me. "Javier is a very talented musician."

"So I've gathered," I say. "I'm excited to see him in action."

We mount the top step and hang a right. I'm torn between ogling exquisite marble inlays on a nearby arch and listening to Javier and Carmen catch up. I'm more curious than I should be about their relationship. They're just so —*hot.* Spanish. Sexy. Things I will never, ever be. It's like catching the world's most beautiful celebrities falling in love right in front of you. You can't *not* watch.

I hear the thrum of an acoustic guitar, followed by a few

claps and shouts, as we head toward a pair of monumental doors at the end of the gallery, one of which is open.

Javier stands by the door, gesturing Carmen and me inside first.

"Thanks," I say.

He meets my gaze. My pulse hiccups. Those *eyes* of his. They are warm and gentle. "You're welcome, Maddie. I hope you're inspired by what you see."

I step inside the church.

My breath leaves my lungs as a tingling awareness moves through me.

I don't believe in fate. Not like I used to, anyway. And whatever faith I had in a higher power's "master plan" pretty much went out the window when my dad blindsided me with his lies.

But stepping inside this theater—this overwhelmingly beautiful theater—I know in my gut that this place, and this moment, are important. This isn't just another church, another historic monument I'm not allowed to touch.

This place means something. I'm not sure what. But I've never, ever seen anything like it. I haven't read about anything like it either—a palace turned monastery turned theater. A theater where this guy I just met is going to play some flamenco guitar. It's fresh subject matter in a field where hidden gems are increasingly hard to come by.

The angles are infinite—I could write about history, the success of restoration work already done, the architecture of acoustics. I just need to be able to come here on a regular basis so I can actually *study* the space. If by some miracle I make that happen, I think I can put together a solid thesis proposal. Maybe I really do have a shot at coming back to Madrid for graduate school.

Goose bumps break out on my arms.

Being inside the theater makes me feel like I am definitely

in Spain. I see Moorish influence in the stylized arches above the doors, lots of Catholic motifs in the sculptures above what was once the altar but is now the stage, more Catholic mythology etched into the stained-glass windows.

Oh, the windows. They're enormous, set high into the walls on either side of the theatre. Colors hundreds of years old still burn brightly, the light warm: purple from this angle, green from that one, now cobalt blue, and red, and yellow. It's like being inside a prism.

The church was obviously meant to impress, with its soaring white walls, sculpture, and heavy gilding. Now that it's a theater, the effect is very much the same. Only these days it's not the nuns' voices that fill the space, rising higher and higher in arias to the Virgin Mary, it's bands like Javier's that crank out the tunes. And something tells me Javier's music has nothing to do with virgins.

"You all right?" Javier asks.

"Yes," I say. "Yeah. Definitely. Just trying to absorb it all."

"That's going to take a while."

I wrap a hand around the back of my neck, which has already started to ache from all my gawking. Javier is right; there's just so much to see. I could look for hours, days even, and there'd still be details I would miss.

I look down to see Javier watching me. His eyes appear hazel in this light, the brown tinged with green.

"C'mon," he says, nodding to the stage. A couple guys are up there, tuning their guitars. "Let me introduce you to the band."

Javier

I remember the first time I visited El Monasterio de los Humildes Royales. I'd been dating María Carmen for a few months and her parents had just gifted a big chunk of change to the foundation for the monastery's preservation. They were season ticket holders, and this was the first time they'd invited me to tag along as Carmen's date. Being the music geek I am, I was stoked to attend a concert given by one of my favorite flamenco bands of all time.

While the band was awesome, it was the monastery that stole the show. Listening to the sound of the guitars echoing off the centuries-old walls was nothing short of a religious experience. Every note, every cry and stomp and clap became its own living, breathing thing, taking on new depth. The stage lights, sparkling in the stained-glass windows, only added to the magic. It was a defining moment in my musical career, and that night I decided I would be up on that stage someday, playing music inspired by the place I call home.

I'll never forget that first time. But now, watching Maddie take it all in, it's like I'm reliving the experience all over again. Her wonderment, the excitement that lights up her blue eyes —I remember feeling those things too. I remember how intensely I felt them, an out of body experience that touched every part of my being.

I had this gut feeling that this spot would mean something to me. Granted, I was eighteen, and I was in love. The world was a very romantic place for me back then. But I was right. The monastery *has* come to play a big part in my life. And I can tell from the look on her face that Maddie feels it too, that sixth sense telling you to pay attention, because something big—something cool—is going to happen here.

Maybe her tagging along with me today isn't the worst thing, after all.

I could watch Maddie ogle the monastery all day, reliving

that excitement vicariously through her. But I'm not a creeper, first of all, and second, my band is waiting.

On cue, I hear a familiar voice call out something filthy that I won't repeat in a church. I know without looking that it's Leo.

Leo Rodriguez an insanely good guitarist and one of my best friends. He's also *that* guy. You know, the guy you love like a brother but are embarrassed to be seen with in public because he's such a mess.

Rolling my eyes, I let out a groan. "So, the band. They're really talented musicians, Maddie, and I swear to you they mean well. But let's just say they don't spend enough time in polite company, yes?"

Maddie smiles, tucking her hands into the pockets of her jacket. "I'm always game to learn new ways to swear in Spanish. What did that guy say?" She glances over my shoulder. "Something about milk? I didn't catch it."

"You don't want to know," I reply. "But in the interest of furthering your cultural education, I'll tell you. Me cago en la leche—literally, I shit in the milk. In this case, my dumbass mate used it as an expression of surprise. As in, 'holy shit, our lead man has arrived.' The Spanish is a bit . . . er, stronger than the English translation, I think."

"I shit in the milk." Maddie nods, trying out the Spanish. Her accent is excellent and a bit cute. "A keeper for sure."

I smile, even as I catch María Carmen cross her arms and shoot me a look of disapproval. I guess she's not as nuts for shitting in the milk as Maddie is. Makes sense, considering Carmen is the epitome of that polite company I was talking about. I actually can't think of a time I ever heard her swear, even something so innocent as cállate—shut up—or culo—ass.

I climb the steps onto the stage, the lights warming the crown of my head and shoulders as I wave Maddie up behind me. I introduce her to Leo, who gets a little handsy for my taste when he leans in to kiss her cheeks.

I blink. The possessiveness that prickles inside my skin takes me off guard.

Maddie isn't mine. Never was and never will be.

Still, I find myself staring down Leo as he touches her.

"Oh!" Maddie says, looking down at his hand on her hip. Her lower, almost-lady-groin-area hip. "Oh, aren't you, um, friendly. Mucho gusto, I guess?"

I quickly untangle Maddie from his grasp, keeping her close beside me lest Leo is feeling especially ornery this afternoon.

"*Ha*-lo, Maddie," he says. "I have enchanted to meet her. You have a yearning for doing it together?"

She blinks. "A yearning? To do—do what? I don't know—um—"

"Doing it!" Leo gestures at the guitar hanging from a strap at his pelvis. "Together! The music. I have played guitar, and you do the singing? The songs!"

"Oh!" she says again, letting out a small trill of relieved laughter. "No, no, I'm not part of the band. I'm just here to watch. To see the monastery." She waves her hand above her head, gesturing at the ornately frescoed ceiling.

Leo, clearly having understood none of what she just said, smiles and nods. He gestures to his pelvis again. I wince. "Watch my part? Yes!"

Maddie looks at me. "Help."

"There is no helping him," I say, shaking my head as I angle my body between the two of them. "I can, however, protect you from that weird Elvis thing he's doing with his . . . you know."

I explain to Leo that Maddie is a friend of Rafa's, which means she's a friend of mine.

I speak Spanish, Leo, Maddie says in that cute accent of hers. *Would that be easier for you?*

"I am the need practice the English," he replies. "If good to you, we speak it together, vale?"

"Sure." She glances at me, a grin playing at her lips. "Of course. I'm happy to help you with your English. So you play the guitar—do you guys write your own music? Are you classically trained too?"

Leo smiles and nods again. I let out a bark of laughter and quickly translate what Maddie is saying into Spanish.

Vale, Leo laughs. *The Spanish is better for this, yes. I help Javier write a little bit, but right now he has not been writing much. He is very good at writing hooks—*

Maddie looks at me, brow furrowed.

"Hooks," I translate. "It's the part of the song that makes it catchy. It could be a turn of phrase, a riff, a chorus—whatever has you singing it in the shower."

She nods. "So basically Taylor Swift is the queen of writing hooks."

"Absolutely," I reply, trying—and failing, quite miserably—not to imagine Maddie singing "Shake it Off" while lathering up in that shower we never got to take together. She'd be all long legs and slippery skin, hot to the touch.

I swallow, hard. Why the hell am I thinking about Maddie when I want to find forever with Carmen? I need to get a grip. *Now.*

With no small effort, I shove the glistening shower image from my head. "T. Swift is a genius in that regard. I've actually studied her songs a great deal."

"I thought you said you didn't like country." Maddie cocks a brow.

"Taylor went pop a while back, didn't she?"

"Point taken," Maddie says. "I'm so excited to hear what you've come up with."

You should be more excited about the acoustics of this place, Leo says. *We're going to sound a lot fucking better than we actually are.*

"Do you guys have a name?" she asks. "The band, I mean."

Leo and I look at each other.

"Yet no," Leo says. "Javi, he has four or six bad ideas."

"They're not *that* bad," I say.

Leo looks at Maddie. "They are very bad. For example, there is the Gods of the—"

"Nope," I say. "Nope nope nope. It's bad luck to tell people our band name before we've officially decided. We have plenty of time to come up with—uh—other options, if we don't like what we have."

"Chicos, chicos," Carmen is saying from the first row, *I only have you booked for two hours, then the next performers have the stage.*

It's two hours we can't afford to waste. Yes, we're paying for the practice time—not even the really famous bands get to practice at the monastery for free. But what really matters is the fact that we would've never been considered for the slot if it wasn't for María Carmen. She did me a solid by putting my as-yet-unnamed band on the schedule this month and next. We have a lot of ground to cover in that small bit of time.

It's stupid, I know—she's got a serious boyfriend, for God's sake—but I can't help but wonder if she went so far out of her way to help me and my band because she still has feelings for me.

A man can only hope.

Chapter Eight

JAVIER

I quickly introduce Maddie to the rest of the band—Sergio, Martín, and Pablo, who, for reasons I don't want to know, insists on being called Ricky B.—before I take off my jacket and flip open my case and duck under my guitar strap, settling it over my right shoulder. A semicircle of chairs is set up in the center of the stage. We sit. My fingers find the strings, moving over them with mindless ease as I tune the guitar. Since this is just practice, the guys and I aren't plugged into any amplifiers or speakers; we're one-hundred-percent acoustic this afternoon.

But even without all that power, Leo may be right. The church is going to make us sound lovely.

I look up, searching for María Carmen in the gaping vastness of the church.

Instead I meet eyes with Maddie.

She's sitting in the front row beside Carmen. Maddie smiles, offering a little wave. A beam of light from the stained-glass windows above stretches across her row, coating her dark hair in a halo of violet. She glances up at the window, that look of disbelieving awe softening her features as her eyes move up, up, always up. There is so much to see here at the monastery.

I'm smiling now. I adore her curiosity.

María Carmen clears her throat. My gaze snaps to her face. She smiles too, that high-wattage, movie star smile of hers that is so beautiful it once upon a time kept me awake at night. She's a gorgeous girl, no doubt about that. But looking into her wide, thickly-lashed eyes, I'm surprised that I don't feel that heady rise in my chest like I used to.

It's probably just that I don't feel things as potently as I did as a teenager. Everything is a big deal when you're that young. And Carmen was my first—well, she was my first everything.

I've missed her. For months I've fantasized about coming back home after the tour and settling down with a girl like Carmen. I know she wants what I want. She wants to commit to someone, to make a home in Madrid with him.

"Estás listo, Javi?" Leo asks. *Are you ready?*

Ready, I say. *Let's start with* "The Girl."

It's my favorite song that we've written so far. I'm still working on the lyrics, but I think I've got the riff down. I ease into the first notes, a complex bit of *toque*—in flamenco, it's the guitar component of the song, in addition to the singing, clapping, and dancing—and the guys join in a beat later.

The music sprawls through the church. Timidly at first, as if the notes are trying the space on for size. But as the song gains momentum, it swells around us, a throaty echo that makes my blood sing. I close my eyes, reveling in the sound, in the feeling of being here, now, playing *my* song with *my* band.

It feels right.

It feels like home.

Finally. *Finally*. I'm here.

I open my eyes. I open my mouth. I start to sing, smoothing out the lyrics as I go. Leo meets my eyes and grins, going to town on his guitar. This, being surrounded by old friends, an old stage, and even older art, is exactly what I needed.

Our nameless band's sound is still evolving. We're not flamenco, exactly; there are no gorgeous dancers twirling in front of us, or old men with big voices trilling about the grief of thwarted love. I'd like to think we're two parts classical Spanish guitar, one part pop, one part rock. I listen to all kinds of music—except, of course, country—and our sound (hopefully) reflects all those different influences.

I'm aware of Maddie's eyes on me as I tap out the beat with my foot. I can't help but get into the song, rocking in my chair, ducking my head in time to the tune. It's impossible for me to hide my passion, especially when I'm on stage. It's one of the things that landed me a spot in Juan's band.

Now, witnessing the way this venue's wildly beautiful acoustics amplify my music, it's all I can do not to leap from my chair and wiggle my butt all over the place.

I'm glad I possess some semblance of self-control. I don't want to make a fool of myself in front of Maddie, even though I think she wouldn't hold my dancing against me. She starts to clap to the beat, a smile splitting her face. Carmen reluctantly joins her a few moments later, her claps contained and ladylike.

I stumble on a note, and like dominoes the guys behind me fall flat too. But looking around at their faces, I can tell they're having a good time. We laugh it off and start in on the next song, loosening up as we go, having fun.

Looks like Maddie's having fun too. She's standing now, hands clasped at her chest. Her smile is still there, bigger than ever. She sways to the beat, moving her hips in a slow circle, shimmying her legs.

Those *legs*. Long, lithe, shapely legs. They go on for days and days, curving into hips that are just—gah. They are everything.

Maddie digs her phone out of her pocket and holds it up, meeting my eyes. She's asking if she can take some pictures. I nod, glad to see that smile of hers stay in place. Before—when she talked about being homesick—I caught a flicker of sadness in her eyes. Deep sadness, the bottomless kind.

I know Maddie has some not so awesome stuff going on in her life right now. I don't need to dig into that stuff. She said she didn't—couldn't—talk about it. But I'm glad I can light Maddie up for a little while at least.

I'm glad I can make her smile. Maybe because her enthusiasm for my band and my city—well, the monastery, at least—makes *me* smile.

Maddie

The second Javier puts his hands on the acoustic guitar, I can tell he knows what he's doing.

His fingers move effortlessly, knowledgeably, along the neck of the guitar, the veins in his forearms and biceps bulging against his skin as he smiles and the band begins to play.

I snap a few pictures of Ricky B. singing, of Leo crooning as he plucks a beat on his guitar. They sound great, if a little rough around the edges, their music a mishmash of rock and pop and more than a little of flamenco. It's impossible not to bob your head to the beat. Their enthusiasm is nothing short of joyous.

Leo was spot on about the acoustics. There may be just four guys and their instruments on stage, but the church makes it sound like there's twice as many guys up there, playing twice as many instruments. It's mind-blowing, listening to a local flamenco-rock-pop band in a five-*hundred*-year-old venue. Definitely one of those "I'm so glad I studied abroad because this would never happen in America" moments.

I aim my phone at Javier last. He comes into focus on the screen, the blurry outline of his shape sharpening, suddenly, into a whole that makes my entire being pulse with awareness. His body sways ever so slightly to the beat while he plucks a complex, flamenco-esque tune. Between notes, his fingers slide up and down the strings, making them gasp.

For several heartbeats I don't take a picture. I just watch him on the screen, my heart working double time, my blood dancing. The features of his face tighten, unfurl, tighten again. It's like he feels every note, feels the song in a way the other guys on stage don't. I've never seen someone look so passionate or absorbed in what they're doing.

And he's good. Like, *really* good.

During the chorus, Leo sings along with Javier. Their voices intertwine, rising and falling as they sing about a girl who left, or maybe it's about them leaving a girl? I'm too distracted to translate the Spanish.

The guys play a slow song, a fun song. A song about the moon and a song about being on the road. I dance, I clap, I take pictures and videos. Beside me, Carmen stands but doesn't dance. Maybe the heels of her boots are too high, and she's worried she'll break her ankle if she tries. Whatever. She's missing out—I don't understand how you could *not* dance to this music. It's sexy and fun, just like the guy who wrote it.

Javier leads the band into a pretty song about a pretty girl (I think). I lower my phone to get a look at the picture I just snapped, lit up on my screen. It's actually all right. Grinning, I look up.

Javier is looking at me. He's grinning too.

The moment our eyes meet, something inside my chest twists.

His gaze is tinged with teasing heat. Desire warms between my legs and squeezes my heart.

I clear my throat, shake my hair from my shoulders. *Stop, stop, stop.* This is ridiculous. I came to the monastery to work on my thesis, not to ogle cute Spaniards I've already slept with.

I don't want Javier. And even if I did, he isn't mine to have. It's obvious he wants María Carmen.

He wants a gorgeous girl who is stable and Spanish. A girl who is capable of giving him el amor—the love—he's looking for.

I am most definitely *not* that girl. Nor do I want to be.

I refocus my gaze on the screen on my phone. Javier is standing now. He rolls his hips, a sassy little smirk on his lips as he works this stripper move. The guy can dance, I'll give him that.

The band plays for a solid hour, but I'm having so much fun it goes by in the blink of an eye. As they step down from the stage, I give them a round of applause so rousing I should be embarrassed—I mean, I'm *this close* to shedding a tear like a pageant mom whose toddler just won her first crown—but I don't care. Javier and his fellow "Gods of Whatever" were awesome.

María Carmen crosses her arms. No clapping for her I guess.

"You enjoying our making music, yes?" Leo asks.

I smile. "You guys were great."

"Photos." Leo points to my phone. "To me show please?"

I slide my thumb across the screen and pull up my photo albums. Leo watches as I scroll through the photos.

"Dios mío." He digs a hand into his hair. "I look like . . . how do you say? Un pendejo."

"Oh, come on," I say. "You don't look like an asshole. You're adorable."

A shot of Javier appears on the screen. Then another. And another. I scroll a little faster. I didn't realize I'd taken so many pictures of him.

"Speaking of assholes—*that* guy is the biggest one I know."

I jump at the sound of Javier's voice. I look to see him hovering at my shoulder, pointing to the picture of him on the screen. Heat returns to my face with a vengeance. I click off my phone, stuffing it in my pocket like I've been caught red-handed.

"Hey," I say, running my sticky palms down the front of my jeans. "Hey, Javier. That was an amazing set."

"We need a lot more practice," he replies. "And a lot more songs. But I'm glad you enjoyed our little jam session. This place is unbelievable, isn't it?"

"I can't get over it," I say. "It's be*yond*."

His forehead is covered in a glistening sheen of sweat. The memory flashes through my mind: him ducking between my legs, my thumb wiping that sweat from his brow as my body rose to meet his mouth.

I bite the inside of my cheek. *Stop.*

I seriously need to stop. Hearing the monastery's other-worldly acoustics solidified my complete and utter fascination with the place. I've been all over Madrid—all over Spain, thanks to a travel class required by our study abroad program —and no palace, garden, or walled city has spoken to me the way The Monastery of the Humble Royals has. I even have the goose bumps to prove it.

I'm also running out of time. In less than two months I'll be heading back stateside, and it will be too late to find the architectural inspiration I came looking for in Spain. I need to focus on my research, *not* on Javier's toe-curling oral sex skills.

Leo and the other guys trickle out a side entrance, leaving me with María Carmen and Javier.

"Really," I say. "Thank you both for having me here today. This place is just . . . there are no words to describe how much I love it here. It sounds kinda cheesy, but I feel like it has so much to say—the monastery. This room. Everything."

Javier sets his guitar case on a nearby seat and ducks into his bomber jacket, flipping up the collar before giving the brass zipper a good tug to get it going.

"It casts a spell on you, doesn't it?" he replies. He looks up, meets my eyes. "I'm glad you were able to come, Maddie."

I look away. That's certainly a change of heart.

"Yes," Carmen says. "We always enjoy welcoming new visitors."

"So, Carmen," Javier says. "Maddie is working on putting together some information on historical preservation for her thesis. I understand the paperwork to apply for research here is something of a bear, but I wonder if we can't help her skirt some of that mess? Perhaps introduce her to your colleagues at the foundation, get her familiar with the work they're doing?"

"Claro." Carmen meets Javier's gaze. "I am happy to help Maddie. I'm the foundation's youngest employee, yes, so I don't have very much influence. But I will see what I can do. Let me make some calls, talk to a few people."

"Thank you," I say. "Thank you so much. I really appreciate your help, María Carmen. Please, let me know if you need anything from me—I have recommendations, term papers, copies of my transcript—I'm happy to hand over any paperwork the foundation wants to see."

Carmen finally looks at me. "I will let you know."

"Awesome." I say.

Javier looks at me, that weird softness in his eyes again.

"You can come here with me," he blurts. "When we're practicing, I mean. The band. Me and the guys. Anytime."

"Wow." I blink. "That's very generous of you."

"We've got practice time here through—what is it, Carmen, December seventeenth? The nineteenth?" he says, looking away.

He palms the back of his neck. Is he blushing? No way he's blushing.

Is he?

"The twentieth," she replies, crossing her arms. "It's the best I could do."

My pulse hiccups. December twentieth is my last day of exams here in Spain. I booked a flight back to Atlanta on the twenty-first, so I'll be home just in time to spend my first Christmas without a family. I have no idea what the holidays are going to look like now that my parents are split, and my dad is . . . well, what he is. We're probably all getting coal and/or therapy from Santa.

The holidays used to be my favorite time of year.

But now, if I could stay in Madrid and just skip the whole damn thing, I would. To say that I'm dreading Christmas is an enormous understatement. My parents put our house on the market back in September. While they haven't gotten any offers yet, there's still a chance they'll sell it before I head back to the States. The thought of waking up Christmas morning in some tiny apartment with only half my family there—ugh, I'd rather run away with the Grinch, to be honest.

"So that means we have a little more than a month's worth

of practices left." Javier is saying. "If nothing else, that gives you quite a few hours inside the church to do your thing, Maddie."

"Awesome," I say. "I mean, I don't want to impose on your practice time or anything—"

"Please." Javier grabs his guitar, and the three of us start walking up the aisle. "The guys and I loved having you here today. Having someone so enthusiastic around definitely helps boost our morale. So far, you're our only fan."

"What!" Carmen says. "Por favor, Javi, I'm a fan too."

"That's right." He elbows her affectionately. "I forget you've been my fan since the beginning."

"And I am an even bigger fan now that you play with Juan," she says. "You're going to go back on tour with him, right, Javi? This new band of yours, it is good, but Juan is *Juan*."

I blink again. *Juan?* Javier was *on tour* with an obviously well-known guy named *Juan?*

"Whoa," I say, falling back. "Whoa, whoa. whoa. Javier, you told me you worked in the music industry. You didn't say you were, like, on tour or anything."

María Carmen throws her head back and laughs. "How like our Javi to be so modest. He does not like people to know he is famous—"

"I'm not famous," Javier grounds out. Oh, he's definitely blushing.

"When you play guitar in Juan Ramos's band, you are too famous."

My heart skips a beat. I stare at him. "Juan Ramos? You played guitar with *Juan* freaking *Ramos?*"

"You know him?" Javier replies weakly.

"Do I know Juan Ramos? Of *course* I know Juan Ramos! The only person more famous in Spain is Jesus. They play his songs, like, nonstop at all the bars and *discotecas* here. Juan's songs, obviously, not Jesus's. I love his stuff. Holy shit, Javier. The concert you said you 'went to' in Atlanta—that was *your concert*, wasn't it?"

I'd pin Juan Ramos as Spain's equivalent of an Ed Sheeran/Adam Levine mashup. He's very talented, a guitarist at heart with a distinct pop-Latin flair. He's a really big deal in the Spanish speaking world, especially in Madrid, where he was born and raised.

Javier shrugs, a small, tight motion. He looks intensely uncomfortable. "It was."

"That's amazing!"

"It was a lot of fun, yes, but I'm glad to be home now."

"If I wasn't so star struck," I say with a sly little grin, "I'd ask you to take a selfie."

"I have a policy against selfies—the angle gives me this ghastly double chin, you see."

"Ghastly. What an awesome word. Although I wouldn't use it to describe your chin."

He arches a brow. His shoulders relax, the stony look in his eyes softening with amusement. "You haven't seen the selfies. Trust me, ghastly is the right word."

Carmen hooks her arm through Javier's as we begin to move again.

"All of Spain talked of nothing but the Juan Ramos tour," she says. "Javier was in the newspapers, on the talk shows. You could not escape his face."

"It was fun," Javier repeats, quickly, "but I'm not that guy anymore. The tour is over. I just want to go back to my life in Madrid. Maybe go somewhere with this new band."

Carmen looks at him. "We'll see," she says.

The way she says it—with quiet, confident possession, her dark brown eyes flashing—makes me think Javier has more than a fighting chance of finding that happily ever after with María Carmen.

Chapter Nine

JAVIER

We wind our way back through the monastery. The light pouring through the windows burns gold now, lending the frescoes on the ceilings and walls a romantic, Ruben-esque air. Outside in the courtyard—a common feature in Spanish architecture, placed squarely in the center of the building—the few leaves still clinging to the branches of adolescent trees shiver in a breeze.

Carmen walks beside me, the warmth of her body seeping into my own. She's just as gorgeous as I remembered—more so, if that's even possible. She's been flirty and forward all afternoon. She's definitely interested in what I have to say, even if she's expressed a lukewarm opinion of my new band.

Why, then, the slight press of disappointment in my chest? Our first encounter after so many years apart is going far better than I dreamed it would. I should be ecstatic with hope.

Only, I'm not.

Not really.

I try to shake off my doubt. I'm probably just annoyed with Carmen for telling Maddie about my C list celebrity past. Not that it matters—if last weekend was any indication, Maddie wanted me for assets other than my bank account and my relationship with Juan Ramos—but still. I kinda liked just being "Javier the scruffy Spanish guy" with Maddie. I *am* Javier the scruffy Spanish guy. I'm not a rock star, a celebrity. Not anymore.

It sounds like María Carmen still wishes I was.

When we reach the exit, Carmen pulls me aside.

"Do you mind if I have a moment only with Javier?" she asks over my head to Maddie.

Maddie nods. "Sure. I'll just peek around for a bit."

"Help yourself," Carmen replies.

I look down at her. "Everything okay?"

"Of course," she says. "You're here. I'm better than okay."

Thank you for helping me get this practice time, I reply in Spanish. *I'm really excited about my new band.*

Carmen smiles. *I'll be excited to see you back on stage with Juan. Seeing you play today made me realize just how talented you are, Javi.*

Javi. Hearing her call me that nickname used to make my heart hurt. In a good way, of course. The intimacy it implied, the comfort, the closeness—God, I loved it.

Now it feels . . . I guess I don't know how it feels.

So how are things with you? I ask.

Job is going well, she replies. *But other things—they're okay, I guess. Pedro works a lot, so I haven't seen him much. It's hard with him putting in so many hours. There isn't much time in his life for other things.*

My pulse trips. So all is not well in paradise with her and the new boyfriend.

I'm sorry to hear that, I say. *I'm sure Pedro will make it up to you.*

Carmen looks up at me. *Maybe. Maybe he will.*

Come on, I say, grinning. *He'd be an idiot not to. And if he doesn't—well, you can just call me, and I'll come kick his ass.*

Oh, please, Javi, she says, cuffing me on the shoulder. *I'm really glad you're home. Thank you for reaching out to me. I'd like to see more of you.*

I'd like to see you too, I reply. *Anytime. Name the time and place and I'll be there.*

She looks up at me, her dark brown eyes framed by long, thick lashes.

There's this new restaurant in Chueca that everyone is talking about, she says. *Want to grab dinner there sometime? Pedro's in New York all month, so I'd love the company.*

I roll my lips between my teeth to keep from grinning. My first encounter with Carmen is going much better than I hoped. A few minutes chatting and we're already making plans to get dinner?

Fuck. *Yes.*

Is it possible she's been thinking about me too? She's a gorgeous girl, accomplished, ambitious, and kind—plus she has a boyfriend—so the chances that she's devoted any time at all to thinking about her ex-boyfriend are slim to none.

Still. The way she's looking at me, intently, warmly, makes me think that maybe I'm not the only one who might want to revisit our shared past.

Yes, I say. *I would like that. Maybe next weekend?*

Maddie

I watch Carmen and Javier from the corner of my eye. They stand close, speaking in warm, happy murmurs.

Maybe Javier is going to find el amor this Christmas after all. I hope he does.

96

I'm about to turn back to a tiny oil painting when Javier looks up, his eyes meeting mine.

He smiles, putting those vagina-slaying dimples on full display.

So his private little interlude with Carmen *is* going well. I resist the urge to give him an air high-five.

"I'm coming!" he says.

"Take your time," I say, waving him away.

"No, no," he replies. "It's late, we should get going."

María Carmen presses a kiss into either of Javier's cheeks. Laughing, she thumbs at a smudge of lipstick she left on his skin.

Until Wednesday, then? she asks. *You have the stage from eight until ten that night.*

"Perfect. Gracias, Carmen."

She turns to me, holding out a gilt-edged card between her first two fingers. "For you, Maddie. Email me your contact information, and I will be sure to pass along any news."

"I really can't thank you enough." I tuck the card into my pocket, pressing my thumb against its pointed edge. *This is real.* This is happening. I might actually swing this thesis thing.

Holy shit!

Javier looks at me, opens the door. "Shall we?"

I wave at María Carmen over my shoulder as Javier and I move into the chilly afternoon. His guitar case dings against the door that closes behind us.

He falls in step beside me on the teeny-tiny sidewalk. "I don't mean to pat myself on the back," he says. "But I believe you fell in love today."

"From what I just saw in there, so did you."

He makes a noise, something between a grunt and a scoff, and moves the case from one hand to the other. "The look in your eyes when you checked out the church—admit it, you're obsessed with the place."

I grin, meeting his eyes. They are glassy from the cold, pools of depthless amber. "I am. I know I keep saying it, but thank you—that was nothing short of magical, listening to you play inside the church. You guys sounded great, and the space is just incredible."

"You're very welcome." His breath puffs around his head in a cloudy halo. "Madrid is my home. I am happy to share its best secrets with anyone who will listen."

The sidewalk narrows ahead of us, disappearing into the side of a medieval building that comes to a point at the edge of the square. I step into the street, not bothering to look, so there's room for Javier and me to keep walking.

"Whoa!" he shouts.

The next thing I know, Javier is reaching for me, pulling me onto the curb. My body bumps into his, and he holds me there against him, fingers wrapped tightly around my arms.

Half a second later a van whizzes by, horn blaring. It misses me by a hairsbreadth.

"Here," he says, a little breathless. He angles himself between the street and me. "Let me walk on the outside, vale?"

He is solid and warm, and he smells like cinnamon mints. His breath, coming fast, tickles the hair at my temples.

"Vale," I say, struggling to catch my breath. "Ohmi*god* I'm an idiot. You'd think that after living here for three months I'd be a little more careful about stepping into the street."

"You'd think," Javier says. "I don't know if you've noticed, but Madrileños drive like lunatics. You've got to take care."

I climb into his car—I move to open my door, but he beats me to the punch—and then he moves to his door and gets in. Javier turns the key in the ignition, coaxing the Range Rover to roaring life.

"Is it just me," I say, teeth chattering, "or did it get colder since we left the café?"

Javier cranks the temperature knob all the way to red. He puts on his aviators. Good Lord those look good on him. I bite my cheek again. *Down, girl.*

"Definitely colder," he replies. "They're saying we're to have a terrible winter this year. Lots of snow."

"Good thing you have this ridiculous safari-SUV thing to plow through the three inches you'll get."

We were told by our study abroad program to expect chilly winters in Madrid but little snowfall. Apparently when it *does* snow, even just a few inches, the city shuts down. Madrid is a lot like Atlanta in that respect. Both cities have relatively warm climates and don't get much snow, so they don't keep many plows and salt trucks on hand to clear the roads.

"Hey." Javier shifts into gear. "I happen to love this ridiculous safari-SUV thing."

"Be honest. You bought it because you thought it'd get you laid."

His grin reveals those dimples again. "You're wrong there. I bought it for the terrible gas mileage and expensive upkeep. Obviously."

"Obviously," I say, flipping down the sun visor against the late afternoon sun.

I wonder how many times, exactly, the Rover has gotten him laid. Probably a hundred. More than that.

Good for Uncle Javier. Maybe one day when I can afford it, I'll buy one for myself.

"Pardon me," he murmurs, reaching across my lap for the glove compartment. He grabs a red tin of cinnamon Altoids —ah, so that's the smell—and opens the lid. He holds it out to me. "Care for one?"

"Sure." I pluck a mint out of the tin. "I've been wondering where that smell came from—the cinnamon."

"I'm a bit addicted," he says around the two Altoids he popped in his mouth. He closes the lid, places it back in the compartment. "I'm trying to quit smoking. I know, I know, it's a completely shit habit. But I picked it up at university, and it's been a nightmare trying to stop. Especially considering the guys I toured with were all smokers. But the mints help—whenever I feel like having a cigarette, I chew on these a couple at a time."

"Is it working?"

"It is. For the time being, anyway." he replies. "I've gone three weeks now without a smoke, so. Yeah. Baby steps."

I settle into my seat, slowly defrosting in the lukewarm heat.

Javier drives through the winding streets with ease. Even when he's driving he's polite: he always gives pedestrians the right of way and patiently waits when an older lady with a cane walks slowly, oh so slowly, across the middle of the street.

The sun burns gold now, the late afternoon light streaming through the windshield. It turns Javier's stubble a coppery shade of brown.

"Why didn't you tell me?" I ask quietly. "About who you are. The Juan Ramos thing. I'd hate to think you assumed I was some sort of sperm-crazed groupie who was out for your child support or whatever."

He scoffs. "Assuming is a terrible thing to do. But it's become a bit of a habit, I'm afraid. I wasn't worried about . . . what you just said, per se, but—"

"It's okay to say that word, you know."

"What word?"

"Sperm. Say it."

"Um."

"Come on. Say it. It's your junk. Why be afraid of it?"

"I'm not."

"Yes you are. Don't you think it's ironic that you have no problem saying *pussy*, but when it comes to *sperm* you go all blushing bride on me?"

"I'm not—what—I'm not blushing—" He's grinning now, chewing on his bottom lip. "Okay, fine, maybe I *am* blushing."

"Yeah you are," I say, grinning back.

"I wasn't worried about my *sperm*. But I do worry, sometimes, that girls only want to hook up with me because I'm a half-assed rocker."

"Half-assed? I don't think playing for Juan Ramos on a worldwide tour is half-assed, Javier."

"Juan Ramos aside," he says, shifting gears. "You know what I'm getting at. I don't like being used."

I nod. "Understandable. It's easy to glamorize that lifestyle, sure, but I imagine it's also pretty isolating. Lonely. Was probably tough to figure out who genuinely enjoyed your company, and who was just in it for the story, or the fame, or the *sperm*."

"Exactly," he says. "A couple of girls—well, let's just say I've been burned more than once. Selling stories to the tabloids, spreading rumors. One day I wake up and find out a girl's filed a paternity suit against me."

"No!" I gasp.

"It was awful. I don't know if I've ever been more embarrassed. The woman and I didn't even have sex. Still. If she had just come to me first—if I had known . . . well. Whatever. She dropped the suit pretty quickly."

"Wow," I say. "Just . . . wow. That'll scar you for life."

"It was awful," he repeats. "So, yeah. I apologize for not telling you about everything sooner. I'm sorry for assuming what I did. That was a dick move. But it was such a refreshing experience with you—being with someone who, you know, was into me for me—I didn't want to ruin it."

"I was into you for your ass, really," I say with a smile, "but I get your point."

"Besides. It's a bit obnoxious, yeah, to introduce myself as Juan Ramos's guitarist. Which I'm not, by the way—I'm not in his band. Not anymore. He asked me to go on tour with him again next year, but I think I want to focus on my own band now."

"Good for you," I say, and I mean it. "I love your new band, even if it has a terrible name and four songs to play. Why haven't you written more, if you don't mind me asking?"

Javier shrugs. "Haven't been very inspired lately. I'm hoping being home for the holidays might make my muse sing."

"Well good luck," I say.

He grins. We stop at a light and he turns to look at me. "Thanks. I'm gonna need it."

The rest of the drive to my señora's apartment is quick. Traffic isn't that bad—it will be much worse tonight, when the city throbs to the techno beat of its infamous discotecas —and Javier zooms across town with ease.

"Up here?" He points to Calle de Villanueva.

"Yep. We're the building toward the end on the left, with the blue door. Hard to miss."

Javier glances out his window as we make our way up the street. "Salamanca. Very nice neighborhood. You girls lucked out—so close to city center, to the parks and museums. It's such a lovely area, isn't it?"

"Lovely." I try the word on for size. "Yes. That's exactly what it is."

The truck hums as Javier slows to a stop in front of a familiar blue door. He puts the truck in park.

"I'm going to say it again." I unbuckle my seatbelt. "Thank y—"

"Don't. It was a pleasure. I enjoyed myself, and hope you did too." A pause. He runs a hand through the hair at the back of his head. "And thank you for your apology."

"Sure," I say. "Yeah. Thank you for yours too."

"So, um. How about I get your number?"

I cock a brow, teasing, even as my heart skips a beat. "My number? That's pretty forward of you, Uncle Pervy. I thought you wanted el amor with María Carmen?"

He laughs. I like the sound of it—masculine, deep, sincere.

"Uncle Pervy just wants your number so he can text you the next time his band has practice."

"Here, I already have my phone," I say, grabbing it from my pocket. "Give me your number and I'll text you so you have mine."

He gives me his number. I save it under the contact name "Uncle Pervy" because, really, it's just too good not to use.

"All right." I type up a text. "Sending it over now."

His phone pings on cue. He swipes his thumb across the screen. "Awesome. Thanks."

He leans over my lap to look at my phone. "Did you save me as Uncle Pervy? Christ, you did! Change it, please!"

This is fun, and part of me wants to stay and engage in more witty repartee with Javier. I'm a little bummed our cultural adventure is over. But I have plans to go out tonight with the girls, and I'd better get a nap in if we're going to stay out until our usual four or five A.M. Which, believe it or not, is pretty early by Madrid standards.

Plus this conversation feels . . . I don't know. A little flirty. And I definitely don't want to be flirting with Javier. He was an orgasmic lay, I'll give him that, but it was a one-time thing.

I don't want anything else. And Javier—he wants *someone* else. Someone to fall for.

So yeah. Flirting with him is stupid for a lot of reasons.

I push my weight against the door, opening it. A gust of chilly November air invades the cocoon-like warmth of the truck. "Really, Javier, thank you so much for letting me tag along today. This was amazing."

"But I'll see you next week, yes?" He rests his wrist on the top of the steering wheel, fingertips brushing the dashboard. He looks at me. "Leo will be terribly disappointed if you don't come to our practice."

"That guy and his—what did he call it?"

Javier shakes his head. "I want no part of that—er, part."

I grin.

He grins, too. "Buenos noches, Maddie. I'll be in touch about Wednesday."

Good night, Javier, I reply in Spanish. I close the door and make my way around the truck.

Javier waits until I'm inside before he drives away. A second later, my phone pings. It's a text from Uncle Pervy.

[praying hands emoji] Please, please change my name in your phone. How old r u? 20? I'm only 4 yrs older than u. Not old enough to b Uncle Pervy [praying hands emoji]

Even as I roll my eyes, I can't help but smile.

I'll b 21 on December 3, thank u very much, I type back. *See u Wednesday, Uncle P.*

Chapter Ten

MADDIE

Wednesday
The Usual Madrileña Spot

I'm the last one to arrive at our weekly Madrileña gathering.

Laura shoulders back her perfectly coiffed waves to give me a kiss on the cheek. "Don't you look cute! I've never seen you wear those leggings before. Are they real leather?"

"Hello no," I reply, taking my customary seat next to Vivian. "I got them at that big department store on Gran Vía for, like, twelve euro. They're actually pretty comfortable. Here, feel them."

Rachel looks me up and down over the rim of her wine glass. "They're super-hot, Mads. You're going to see a boy after this, aren't you?"

"Not a boy," I reply. "A band. It's for my thesis."

"Anonymous sexual encounters with members of a band are part of your thesis?" Katie asks. "If I had known that topic was up for grabs, I would've nabbed it myself. Your research must be quite . . . explosive."

"Earth shattering," Laura adds with a smirk.

"Mind blowing," Rachel says.

Vivian wags her brows. "Oh, there's blowing all right."

I bite back a grin. I don't remember whose idea it was to start calling ourselves the Madrileñas—literally, the Madrid girls—but the name stuck. There's five of us from the Meryton in Madrid program—me, Vivian, Rachel, Katie, and Laura—and while most of us didn't know each other back at Meryton, we've bonded over the trials and triumphs of studying abroad. We meet every Wednesday evening for wine and *tapas* at a cute little restaurant down the street from my apartment. We bitch, we laugh, we drink too much vino tinto de la casa (red wine of the house).

If it wasn't for the Madrileñas, I would've drowned months ago. Just when I think I can't carry the weight of my hurt—just when I think I'm about to go under—they come to the rescue. They're great girls—smart, loyal, and just about as obsessed with sexual innuendo as I am.

"No blowing," I say, waving down the waiter. "Not tonight, anyway. Rafa's uncle has a hookup at a really cool historical venue where his band plays. I don't know if any of you have heard of it—El Monasterio de los Humildes Reales? It's basically a medieval castle that got turned into a monastery, which got turned into a theater. Javier's helped me gain access to it—a friend of his works there. I'm hoping to do some research there, maybe come up with some ideas to use in my thesis."

The Waiter with the Wandering Eye, as we call him, sets a heavy pour of red wine in front of me. I thank him, but like most men with two eyeballs and a penis, he ignores me and stares at Laura instead.

"That still doesn't explain why you're wearing pleather leggings," Viv says. "You sure you don't have a little crush on Uncle Javier? He's really cute. Like, *really*."

Rachel wrinkles her nose. "Uncle Javier? I didn't know you were into older men, Maddie."

I take a sip of my wine. God that's good—a little spicy, deliciously fragrant. I came to Spain never really having drunk wine. We started drinking it because it was the cheapest thing on the menu—cheaper even than water. A couple months later, and now I'm totally obsessed.

"Javier is twenty-four," I say. "Not much older than we are. And I already did some 'research' with him, as you ladies call it, a couple weeks back. Which of course means I *don't* have a crush on him."

"Why? Was it bad?" Katie nibbles on a triangle of manchego cheese. "The boning-slash-research, I mean."

I take a long pull of wine, a pleasant tingle in the back of my knees beginning to stir. "No. It was good. Really good, actually. But he's into this other girl, and I'm—well. I don't go back for seconds. It was definitely just a one-night stand."

"A one-night stand? Really?" Rachel says. "From what you're telling me, this guy is not only super-hot, he's super nice too. I mean. He was a great lay, he's in a band, *and* he's helping you with your thesis? What's not to like? If I were you, I'd be seriously crushing on this hombre, whether or not he's digging someone else."

"Javier got drunk and told me he's 'looking for love.'" I curl my fingers into air quotes. "I'm looking for orgasms. Two completely different things."

Viv tilts her head. "Are they really?"

"For me they are, yes."

"Orgasms are the best," Laura says, holding up her glass. "I had three this morning."

"Three!" We clink glasses. "That soccer stud of yours has a gift."

"The man's got magic hands. And a magic tongue, now that I'm thinking about it."

Ever since the start of the semester, Laura's had this thing for a star soccer player on the Madrid team. "It's the man bun," she said. "I have a weakness."

She also has balls. When she saw said footballer at a bar a couple months back, she had just enough liquid courage to go up to him and say hello. They've been fuck buddies ever since.

"Well," Rachel takes a long pull of wine, "best of luck on your thesis, Maddie. I know you've been stressing about it lately. I have no doubt this monastery place is going to be the break you've been waiting for."

"Let's hope so," I say. "Can you believe we have, like, a month left in Spain? It's flown by."

"Hard to believe we *wanted* it to fly by at the beginning of the semester," Vivian says. "Remember what a head case I was? I couldn't speak the language, I was failing my classes. I just wanted to go back home."

"And now you're staying another semester in Madrid," I say. "A whole year in Spain. Good for you."

Viv smiles. "It's not too late for you sign up for the spring semester, you know. The deadline is the first week of December."

"Trust me, there's nothing more I'd rather do. With everything going on back home—well, let's just say I've enjoyed being a world away from all that shit. But I've gotta get back to Atlanta to check up on everyone, especially my mom. My parents are trying to sell the house, and we have to start packing it up. Plus I don't think my dad is going to pay for me to spend another semester here. I mean, I'd love to come back for grad school when I'm on my own dime. But until then, I don't think I'll be studying in Spain. Which means I have to cram as much research into the next month as I can. The clock is ticking on getting my thesis right."

Katie wiggles her eyebrows. "Then let's hope this Uncle Javier situation works out."

I almost jump when my bag, hanging from the back of my chair, vibrates.

"Speaking of," I say, digging out my phone. Not gonna lie, I thought Javier might've forgotten about me. I haven't heard from him since I saw him last weekend at the Monastery.

Buenas noches, Maddie. My heart does this weird fluttery thing as I read the message from Uncle Pervy. *I hope u r still up for band practice 2nite? I can pick u up.*

I'm actually out with some friends for a quick glass of vino, I text back. *I can just take the Metro and meet u there?*

He responds right away.

Don't want u taking the Metro alone at nite. Tell me where u are and I'll come get u.

I should've known Javier would be a gentleman—he's been nothing *but* a total stud when it comes to manners and kindness—but still, his thoughtfulness takes me off guard.

"Anyone know the address here?" I say.

Rachel looks over her shoulder at the door. "We're on— wait, I think I remember it—Conde de Aranda? Something like that. Why, dear friend, do you ask? Is this Uncle *hombre* of yours coming to join us?"

I roll my lips between my teeth to keep from smiling. "He's coming to pick me up, actually. He has a car, so . . ."

"So," Katie says. "That means you're going to bone in the backseat?"

I let out a sigh of resignation. "I don't go back for seconds, remember?"

Vale, I reply. I type out the address. *Thank u very much 4 coming 2 get me.*

I'll be there in 30, he replies. *Thank u for coming.*

For the next twenty-five minutes I can't sit still. The girls chat about their plans for the weekend—a trip to the Royal

Palace, some clubbing—and we moan about a bullshit paper due Friday in our cultural experience class.

"Whoa," Laura says, looking over my shoulder out the restaurant windows. "Mads, is that him?"

My pulse drums in my ears as I turn around in my seat.

A sinister black Range Rover is pulled up in front of the restaurant, its headlights cutting a lane of yellow through of the darkness. I can hear the hum of the engine, that throaty, slightly threatening rumble.

The light inside the truck is on. A guy is bent over the passenger seat, digging something out of the glove compartment.

His mints. The cinnamon Altoids, the ones that smell like him.

He sits up on his seat and turns his head. His eyes latch onto mine.

My blood jumps, a tingly leap.

Oh, it's Javier all right.

And he is even more handsome-hot than I remember. Hotter even than he was in the videos I took of him playing guitar. The videos I may or may not have replayed a few—er, more than a few—times since this weekend.

He holds up his palm in greeting, a tin of Altoids tucked between his thumb and forefinger. A small smile curves at the edges of his mouth. His stubble—his dimple things—the slick hipster wave of his hair—they are out in full force.

"Ho-ly *shit*," Rachel breathes. "Maddie, if you don't want him, I'll take him. Gladly."

I slide out of my chair, tucking my hair self-consciously behind my ear.

"I'll see you guys in class tomorrow," I say.

Katie shakes her head. "I sincerely hope we *don't* see you in class. Because you're still tied to Uncle Javier's bed, obviously. Vaya con Dios, amiga." *Go with God, my friend.*

"Not gonna happen!" I call over my shoulder.

Javier

Maddie's face is flushed from the cold as she climbs into my truck. I look and see her girlfriends staring at me—us—through the windows of the restaurant. I offer them a smile. They turn away, giggling.

"Hola, Maddie," I say.

She meets my eyes. "Hola," she replies. "Qué tal?" *How are you?*

"I'm very well, thanks," I say. "How about you?"

"Sorry about them." She nods at her table of friends. "They were very intrigued by Uncle Pervy."

"Who wouldn't be?" Turning my head, I lean toward her and brush my lips against her cheeks. I bite back a grin when she shivers, digging her hands into the pockets of her huge puffer jacket. I can smell the red wine on her lips, a spicy, sweet scent.

I'm inundated by a warm awareness of her body. Its shape. The way it moves. The nervous excitement running through it, making her ever so slightly jumpy.

The way my body responds to it, her body. The desire that curls between my thighs. I shift in my seat, suddenly uncomfortable.

I've been looking forward to this evening all week. I'm excited to play with the band, of course.

But the more I thought about it, the more I realized my excitement had a lot to do with Maddie. *Her* excitement is contagious, and even if I was a bit annoyed at first to have her tagging along, now I'm happy to help her. Turns out she's an absolute joy to be around. I loved watching her fall for the monastery, a place *I* fell for years ago. I loved that she loved my new band. I loved how she danced to our music and laughed with Leo. I am all too eager to have her at practice again. If she were a part of this new life I'm building here in Madrid—which she's not, obviously—she'd fit in with my crew pretty well. I dig that about her.

I don't *dig her* dig her, of course. Whether or not she'd fit in in my life here, she has no interest in being a part of it. I may be looking for my happily ever after, but she told me point blank she isn't. And I've had my sights set on María Carmen for so long—I've thought about her so often—I know there's no better girl for me.

Maddie is fire. Hot to the touch, wild. Unpredictable. I've been burned by girls like her before. I've learned my lesson the hard way.

I don't want fire. I want comfort. Connection. Things I know a girl like Carmen is capable of sharing with me, her bougie boyfriend aside.

But judging by the tent I've just pitched in my pants, my traitorous dick begs to differ. Today I woke up with raging morning wood—I don't know why, I felt like I was fifteen again—so I climbed in the shower and began to rub one out. Lately I've been concocting some explicit fantasies about Carmen's curvaceous body, so I thought I'd revisit one or two of them.

But when I closed my eyes and leaned my forehead against the cool tile, I didn't see Carmen.

I saw Maddie. The sated look in her deep blue eyes as she surrendered to her orgasm again and again and again. Her strident confidence in bed. How she met me stroke for stroke. How unafraid she was to say what she wanted, and how unafraid she was to take it.

Take me. And I gave to her, willingly.

I saw her smile, the way her eyes lit up, as she clapped to the beat of my newest song.

My orgasm hit me like a ton of bricks. When the shock-waves subsided, I felt so guilty for thinking about Maddie instead of Carmen, and so fucking confused—I don't want Maddie, and she doesn't want me—I turned the spigot all the way to the right and let the water singe my skin. A punishment, I guess, for indulging in another dead end with another girl who isn't right for me.

Another girl who has no interest in who I am or what I want.

"I hope this wasn't too far out of your way," Maddie says.

I blink, the dark interior of my truck materializing around me.

It was pretty far, actually—with traffic, an extra twenty minutes or so—but I don't mind. It bothers me, thinking about the weirdos and the drunks on the Metro giving her a hard time. I have no doubt Maddie can take care of herself. Still. It makes me feel better knowing she's safe with me. Plus it's freezing outside, and taking my car is a much warmer route than the Metro.

"Not at all," I say, chewing through the mints I just put in my mouth. "I'm always happy to come grab you. Keep you out of the cold a bit longer. Being from Georgia, I bet this weather is something of a shock."

"It's freaking ridiculous," she says. As if to drive her point home, she shivers again. "The heat feels delicious. A little red wine buzz doesn't hurt either."

"Nothing quite like a good vino buzz," I say. "A warm liquid blanket is necessary in Madrid this time of year."

"I brought my big camera." She glances at her bag. "María Carmen and I have been emailing this week. Apparently she has more influence than she let on—she got permission for me to take photographs of the church. I'd like to take some of the band too, if that's all right with you?"

Reaching up, I turn off the light. I shift into first gear. "Of course it's all right. As long as you don't mind making a quick stop at my flat. I've been at the airport all day—my plane needed some work—and I need to grab my guitar."

"Your plane!" she says. "That's right. You have a freaking plane. As if being Madrileño and playing in a band weren't cool enough, you're also a pilot."

I shrug. "My dad was a big aviation geek—he passed on his love of flying to me. I love it, I do. It's very relaxing up there. Peaceful. Kinda neat to see Madrid from another angle, you know?"

"I bet it's so, so cool. You're lucky you get to go up whenever you want. Madrid is so beautiful from the ground—I can't imagine how gorgeous it is from above."

I swivel my head, just a little, and catch Maddie's eye. They're lit up again, her eyes, the blue fiery somehow, like a white-hot lick of flame. She's so passionate in her adoration of Madrid. Madrid, my home, my city. She loves it as much as I do.

She may be a mess. She may have run out on me. But this girl—this fucking girl—there's something wonderful about her, and I can't get enough of it.

It's stupid.

It's a waste of time.

But the thought forms anyway, and suddenly it's the only thought inside my head, big and loud and demanding to be heard.

"Come with me," I say. "Next time I fly, you should come with me. My plane will be ready next week, I think. Maybe you could take some pictures for your thesis—we could fly over the monastery . . ."

"Really?" She draws back, nose scrunched in surprise. It's

cute. "That'd be awesome. I mean, I don't want you to feel obligated—"

"No," I say, too quickly. "Of course I don't feel obligated. I want to. Take you flying, I mean. Of course, if you don't feel comfortable, or you don't want to come or whatever . . . you, um, don't have to. Come with me. Flying. I meant you don't have to come flying if you don't want to."

Christ I'm making a mess of this. I shove a hand through my hair, hoping she can't see the heat creeping up my neck.

Maddie

I bite my bottom lip to keep from smiling. Javier is usually so eloquent, so well spoken in both English and Spanish. I've never seen him flustered like this.

I kinda like it.

"Yes," I say. "I would love to come flying with you, very much. Thank you for offering."

"All right," he says. "This weekend?"

I grin. "All right," I say.

I tell myself I agree to go flying with him for my thesis. Seeing the monastery from above might reveal something about its architecture I haven't picked up on from the ground. It could be the missing piece that makes the whole project come together.

But there's a niggling thread of lightness in the back of my chest, right between my shoulder blades, that has nothing to do with my thesis or the monastery.

It does, however, have a lot to do with Javier's kindness. His adorable shyness as he offered the invitation.

I close my eyes.

Stop it. I need to stop being so stupid.

I take a warrior breath, hoping it extinguishes that light-ness in my chest. It does.

Good.

A few minutes later, Javier pulls up in front of his apart-ment building. Vaguely familiar, it's a cool spot. The flat itself is in an old building, with tall ceilings and huge windows. The neighborhood is just on the edge of fashionable, with tree-lined streets and great bars, restaurants, and shopping.

I wait in the car while Javier runs up for the guitar. When he comes back out a few minutes later, he sees me through the window and smiles. My head's been on swivel, watching people as they pass by with their dogs, their kids, their groceries. I was way too much of a mess that morning I left Javier's to appreciate his 'hood.

"I love it here," I breathe when he climbs in beside me. "What neighborhood is this?"

"Malasaña," he says. "I actually bought the flat sight unseen while I was on tour. I knew I wanted to live in this area, so I jumped when I had the chance. It's turned out to be quite lovely. Sounds a bit cheesy, but there's no place on Earth I'd rather be. When we have more time, I'll show you around."

I look down at my lap, smiling tightly.

Javier will never show me around Malasaña. Not because his offer isn't genuine—he's a gentleman, any offer he makes is genuine—but because I won't ever take him up on it. Touring his neighborhood together sounds pretty date-y to me. Something out of a romantic comedy. I don't do dates, and I definitely don't do romance.

Romance—falling in love—it requires you to stand still. To abandon distraction and face your fear and surrender to it anyway. The last thing I want to do is stand still right now, because then I'd have to face some pretty awful facts. Like the fact that my dad may not love me or my family. Like I may not be loveable at all. I mean, not to hark back to the whole Rafa thing (he *did* fall for my roommate, not me), but what else am I supposed to think?

Moving, doing, coming—they keep me from thinking about that stuff. I need the distraction to keep from hurting. It hurts too much to think about those fears, much less face them.

Still. I can't help but imagine how wonderful touring Javier's neighborhood with him would be. Walking beside him on a pretty afternoon, the low rumble of his voice filling the space between us as he tells me why this hole-in-the-wall bar is his favorite, showing me where he buys his groceries, where he takes his mom for gelato, all while explaining in languid Spanish why he's so in love with this place, the place he comes from.

He's so sure about who he is and where he belongs.

So sure about the beautiful life he wants. The beautiful life he deserves.

I look up at the window. The nighttime rush of Madrid passes by: twinkling lights, pedestrians huddled against the cold, fountains lit up like shimmering beacons in the darkness. My heart swells in my chest. It's so gorgeous here, even at night when it's negative fifty degrees outside and it's a gloomy Wednesday in November. That's the magic of Madrid —even when you're cranky and you're cold and you're confused as hell about who you are and where you're going, it can stop you dead in your tracks with its beauty. Its ageless elegance.

I used to think I deserved a beautiful life too. I wanted to marry the guy of my dreams. I wanted the white picket fence and the pretty dream house and the family.

But now, after my dad set fire to my sense of self, my sense of trust? I'm not so sure. That life seems more like a fantasy —something that doesn't exist, something that could never come true—than a dream. A dream is something that *could* come true with a lot of work and a little luck.

But right now I'm overwhelmed by the amount of work it takes just to keep my head above the water. My dreams—well.

I don't know if I even believe in them anymore.

Chapter Eleven

JAVIER

Traffic is still pretty bad, and it takes us a while to weave our way to city center.

Maddie watches out the window as we drive up to the monastery, lips parted in breathless wonder. I'm worried the dazzle of seeing it for the first time might fade, but Maddie appears as enrapt, as passionate, as she was last weekend. More so.

I hurry to open the door for her, but she's already climbing out of the Defender, her boots landing on the cobblestones with a small *thump*.

"*Balls* it's cold," she says, inhaling a sharp breath through her teeth.

I take a step back, allowing her to walk forward before I move to her right. "I'm on the outside, remember?"

She tugs at her bottom lip. "Right. That time I almost got run over by a van."

"This way they'll hit me first," I reply. The sidewalk is very narrow here. My elbow brushes hers.

"Sorry," I say.

"It's all right," she says. She steps back, putting a bit more space between us.

It's none of my business, what's going on inside Maddie's head. It's none of my business, and I tell myself I'm not interested in digging deeper anyway.

But why does the girl who came apart quite loudly, quite freely, in my arms that night at Ático—the girl who let me touch her and tongue her, the girl who seemed to enjoy every second of it—why does that girl back away when our arms touch?

Leo is waiting for us at the side entrance to the monastery. He's running through the last bit of his cigarette, inhaling deeply. I inhale myself. The second the smoke fills my lungs, I'm hit with longing so potent it makes me dizzy.

Staring down the cigarette, I run my tongue along the inside of my cheek. It's all I can do not to reach out and pluck the cigarette from his mouth, taking it for myself.

"Put. That. Out," I manage through gritted teeth. "For the love of God, Leo, you know I'm trying to quit."

"Sorry, mate," he replies, tossing the cigarette on the ground. He grinds it out with the heel of his boot. "Maddie! Ha-lo! Nice very to have you!"

Maddie allows Leo to wrap his arms around her with a smile, squeezing her eyes shut when he plants an audibly wet kiss on either of her cheeks.

"I wouldn't miss it, Leo," she says. "You guys sound so great up there. The perfect soundtrack to do some research to."

Leo meets my eyes, wags his brows. "The research. Yes. So much of the doing research together."

I step inside the monastery after Maddie, her shoulders relaxing at the sudden burst of heat.

I help Maddie out of her jacket, and when she tries to take it from me, I wave her off, and tell her to start taking her photographs. As we head farther into the monastery, I grab Leo by the arm, letting Maddie walk a few steps ahead of us with her enormous camera in hand.

Leo, I murmur. *What the hell was that? You're scaring Maddie with your weird innuendo.*

He looks at me with a teasing gleam in his eye. *I see the way you look at her, Javi,* he says in Spanish. *She's beautiful. I hope you get to do a lot of* ree-search *with her, whatever that is. It sounds dirty. Is it dirty?*

I hold my head in my hand, letting out a small sigh of exasperation as we climb the stairs. *I wasn't looking at her like . . . like that.*

You can lie to yourself, Javi, he says. *But you can't lie to Leo.*

I came back to Madrid for Carmen, I say. *I want Carmen. That's who I've been looking at. Didn't you notice last time at practice?*

He shrugs. *No. I didn't.*

The gallery is lit up like there's an honest to goodness concert tonight, the frescoes and sculptures and six-hundred-year-old tapestries taking on new dimension in the soft gilding of the chandeliers above.

Maddie is already at the top of the stairs. She holds the camera to her face, one hand curved around the lens while the first finger of the other clicks away, the camera emitting a snap every time she takes a photo. Right now she's getting up close and personal with a green marble column that supports a monumental gilded arch, bending her knees to get a better shot.

Her legs. My gaze moves up and down, down and up the shapely length of her legs. Her heeled booties make them look even longer. She's wearing these super tight leather legging things that leave literally zero to the imagination. I can see everything. *Everything.* They make her ass look— Christ help me, it's perfect.

María Carmen, I tell myself. Think of Carmen. Carmen, the girl you've been fantasizing about for the past six months.

The girl you came back to Madrid for.

Think of Carmen and stop staring at this American chick's ass.

Maddie looks up, meets my eyes. Smiles. Excitement lights up her face, her eyes glittering with that heat again. I tighten my grip on the plastic handle of my guitar case.

"Incredible," she says.

"Yes." I mount the top step, my gaze sweeping up the length of her legs one more time. "Incredible."

I'm glad I have the band and practice to distract me. Otherwise I'd have a tough time fighting an inconvenient boner right now.

I swallow, hard, and hold my guitar in front of my crotch as I make my way toward the church.

Practice goes much more smoothly this time around, thank God. I actually put my music to paper for the first time in forever—before, we were using recordings I'd made on my phone while I was on tour—so now the guys have something solid to work from. We even manage to write the riff of a new song, with sexually explicit lyrics provided by—who else—Leo.

Every so often, I look out into the church, dimly lit, to see Maddie taking notes in front of the organ, a side chapel, a window.

It's fun watching her. She taps her foot in time to the beat as she scribbles in her notebook. I even catch her mouthing some of the lyrics, bobbing her head as she sings. I wonder what she's thinking, if the monastery is capturing her imagination the way it captured mine when I first came here.

I guess I watch her for a while, because all of the sudden

Ricky B. is banging on his drum, a sharp, startled sound, and I look back to see him and the rest of the band scowling at me.

"You are doing the look again," Leo says, a smug little smirk curling at the edge of his mouth. "And it is the look *like that*."

"No, it's not," I growl. "I don't know what you're talking about."

But ten seconds later, Maddie catches me looking too and she smiles, shouting something in Spanish about how our music is inspiring her thought process, can we please keep playing?

I smile too. I smile so hard I feel like it's splitting my face in half. She really does dig my music.

I can't ever imagine Carmen calling to me from across the church for more of my music. My old music—the music I played with Juan—maybe. But my new stuff? No way. During our chat on the phone the other night—I've been calling her a bit lately—she made clear she's less than enthused about me and my nameless band. I even invited her to come watch us again, but she declined the invitation—politely, of course. I told her I'd call her at ten tonight after practice is over.

We wrap up with "The Girl" and after that the guys pack up their instruments and head out with promises they'll learn the new music by this weekend. Leo lingers a bit until his kinda-sorta booty call texts him, and then he exits the building like it's on fire.

Maddie is standing by the organ, clutching her notebook to her chest as she looks up at it.

"I can play that, you know," I say, stopping to stand beside her.

She jumps at the sound of my voice, dropping her pen.

"Sorry!" she yelps. We bend down at the same time. Our fingers brush as we reach for it, a small, singeing touch. It's fleeting, our contact, but my skin pulses with the heated aftershocks of it nonetheless.

Heat I haven't felt in a long time.

I look up. So does she. We're crouched on the floor, our faces less than two inches apart. Her eyes flick to my lips. I could be imagining it, but her gaze darkens, gleaming with a sharp edge of interest.

Her nostrils flare. She breathes in. Breathes out. It sounds like the ocean, her breath, battering against the bulkhead of whatever it is she resists inside her.

The scent of her coconut shampoo fills my head, blocking out anything else. Any rational thought.

Any thought other than *holy shit I want to kiss this girl. Now. I want to kiss her hard and I want to kiss her well and I want her to cry into my mouth when she comes. When I make her come again and again and again.*

Maddie is wearing pink lip gloss, the same shade that clung to her lips that night at Ático. She's as sexy tonight in her leggings and sweater as she was in that teeny-tiny joke of a dress.

Sexier, because I know her now. I know she loves this monastery and she loves my band. I know how much she's enjoying my world here in Madrid.

Is there anything sexier than that?

But then she blinks and I blink and suddenly I'm aware of how close we are. We're way too close. I'm too close to a girl who is definitely not the girl I want.

I want Carmen. I want a forever girl. And I'm not doing myself any favors by indulging in a little heated eye contact with a twenty-year-old American who's leaving Madrid in a month's time. Not when I'm determined to settle down here, make a home with someone who's in it for the long haul.

I also told Carmen I'd call her at ten, so I really should get going. You definitely don't want to be late for any kind of date with her.

"Got it." I swipe the pen off the floor and leap to my feet a little too enthusiastically. I hold out my hand to help her to her feet. She doesn't take it.

"Thanks," she says. She grabs the pen, careful not to let her fingers touch my hand.

Good. It's a good thing Maddie keeps her distance.

Even if my pulse thuds in disappointment, I know it's a good thing Maddie and I stick strictly to business. The thesis-kind of business, obviously, not the kind you engage in without your pants on.

But yikes we were really good at that kind.

Not that it matters.

I want Carmen, and Maddie wants . . . well. She wants what she wants. It's not me, and it's not love.

I clear my throat. Maddie crosses her arms. A beat of awkward silence passes between us.

"So you can play this thing, huh?" she asks at last, glancing up at the organ.

"No," I shake my head, scoffing, and shove my hands into the front pockets of my jeans. "I was just fooling with you. I definitely can't play the organ. I mean. Wouldn't learning it be kind of a bad idea? It'd be like picking up Latin. Completely pointless."

"Not pointless." Maddie meets my eyes, fighting a grin. "They still use these things a lot, actually. I'd learn how to play it for sure."

"Yes, but you're a history nerd, so you don't count."

"Point taken," she says. She looks back up at the instrument. "It's just so . . . big. Monumental. Ha! That's what she said."

I grin. "Now who's the perv?"

"Oh, you're not getting off the hook that easily, Uncle P."

I glance at her notebook. While her handwriting is so pretty it looks like a computer font, the notes themselves are a bit messy. Lots of circled passages, arrows pointing up, arrows pointing down, arrows connecting a line at the top of the page with one at the bottom. There are a few drawings too, rough but well-constructed. It's very Word-document-meets-Jackson-Pollock, if you will.

I should go. I have to call Carmen.

But I realize I want to linger with Maddie a bit longer.

"Any light bulbs go off tonight?" I ask.

Maddie lets out a sigh, shaking her head. "Nothing yet. I'm still absorbing it all. It's really wonderful that there is so much to see—so much to talk about, you know? But at some point—if I want to use the monastery in my thesis—I'm going to have to narrow my focus. Pick one thing and run with it."

"Right. The picking isn't going to be easy," I nod. "I'm a bit of a history nerd myself—"

"I've noticed." She smiles.

"And I've noticed that everything in this building fascinates you. The architecture. The acoustics. The music played here. The art and the sculpture and, well . . ." I look up at the organ. "This dinosaur of an instrument. It's all worth studying, but you'd need several lifetimes for that. So you have to choose. Only once you pick, it will be difficult not to imagine being more inspired by what you didn't pick."

"Yes. Exactly. Grass is greener kind of thing."

I meet her gaze. My pulse skips a beat at the flash of interest in her eyes.

Carmen. I need to think about Carmen, dammit! Her eyes are pretty too. Really pretty.

But I've never seen them light up the way Maddie's do.

"We should get going," I blurt.

"Oh. Yeah, yeah, definitely," she says, the faintest blush

reddening her cheeks. "Sorry. It's easy for me to forget myself when I'm—um. When I'm here. At the monastery, I mean. With you—you and the band and everything . . ."

"No worries," I say.

That's a lie. I am worried.

Worried about the way Maddie looked at me. Really *looked*. With intention and interest.

I'm worried she might have seen the same things in my eyes when I looked back.

Which is ludicrous, because there are several very good reasons why I shouldn't be looking at Maddie like that. Maddie, the girl who prefers drama and one-night stands. Maddie, the girl who doesn't care to know who I am or what I want.

Maddie, the girl who couldn't be more different from Carmen, the girl I *do* want.

I came back to Madrid to build a home.

Maddie came to Madrid to run away from hers.

Even if I wanted her—which I don't—we'd never work. Period.

End of story.

Maddie

Javier and I are both quiet on the way home. I'm glad it's dark so he can't see how red my face is; it's practically on fire.

Something happened between us tonight at the monastery. Something changed, shifted.

And it's my fault.

I told myself I wasn't interested in Javier. I'm not interested in *anyone*. I'm definitely not interested in letting anyone in—letting them see how shitty I feel about myself and my life in general these days. No one wants to deal with that ish.

Least of all Javier Montoya, señor-I'm-looking-for-love sappypants. I have no doubt he and María Carmen will ride off into the Spanish sunset in the very near future to make beautiful memories and even more beautiful babies.

Javier's got his shit together. He knows what he wants, and it certainly isn't me.

Tonight I kept my eyes on the prize and focused on research for my thesis. But then Javier started opening doors for me and laughing at my jokes and checking me out when he thought I wasn't looking. He smiled at me from the stage and protected me from Leo's pelvis and asked me to go flying with him.

He made me feel like a million bucks. Like I was *worth* a million bucks. Like I was interesting and intelligent and sexy.

I haven't felt that way in a really, *really* long time. And honestly? It was wonderful. So wonderful I allowed myself to bask in the feeling longer than I should have. I let down my defenses, and somehow, in the space of two freaking hours, Javier managed to work his way inside my skin.

He saw it in my face—I know he did—when I looked at him after we almost-nearly kissed. He saw the longing I feel, stupidly, for him.

Longing I knew he doesn't feel for anyone but Carmen.

I embarrassed him, and I embarrassed myself too. He's just trying to be nice, just trying to do his nephew a favor. And here I am, mooning at him like a lovesick teenager. Ick.

I leave Javier with a quick "hasta luego" ("see you later") before bounding up the stairs to my señora's apartment. My heart pops around inside my chest like a panicked ping-pong ball. Viv is gone. Rafa's parents are out of town, meaning she'll be spending the night at his apartment. It's just me and our tiny trundle that Vivian and I affectionately dubbed "the marital bed."

I set my stuff down, pace the room as I shoot off some texts, then fold some clothes. I can't sit still. I can't stop thinking about Javier, the way he smelled like cinnamon mints and soap. The way he made me feel like . . . like everything was possible, I guess.

Finally I throw open my laptop and sit down at the rickety desk beside the bed. I pull the notes I took tonight out of my bag and set them next to the laptop. Then I open a blank Word document and pluck the cap off a pen with my teeth.

The only thing that might take my mind off Javier is writing this goddamned thesis. Medieval architecture thrills me *almost* as much as Javier's deliciously broad shoulders do.

Almost.

I begin to type.

I slipped up tonight. I can't—I won't—let it happen again.

Chapter Twelve

JAVIER

Saturday Night

María Carmen slides into the chair I hold out for her, offering me a high-wattage smile in thanks. Making my way around our table, I glare at the man across the aisle who's been ogling Carmen since we arrived an hour ago for cocktails.

I'd forgotten what it's like being out with her. The stares, the cat calls, the universal and voracious interest in her every move. I lost count how many fistfights I'd gotten into over Carmen at bars and discotecas when we were younger. I hated the way men felt it was their prerogative—their right—to look at my girlfriend like she was a piece of meat.

Even now my hands curl into fists underneath the table, the hair at the back of my neck prickling with testosterone-laced awareness. I don't fight anymore, but that doesn't mean I can't shoot a "back the fuck off" look at every guy who passes.

"Javi," Carmen is saying. "Javi, you don't have to do that."

She's still smiling as she watches me, her bright red lipstick making her teeth appear fluorescently white.

"Do what?"

"Toss those daggers in your eyes at everyone in the restaurant. Really, it's all right."

"It's not all right," I growl, picking up my menu. "How does Pedro feel about the way other men look at you?"

She shrugs. "I'm not sure he even notices."

That's bullshit, I say in Spanish. *He's your boyfriend. How could he not care?*

Javi, the cursing—please. She frowns at me.

Sorry, I murmur. *I just don't understand how it doesn't drive him crazy.*

I remember it drove you crazy, she says. She's smiling again.

What can I say? I smile back. *I was crazy about you.*

In the low light of the restaurant, her eyes are soft, almost black. *I was crazy about you too. I miss those days. We had a lot of fun together, didn't we?*

I feel myself leaning into her pull, and for a second I think she's leaning toward me too, her perfume—*orange blossom*, she'd called it, some fancy stuff from London—tickling my nose.

Some of the best times of my life, I say.

Me too, she says.

I pass Carmen the wine list, and she orders a bottle of something French that sounds very expensive. I guess I also forgot how . . . well, pricey her taste is. Even when we were teenagers, she liked her fancy things. I remember blowing every single Euro I earned one summer as an usher at a local cinema on a sapphire and diamond necklace for her. I don't think she even liked it—I saw her wear it maybe once—but I remember how proud I was, how nervous, to buy something so nice for my girl.

The restaurant is packed and gets louder and louder as the hours pass. By the time we finish with our food and the wine, we're leaning so far over the table Carmen and I are practically in each other's faces, the only way we can hear each other. We talk about our jobs, our parents, our past. I make her laugh, the familiar sound making my chest swell.

I've been thinking about you, I say, my sudden bravery egged on by a pretty decent buzz. *While I was on tour, I mean. I thought about you. I'm glad you're doing so well at the monastery— I'm so proud of you for pursuing your passion. And I hope Pedro is making you happy.*

Carmen looks at me for a long minute. Her eyes darken. My heart thumps in my chest.

I am very happy at the monastery, she says. *But Pedro . . . he tries. He does. But I don't know if we'll ever be happy together. It's strange, but being with him has made me feel lonely. He's gone so much, and when he's with me, he's so preoccupied with work . . .*

Carefully, slowly, she trails her hand across the table and places it over mine.

I look down at her hand, the perfectly manicured nails, the pretty rings on her fingers. I wait for my pulse to leap, for sparks of energy to ignite from this place where skin meets skin.

I wait, in other words, for overwhelming need to bowl me over. The kind of need I felt when I woke up to find Maddie, naked, flushed pink with sleep, in my bed. Need so powerful, need wound so tightly, it swallowed me whole.

I wait.

And keep waiting. And while I wait, I find myself thinking about Maddie.

Stop being a dickwad, I tell myself. *The girl you've been pining over like a lovesick idiot is sitting right across from you, telling you exactly what you wanted to hear, and all of the sudden you're thinking about someone else?*

What the hell is wrong with me?

"Javi," Carmen asks, "are you all right?"

I blink, looking up. The image of Maddie's fiery blue eyes

dissolves into Carmen's brown ones. They're wide with concern.

Sorry, I say. *I'm sorry about Pedro. I hate that you feel that way.*

Her fingers curl around the edge of my palm. *I've thought about you too, Javi. Ever since you called me that first time a few months ago, I've thought a lot about you. I've missed you. I can't tell you how happy I am you are home.*

I swallow, hard. I'm not a homewrecker. Never have been. It's wrong to steal another guy's girlfriend. That definitely wasn't my intention when I agreed to come to dinner with María Carmen. She's taken, and I intend to respect that.

But what she's saying—the things she's doing—they make me think she might not be Pedro's girlfriend much longer.

Which means I might have the opportunity to make her *my* girlfriend. To settle down with her in my flat in Malasaña and build the home I've always dreamed of with her. This is what I came back to Madrid for.

I should be thrilled.

I should be smiling so hard my eyes water.

But I'm not, and I don't understand why.

"My plane is fixed," I blurt like an idiot. I resist the urge to pull my hand away from her grasp.

Carmen's grin fades. "Your plane? You mean that rickety death trap?"

"I've had it completely refurbished," I say. Her disdain stings more than it should. "I could take you flying if you'd like."

No thank you, she replies in Spanish. *I have too much to live for! Especially now that* you *are back in Madrid. So tell me more about being a rock star on tour with Juan Ramos. I bet you can't wait to get back on the road together. He's already announced his next tour, right?*

I drain my wine glass.

It's stupid and it's rude, I know, but I can't help but wish it were Maddie sitting across from me instead of María Carmen. She wouldn't want to talk about Juan, or the tour, or my interview with Ellen (yes, *that* Ellen) a few months back. She'd want to talk about my new band. Art. Architecture. All things Madrid.

I'm starting to think that Carmen loves what I was. The rock star. The celebrity.

But Maddie—Maddie couldn't care less about that guy. She loves who I am. Except Maddie doesn't love me at all.

I look up and meet Carmen's eyes. They blaze with interest. Arousal. Things I'm not sure I feel for her.

Fuck.

I am so fucked. I don't know what's happening to me.

Maddie

The Next Day

Javier guides the Range Rover into a lot at El Aeropuerto de Cuatro Vientos—Four Winds Airport—and pulls up the parking brake.

I glance out the window to see a wide concrete expanse dotted with a few jets and dozens of planes. Very small planes. Some of them are downright tiny.

I've always liked to fly. But I have enough sense to know a ride on one of these hobbit-sized prop planes is a much different experience than cruising at altitude on a commercial jet.

"You all right?" Javier asks, hand stilling on the door handle.

I swallow. "You know what you're doing, right?"

"I do," he says. "People tend to get a bit nervous when they see how small the planes are. But the weather is excellent, and we'll have a nice, smooth ride. I promise you're in good hands."

I look at him for one beat too long. Sure, I'm nervous. Nervous about flying in a plane that looks like it belongs to Barbie and Ken.

But I'm also looking because I really, really like what I'm seeing right now. It's all lovely, and enticing: the sinews of Javier's neck, the pointed indent that bisects his top lip, the way the rounded frames of his aviators set off his square jaw.

So lovely it's making me dizzy.

I take a warrior breath, let it out. I promised myself I wasn't going to slip up today. Not again.

But my body's reaction to him, to *his* body, to the things he's saying, keeps getting away from me. Everything is just so easy with him. Comfortable, deliciously so, like my favorite pair of broken-in jeans.

"All right," I say, shoving open my door. "Let's do it."

The sun, a pinprick of blaring white in a wide-open November sky, is warm on our faces as I walk beside Javier. I'm not a petite girl, not by any means, but being next to him makes me feel a lot smaller than I usually do. It's not uncommon for me to be taller than a guy, especially in heels.

I could wear six-inch hooker heels and still I'd be shorter than Javier.

After a quick stop in an office cluttered with maps and computer screens, Javier and I head for a bright blue hangar. A *very* small plane—like, the smallest I've seen yet—is parked outside the hangar, its white paint gleaming in the early afternoon sunlight.

"Is that yours?" I ask.

A proud smile splits his face. "It is."

I take one warrior breath, then another.

"You sure you're all right?" he asks, opening the door for me.

"I don't know, Maverick." I look at him, squinting through my sunglasses. "Are you as good at flying planes as Tom Cruise is?"

Javier's smile deepens, a devastating, boyish flash of white teeth. "Trust me, Goose, you have nothing to worry about."

Oh, oh, *oh*. I have a lot to worry about when he smiles at me like that.

I look away.

He does a pre-flight inspection of the plane, lowering flaps, running his palms along its sides and underbelly. He motions me over and together we peer into every crack and crevice, his voice steady as he explains each part and its function.

"What year is your plane?" I say. "It looks pretty new."

"It's a 1965," he replies. "Just gave her a bit of a makeover. New paint, new interior."

"1965," I say. Another warrior breath. "Wow. That's vintage. Like, really vintage."

I climb into the plane's miniscule cockpit, my hands shaking as I tug my seatbelt across my chest. Javier climbs in beside me. In the tiny space he looks even bigger—his thighs, thick, muscled, seem to take up the whole cockpit.

Speaking of cockpit—I try to think of a lewd joke to keep my mind off the fact that I'm leaving the Earth in a tiny tin can that is older than my mother, but no dice. I'm too nervous.

Javier's eyes move over me, my jacket. "Are you warm enough? I've got extra blankets in the back."

"Um," I say, heat spreading through my chest at his sudden attention. "I think I'll be all right. Thanks though."

"Vale. Let me know if you change your mind—it can get a little chilly up there."

He reaches across the cockpit and clips a map onto the dashboard in front of me. His arm brushes my knee.

Sorry, he says in Spanish. *It's a little tight in here.*

Don't worry about it, I reply.

Your Spanish is very good, he says. *Are you majoring in it?*

Minoring, I reply in my best Madrileño accent. *In high school, I spent a summer in Colombia. I was pretty fluent then. I'm rusty now, but I'm getting there. Slowly.*

I think you're being modest. You're definitely fluent. Your Spanish is excellent. Here, he hands me a pair of enormous headphones with a Madonna-esque microphone attachment. *Put these on and let me know if you can hear me.*

I slide them onto my head. They're too big. I reach up to adjust them, but Javier is already there, his fingers working to tighten the plastic headband at the crown of my head.

"Better?" he asks, pulling away ever so slightly away.

He's already got his headphones on, and his voice sounds even deeper through my own, punctured by a small, radio-like cackle. His hands are still on my head, waiting for instruction.

My heart skips a beat. His face is mere inches from mine, close enough for me to duck my head and press my lips to his if I wanted. I can see a tiny ragged scar that puffs up between stubble in his left cheek, just where jaw angles into chin. He's so close.

And he smells *so* good. Like cinnamon, a hint of clean, simple man-soap.

I remember the taste of his kiss, the patience and the thoroughness of his lips as they moved over my mouth, my body. I'd have to be dead not to want another kiss like that.

Stop. I don't want to feel these silly, squishy things. I really, really don't.

"Yes," I say, turning away from him. "Thank you."

"Goose." Javier drops his hands, a grin playing at his lips. "It's going to be all right."

It could be all the warrior breaths I've been taking, but my pulse slows, just a bit. His confidence is calming.

"I'm ready," I say.

"C'mon. Let's have some fun."

Javier proceeds through a complex scheme of pressing buttons and clicking dials into place. The computer blinks awake. At last he pulls on a red lever at the bottom of the control panel, and the propeller at the nose of the plane cranks to jerking, heaving life. The little steering yokes—there are two of them, one in front of Javier, one in front of me—surge forward, jiggling. The entire plane throbs in time to the engine.

Murmuring to flight control, he puts his hands on the yoke. I put my hands in my pockets, my sweaty palms sticking to the fleece lining.

Javier guides the plane onto the runway using the pedals at his feet. I listen as the guys in the tower give us the go ahead for takeoff.

My heart, meanwhile, takes off at a sprint.

I lied. I am not ready. I do not want to fly the friendly skies. I want to hole up in my bedroom, safe from certain death, safe from Javier and his smile and his general excellentness, and work on my thesis.

"Javier—" I begin, but he's already begun to accelerate the plane, the runway widening before us with increasing speed. We hurtle over bumps, my thoughts growing more frantic with each passing thump.

Ohmigod what was I thinking, ohmigod I am going to die, ohmigod, ohmigod, ohmi*god.*

Javier tilts the yoke toward his chest, and I close my eyes as the plane leaves the ground, the engine groaning with effort. A shudder jolts the plane as gravity pins me to my seat, the combination causing my stomach to drop.

"Ohmigod!" My eyes fly open. My hand jerks out of my pocket, possessed, and latches onto Javier's knee, giving it a tight squeeze.

Smiling, Javier turns to me. "You all right?"

I can hear my breathing in my headphones.

"Getting there," I manage.

"It'll smooth out in a minute. Look." He points over his shoulder. "There's Madrid. Once we get a little higher we'll have a better view."

I sit up in my seat and lean a little toward Javier. I watch through his window as the city begins to take shape, buildings rising out of an arid landscape.

For a minute I forget my hammering heart and my academic agenda. Instead I marvel at the raw beauty of the Spanish countryside, at the fact that I am on a *plane* with a handsome-hot Madrileño on a Sunday afternoon. That I am here, now, hundreds of feet above the earth and all the unpleasant things that wait for me down there.

The plane levels out and so does my heart rate. When I was little, I was terrified of natural disasters—too much CNN, I guess—and I lived in fear of earthquakes, tornadoes, even forest fires. I loved to fly because I imagined I was safe from all those things so high up in the air.

I feel like that now—that sense of lightness, of relief. Surrounded by the hum of the engine and the scent of Javier's cinnamon Altoids, I relax for the first time in what feels like forever. No forest fires to worry about, or warring parents.

It's really nice.

I let go of Javier's leg. "Sorry," I say. "That was definitely weird of me."

"What? The groping?" he replies with a grin. "Not weird at all."

"It wasn't a grope. It was more of a squeeze."

"A squeeze. Wouldn't that be worse? Or better. Probably better, right?"

I level him with a mocking glare. "Okay, Uncle Pervy, back to the controls."

He laughs, a sound that fills the tiny cockpit and makes what's left of my anxiety evaporate. I melt into my seat, the warmth from the sun seeping through my jacket.

"It's so beautiful." I sigh, turning to look out my own window. "And so big. You really appreciate how huge Madrid is from up here."

"I am from Madrid," Javier replies, "born and raised, and I still don't know half of it. There's always a new neighborhood to explore."

The sky is poignantly blue, a striking contrast to the rainbow of reds and creams and yellows that make up the city below. I pick out Retiro Park, a large green square, the water of its enormous artificial lake glittering in the sun. And there, one street over from the park, is my señora's apartment building.

Javier guides the plane in a long, low swoop, giving me an even closer view of the building. I can't see its signature blue door—we're too high up for that—but I can see people, tiny, slow-moving ants, making their way up my street. Couples holding hands, a woman pushing a stroller, children racing in front of their parents. All these families—they look so happy from up here. So connected, so engaged in a way I haven't seen before.

"Who knew that people watching from five thousand feet was so fun?" I say, turning around to grab my camera out of my bag.

Javier turns his head, nodding at my window. "Over there —do you see the steeple roof of the church? That's the monastery."

My heart skips a beat when, looking out the window, I see a familiar roof glinting in the sunlight, its spire no bigger than a toothpick from up here. I aim my camera at the rambling group of connected buildings that compose the monastery and begin clicking away, each frame telling a different story, a new story, one I don't know yet.

"It looks so much bigger from above." I squint through the viewfinder. "Much more medieval, with the irregular angles and all the different buildings. There are no straight lines!"

"Not back in the fifteenth century, anyway," he says.

I keep clicking. "This is unbelievably cool, Javier. I mean —look at the layout of the different courtyards. I wonder what they were all used for? Perhaps some of them were kept private. You know, for the nuns' private meetings."

"You've got quite the imagination."

I look at him, still grinning. "I do." Turning back to the window, I take a few more photographs. "You can really see the progression of architectural styles as they added on to the original medieval structure—see the dormers there, and the domed roof of the gatehouse? Be still my beating heart!"

Javier laughs. He circles around the monastery a few more times. Assured that I'm done taking pictures, he asks, "Do you want to lose gravity?"

I tuck my camera back into its case. "Lose gravity?"

"Yes. Like this." He makes a swooping motion with his hand.

"Um," I say, stowing the case behind my seat. "That sounds . . . interesting?"

"Let me try it just once. If you don't like it, I promise won't do it again."

"Is that what you tell all the girls you hang out with?"

"Only the pretty ones," he says with a wink.

"I'll let you try it if you promise never to wink at me again."

"I promise," he says, and does it again anyway.

Javier pulls the yoke towards him, the plane nosing up, up, the blue sky filling the windshield as the blood gathers at the base of my skull. I grip the seat on either side of my legs, holding on for dear life when Javier guides the yoke back down.

The plane rolls forward, like we're cresting a big hill.

Then it plunges down, my stomach pressing against the back of my throat like a fist as the seatbelt cuts a fiery sash across my torso. My hands dart above my head, pressed to the ceiling as if I can slow our fall. I scream, I curse, I make garbled drowning noises. In my headphones I hear Javier say *wooohooo,* followed by deep, gleeful laughter.

We keep falling, and I keep screaming. There's a rush inside me, a great gust of feeling that scatters my thoughts in a thousand different directions. For a minute I feel weightless, suspended in time, my mind a blessed blank.

Javier pulls the yoke back toward him, and we are suddenly level again, cruising pleasantly through smooth air.

And then something strange, and wonderful, happens.

I burst into giggles. Careless, skipping giggles, the kind that make you feel light as air, that make your ribs hurt.

"You all right over there?" Javier asks, ducking his head to look at me.

"That was terrifying," I wheeze. "And fucking awesome. Can we do it again?"

He grins, the light catching on his stubble, burnishing it red. He pulls the yoke toward him, and the plane starts climbing.

Chapter Thirteen

MADDIE

By the time we land, I can barely breathe, my face hurts from so much smiling. We flew until the plane was practically out of gas, talking and laughing and losing gravity the whole time. The late afternoon sun is dimming, our shadows long and dark as Javier and I walk across the parking lot. His is longer than mine, broader. The flaps of his bomber jacket, unzipped, move in a small breeze. His aviators are hooked into the collar of his shirt.

Good *Lord* is he sexy.

I bite my lip. Look away.

"I hope you enjoyed yourself, Maddie," he says. "I was starting to feel a bit queasy at the end there, but it was worth it, don't you think?"

"Totally worth it. Really, thank you for taking me up with you. I haven't had that much fun in a long time. The losing gravity thing—oh my God, I loved it." I focus my gaze on my feet. "I bet María Carmen loves it too, doesn't she?"

Javier's boots strike sharp notes on the concrete as he walks. "She doesn't, actually. I took her flying once, back

143

when I first got my pilot's license—I was twenty—and she never wanted to go back up with me again."

"Oh," I say.

"Yeah," he says.

He opens the door of his truck for me. It's a simple gesture, but warmth fills my chest nonetheless. Why does he always have to be so excellent?

"You know, I can open doors for myself," I say. "I've been doing it for twenty years now. I think I have the hang of it."

"Of course you can open doors for yourself. I'm sure you do it all the time when I'm not around."

I bite back a grin.

"Which means when I *am* around," he continues, grasping the edge of the door and leaning over me, "you should let me do it for you. If only so I can make you uncomfortable with my kind and gentlemanly ways."

"I'm not—" I roll my lips between my teeth. "I'm not uncomfortable."

"Yes, you are. Do guys back at Meryton not hold doors for you?"

I scoff. "Yeah freaking right. I mean, there are definitely exceptions. But no. Guys are not that nice."

He holds out a broad, blunt-fingered hand. "Some of us are."

Without thinking I take it, stepping up onto the baseboard before I climb into the truck.

Tus manos, he says and steps toward me, brow furrowed. *Your hands*. He clasps the offending appendages in his and squeezes them, gently. *They're shaking. Are you all right?*

I shake harder now that he's touching me. Now that he's speaking in that sensual Spanish of his. It makes me think of that morning in his flat, when he took my hands in his and held them over my head and moved inside me with ardent, patient passion.

"Yeah," I say. "Yeah, just, um. Just the adrenaline. Falling through the air will do that to you, I guess."

Javier meets my eyes. Their warmth is so honest, so inviting, I am sinking into it—into *him*—before I can think better of it.

"You need a drink," he says. "How do you feel about grabbing a copita or two on the way home?"

I blink.

I should say no.

I should go back to my señora's and lock myself in my room and work on my thesis until I go cross-eyed so I can forget Javier. Everything, everything Javier.

He's getting too close, I'm letting him in when I should be pushing him away. Letting him in is only going to hurt in the end. He's only going to hurt me, the way my dad did. Javier may seem perfect right now, but so did Dad—and we all know how that turned out.

Besides. Javier wants Carmen. I've already done the love triangle thing, and I have absolutely no interest in revisiting that particular nightmare.

I should say no.

But I don't. I can't.

Not when Javier's looking at me like he is now, the kindness in his eyes tugging at my heart. There's something else there too. Something bold.

Want. Only he wants Carmen, so there's no way that he's looking at me like . . . like that.

But he is. And I love, I *love* it.

"A drink," I say. "One drink."

"Vale," he says and smiles.

Javier steps into the restaurant behind me.

"This is one of my favorite places in Madrid," he says. "The wine is good, and the food is even better."

"Awesome," I say. "I love trying new places."

The high-ceilinged place is bustling, long-stemmed glasses of tempranillo and albariño wine lining the clean-edged bar. People sit, they stand, their laughter and chatter echoing off the stylishly weathered wooden walls and ceiling.

Javier helps me with my coat—of course—and we check our jackets with the hostess. I'm inexplicably nervous as we belly up to the bar. Maybe because Javier is blazing hand-some-hot today. He's wearing a black sweater over a white button-down shirt, his hipster wave slicked back from his forehead in a devastating swoop. His stubble is on full sexy-mechanic display.

Dear Lord. I need a drink. Now.

"Would you like a cocktail?" he asks, passing me a menu. "Or are you in the mood for some wine?"

"Wine, definitely."

"You like red, right?"

I blink. "Yes. How did you know? Didn't we drink gin and tonics at Ático?"

Color creeps up his neck as he looks down at the menu. "When I picked you up from that restaurant, you know, the one where you were chatting up your girlfriends—you said you had a red wine buzz."

I try to squash the rise in my chest before it gets out of hand.

But it overwhelms me anyway. He needs to stop. Stop making me feel like everything I do or say is important. Interesting.

It's not. *I'm* not.

"You remember," I say.

He looks at me for a long minute. His eyes darken, flash with that *something* again. "Of course I remember."

The bartender appears, and Javier looks at him, ordering a bottle of Rioja—one of Spain's more famous red varietals.

"A whole bottle?" I say, arching a brow. "I agreed to *one* drink."

Javier digs a money clip out of his back pocket. "I think I can convince you to stay for a few more."

"No, wait," I say, scrambling for my bag. "Let me treat you to some wine. It's the least I can do for helping me with my thesis—I mean, the gas alone for today's flight—"

But he's already passing the bartender a few bills. When I try to offer him money—"Please, Javier, take it!"—he gently curls the Euro bill into my palm.

"Perhaps next time," he says.

His fingers are still curled around mine. They are warm and calloused. Threads of heat unspool inside my skin, releasing the tension in my shoulders, loosening the stubborn knot of worry in my head. He's looking at me, I feel it, even though my eyes are glued to our hands. He's waiting for me to pull away, but I don't.

Something about his touch makes my throat contract.

"Thanks," I say, swallowing.

"You're welcome," he says. He holds up his glass. "I admit, I wasn't thrilled about bringing you to the monastery the first time."

"Really?" I grin. "I didn't notice."

"Sorry for being surly," he replies. "But now—now I'm glad I brought you along. Really, really glad. It's worked out well, don't you think?"

I touch my glass to his. "I do."

Javier grins too. He stands, scooches his stool closer to mine to make room for another couple, then sits.

We take a sip. The wine is very good, fruit-forward, jammy on my tongue. Warm.

"You like it?" he asks, hopefully.

"I love it," I say. Of course I love it.

An awkward beat of silence passes between us. I finally pull my hand from Javier's, tucking the money back into my wallet.

"So how's the writing going? The thesis?" he asks.

I nod. Take another sip of wine. "It's going well. Really well, considering all the material I've seen at the monastery. At this rate, I'll be able to put together a pretty amazing paper. If, of course, all goes well with my research."

"I'll do everything I can to see that it does."

I tuck my hair behind my ear and look at him. "C'mon, Javier, you *have* to stop being so fucking great." He's sitting close now, so close I can smell the cinnamon on his breath. My gaze flicks to his lips. Oh, those lips. I remember what those lips can do. "It's getting a little annoying."

He's grinning again, his dimples making a delicious appearance. "Sorry not sorry. I like helping you."

Oh, God, it's like an arrow right through my heart.

"You help me too, you know," he says. "The fact that you like my nameless band so much keeps me motivated. I've written more songs in the past few weeks than I have—well, ever."

I feel like I'm going to cry.

Stop it stop it stop it right now.

"Your new band is awesome, Javier," I manage. "I will be first in line to buy the album."

He looks at me. "I know."

He pours us each another glass of wine. So much for the one drink thing.

"And how are things besides?" he asks, his voice low. "With you. With your family."

I look at him. And look at him. It overwhelms me, suddenly, the need to tell him. To share with him what I haven't shared with anyone else. I can't keep pretending. It's exhausting, for one thing, and it's not fair to Javier for another. He's been so good to me. So patient and understanding.

He already knows I'm hot a mess anyway. That's certainly no secret, not after I tumbled out of his bed in tears following a horrible conversation with my dad.

Javier is kind. He is a good listener. And he cares. I don't get it, I don't understand *why* he cares. But the fact that he does makes me feel . . . safe, I guess.

And if telling him my deepest darkest fears somehow blows up in my face, it really doesn't matter, does it? I go back to the States in a month. Even if I am lucky enough to come back to Spain for graduate school, Javier will probably be married to Carmen by then. Whatever the future holds, I'll never see him again.

That thought makes my heart twist painfully inside my chest.

I set down my wine and I take a warrior breath and I face him.

And then I tell him everything.

Javier

As I listen, I resist the urge to slide my palm beneath the curtain of Maddie's hair, to wrap my fingers around the warm nape of her neck, gently, a reminder that I'm here, she's safe with me, and it's okay to cry.

But I don't want to scare her. She needs to tell her story, and I am more than happy to listen as she does.

I watch her struggle not to cry, to stay strong as she tells me her heart's been ripped out and stepped on and torn to pieces by her pendejo of a father. *You don't have to be*

149

strong with me, I want to tell her. *You don't have to pretend with me.*

Maddie talks, I listen. It all makes sense now. She's not looking for "happily ever after" because it doesn't exist in her world. She thought it did. She thought her parents found happily ever after. But they lost it when her dad betrayed their family. Maddie lost her sense of self—her sense of worth —when her dad treated her like a piece of shit.

What's that saying? It's better never to have had something than to have it and lose it?

Maddie had everything, her family had everything, and then she lost it all.

I can't imagine how eviscerating that loss must be for her.

Disappointment seeps into my chest, a wet, cold weight. Maddie is far too young, and far too lovely, to believe her dreams are dead. I hate the idea of her closing herself off to the world, to the possibility of happiness, just because her parents didn't find it with each other.

I hate that she won't give me a chance to prove her wrong.

My heart feels made of glass, suddenly, and Maddie—Maddie keeps coming at me with the hammer of her sadness and loneliness and anger. I'll let her shatter my heart, I will, if only because I can't stand the idea of her being heartbroken alone.

"Is this why your thesis is so important?" I meet her eyes. "Your way of running from home? Getting into a graduate program in a foreign country so you don't have to go back?"

A single tear spills over the ledge of her thick, dark lashes. Maddie lifts her shoulder, dashes it across her cheek. "Something like that. The opposite of what you're trying to do, basically, after being on the road for so long. I'm trying to get away from home. You're trying to get back."

Her words hang between us. She might as well be saying, *See? See why we'd never work?*

It makes sense. We're looking for wildly different things. I believe in home. Maddie doesn't.

Why, then, do we get on so well? Why do I want to wrap her in my arms and hold her right here, in the middle of a crowded bar?

And why does she have to fall in love with my world when she can't—she won't—fall in love with me?

I dig a hand through my hair, giving it a good tug.

I want a cigarette. Badly.

"I'm sorry," I say when she finishes. "I don't know what to say except that I'm really fucking sorry you're going through this. You don't have to do it alone, you know."

"I know." She finishes her wine. I pour her another glass. "But I want to. I should. For God's sake, Javier, do you not see what a mess I am? No one deserves to be subjected to all this baggage I'm carrying around."

"You deserve some help with that baggage," I say. "Everyone deserves some help from their friends. Their family."

She shrugs, sipping her wine. She doesn't believe me, but I don't want to press her. Not when she's so vulnerable.

"Anyway." Maddie sighs, her shoulders slumping. "Thanks for listening. I really appreciate it, Javier. You're a really, really wonderful friend."

I furrow my brow. "Whoa whoa whoa. Don't get ahead of yourself, cowgirl. We're *friends* now?"

"Yes." She nods. "Friends with a mutual interest in Spanish history and good music."

I look at her from the corner of my eye. "As long as that music isn't country."

"Just you wait," she replies, the sadness in her eyes replaced by a mischievous gleam. "I'll make a believer of you yet."

I grin. "We'll see. In the meantime, let's order some food —your stomach's been growling for half an hour."

"Oh!" Maddie wraps her arms around her middle. "Oh, *eff,* that's embarrassing. I forgot to eat lunch. Which worked out, actually, because otherwise I would've narfed all over your plane."

"Narfed," I say. "That's one I haven't heard. It's like barfed, right, but better?"

It's her turn to grin. "Exactly."

———

The restaurant is close to Maddie's apartment, so we walk the few blocks to Calle de Villenueva together, huddled against the cold. The city has come alive for the holidays, the avenues decked out in twinkling lights that form a cathedral-like ceiling above our heads.

"You guys really go all out for Christmas," Maddie says, teeth chattering.

I move a bit closer to her, and I bite back a smile of surprise when she curls closer to me too, our breath mingling in a pale cloud in front of our faces. I pop a few more mints in my mouth, chewing through them in half a second.

"It's brilliant, isn't it?"

"It is," she says. "More than that. It's magical."

My smile widens. She really is head over heels in love with Madrid. The place I come from, the place I love too.

We slow our pace when we reach her street.

"Javier," she says softly. She loops her arm through mine, burying her face into the sleeve of my jacket. "I appreciate you listening tonight. That was really awesome of you. I understand if you want to run away screaming, though. It's . . . a lot, I know."

My heart begins to pound.

"I mean, *you* practically ran screaming from *me*. So I guess it's only fair if I return the favor," I say.

I resist the urge to wince at my terrible joke. I'm a fucking idiot.

But Maddie just laughs. "Seriously, Javi, I wouldn't blame you."

Javi. She's never called me that before. I like the sound of my nickname on her lips; it's what my family calls me. My good friends too.

It rushes over me then, a tidal wave of lust and like and holy fuck I want to reach out and pull her to me and kiss her until the tears come, tears of release, of overwhelmed relief.

I want to hear that name on her tongue again, this time breathless, a plea.

My heart turns over in my chest, and in that moment, I know, I *know*, that I'm in over my head. It isn't supposed to happen so fast, and it isn't supposed to happen with someone who's on the run.

But it's happening between us, Maddie and me, and there is nothing I can do to stop it.

She draws to a stop a few feet from her door. The soft light from a nearby street lamp gilds her skin, turns her eyes into translucent pools of blue. Tonight they're very full. More beautiful than ever.

A hand grips my heart and squeezes.

Maddie is still curled close against me.

Come home with me tonight, I want to murmur into her hair. *Be with me, Maddie. Let me have you. Let me in.*

She looks up at me. "Thanks again for today. I had a really, really great time. Whenever you want to lose gravity again, you know who to call."

I let out a half-hearted scoff as I meet her eyes. "Is tomorrow too soon?"

"I have class," she says, smiling. Her mouth is inches from

mine. My body throbs with the desire to pull her to me, claim those lips as my own.

That's right, I say in Spanish. *I forgot today is Sunday.*

Maddie bites her lip. *You're using your Spanish. What are you trying to do, seduce me?*

The laughter fades from her gaze as I look down at her.

"No. No quiero seducirte, Maddie." *I don't want to seduce you.*

She wrinkles her forehead. "Then what *do* you want?"

I search her eyes.

And then I take her face in my trembling hands and duck my head and cover her mouth with mine.

This.

This is what I want.

Chapter Fourteen

MADDIE

My pulse blares through my body, a sensation that fills my ears, my limbs, my lips. My thoughts scatter in a thousand directions, my mind captured by the rush of his kiss.

Javier's kiss. It's slow and it's patient and it's thorough, not at all like the hurried, almost violent kisses we shared the night we hooked up. This kiss is different.

This kiss makes my heart sing.

There's a tug in the back of my head, a warning that I shouldn't let Javier kiss me like this. I definitely shouldn't kiss him back.

But I do. Oh, I do, I sink into his kiss, I surrender to the gentle pull of his mouth and the press of his lips and the sting of cinnamon on his tongue.

His hands are shaking on my face. I reach up, cover them with my own, curling my fingers into the crook between his thumb and forefinger. They stop shaking, his hands.

Javier smiles against my mouth, pulling back. He brushes his nose against mine. I suck in a breath as a shiver moves through me, a tremor that tightens the muscles in the small of my back.

"Gracias," he murmurs. *That's better*.

Much, I say, and touch my lips to his, slipping my tongue into the velvet seam of his mouth.

His kiss is kind but deep, considerate but hungry. His stubble scratches my chin as he angles his head, but I don't care, I'm losing myself in him, forgetting all the things that weigh me down, forgetting the hurt and the dread that sit like a stone inside my chest. His kiss makes me feel light.

He makes me feel like I can fly. And considering I've crawled my way through these past few months, that's a heady proposition.

Keep kissing me, I beg with my lips. *Please, Javier, please don't stop*.

I know the things happening inside my head and my heart are dangerous. I haven't allowed myself to feel them for a while now, and there's a reason for that. Many reasons, all of them good.

But I couldn't stop kissing Javier if my life depended on it.

It takes me a few heartbeats to gather the courage to slide my hands onto his waist. I mean, I'm touching him now. Really *touching*, my fingers slipping underneath his leather jacket. With intent, with unabashed curiosity.

I pull him closer, the warm press of our bodies a delicious counterpoint to the frigid air.

Feeling the fleshy of warmth of his body beneath my fingers—the strident pull of his hardened muscles against over me—oh, God help me.

This boy can *kiss*. He moves with feeling. Equal parts salty and sweet. Add to that the slow, soft grind of his groin as he works a thigh between my legs, and I am on. Freaking. Fire.

He tugs my bottom lip between his teeth, running his tongue along the swollen inside of that same lip. My body feels warm. Cherished, as stupid as that sounds.

His hands move into my hair, move to my throat. His

touch is delicious, kind and possessive and confident all at once. I love the feel of his hands on me, my body coming alive from this smallest of touches. Currents of electricity move through me from the five contact points of his fingertips, his thumb toying with my earlobe, his fingers finding purchase in the nape of my neck.

I kiss him with rising passion, our breaths becoming labored, noisy gusts through our noses, the beat between my legs too loud and too needy to ignore. He kisses me deeply, long strokes of tongue and lips, the kind of kiss you only see in the movies.

The kind of kiss you dream of when you're thirteen, wondering what Frenching *really* feels like while practicing on your pillow.

We're really putting on a show now. If little kids passed by, they'd probably be scarred for life by our very passionate, and very public, make-out sesh.

We have to stop. This—whatever *this* is—it can't go any further than this kiss.

But oh, I could kiss Javier like this for hours, days. Weeks. And still I'd want more.

I want so much more. But I don't think I deserve it. My dad sunk his dagger deep, and I'm still figuring out what the damage is, and how to triage it. *Did* I cause my parents' divorce? Am I dumb, ugly inside and out, unlovable? Am I missing some essential thing that everyone else has—something that makes them worthy of respect, of love?

And then of course there's the fact that Javier wants someone else. Yeah, he's kissing me after a couple glasses of wine. But he made it sound like he was kind of in love with Carmen. He wants forever with her, and I want one-night stands with anonymous Europeans. Maybe Javier just wants another one-night stand with me.

Javier and I have to stop. Stop before we do something we'll regret. Before someone gets hurt.

I never go back for seconds, remember?

I break the kiss, keeping my eyes closed as I struggle to catch my breath. I hate this, I don't want to stop. I want Javier.

But he was never mine to have.

He rests his forehead against mine.

"Maddie," he says. "I like you. I like you very much."

I meet his eyes, our lashes tangling in the tiny space between us.

I don't do this. I don't do *like*. The squishy, romantic kind of like.

What in the world was I thinking?

"I can't." I step back. "*You* can't."

"Maddie," he says, reaching for me.

"Don't," I say. "Please, Javier, don't."

Javier looks at me. Looks away, spearing a hand through his hair as he lets out a long, hot breath. His hipster wave is mussed now. I resist the temptation to reach out, smooth it back with my fingers.

"You can't kiss me like that," I say.

His head snaps back, gaze searing. "Why not?"

"A lot of reasons," I say. "Starting with Carmen."

He steps toward me, erasing the space I put between us. Jesus, he's handsome. Huge. I sway on my feet. If I don't get out of here soon I'm going to motherfucking *swoon*.

He sees me moving. He reaches out again but stops himself.

"I'm okay," I say, waving him back.

"You sure?"

"I'm sure."

He looks at me, his brown eyes burning amber in the light of the street lamp. "As for Carmen—I'm interested in you,

Maddie. I have been all along. Carmen is . . . she's a lovely girl. But I'm realizing she isn't the girl for me."

My pulse flutters. "You told me you were looking to put down roots with her. You said that's why you came back to Madrid," I say.

Javier runs his tongue along his bottom lip. That delicious, slightly swollen lip.

"It's a long story," he says. "A story I'll tell you when we're not freezing our asses off. But I want you, Maddie. Carmen is my past. And you . . ."

I look away, swallowing hard. "There is no future for us, Javier. Not the kind you're looking for. I'm leaving in a month, remember?"

"I do. I do remember, Maddie, of course I do, it's just—Christ." He runs his hand through his hair again. "Would you believe me if I told you that Carmen doesn't like the real me? But you—I think you do, Maddie. You don't care about what I did or who I toured with. And you're so passionate about everything, you—"

We both look up at the sound of familiar voices.

Vivian and Rafa are strolling hand in hand down the sidewalk toward us, smiling like idiots. Her eyes catch on mine and she slows her pace. Her approach is cautious, like Javier and I are standing in the middle of a crime scene.

"Hey guys," she says. Her eyes dart from me to Javier and back again. "Everything all right here?"

I step toward them, away from Javier. "You two look like you had a lovely evening. Did you go out to dinner?"

"We did." Rafa gives his uncle a funny look. "What about you, chicos?"

The heat of Javier's gaze spreads across my back, making me shiver. Even though I can't see him I'm acutely aware of his presence behind me. My heart races.

He is not yours to have.

I'm just torturing myself, wanting him like this. Kissing him back. We're torturing each other.

"Just working on some thesis stuff," I say. I nod at the door. "Ready to go up, Viv?"

She blinks. "Um. I guess so, yeah."

I turn my head, meeting Javier's gaze. His face is dark with anger, anger and arousal, and he's breathing hard through his nose. "Thanks for today, Javier."

He doesn't say anything. He shoots me one last pained look before he turns and stalks into the darkness.

Chapter Fifteen

JAVIER

The Next Day

I pace the length of my living room, my shuffled footfalls muted on the rough pile of an antique Oushak rug. It was a gift from my father, the rug, given to me years ago, before he died. Along with my watch, it's one of the few items he passed down to me, priceless treasures that connect me to my past.

That connect me to my family.

Only the rug wasn't making me feel any less lost this morning. I kept waiting for some sign, some ghostly voice to rise from the wool, telling me what to do. I thought I knew what I wanted. I wanted María Carmen. I wanted to make a home with her.

Then a one-night stand with a passionate American changed everything.

I want Maddie.

Only she doesn't want me. Or maybe she does, but she's way too scared to ever give me a chance.

I can't stop thinking about her.

I've been pacing all morning. When my father's ghost failed

to materialize, I had to fall back on plan B. Which is why Leo is currently parked on my sofa, a guitar in one hand and a bocadillo, or Spanish-style sandwich, the size of his head in another.

I thought she was into it, I tell him, my jeans swishing as I move. *I mean, I'm not going to give you all the details, but I'm pretty sure she was having a good time.*

"In the English please," he replies around a mouthful of bocadillo. "I am in the practice, he remembers?"

"Right. Your terrible English. Can't we work on that another time?" I curl a hand through my hair, stopping to cup the nape of my neck.

He shakes his head, spewing crumbs across his lap and onto the sofa. "No. What if Maddie has the friends? Friends want me. I need to speak to them to tell them I am in love."

"I think you'd have a better chance if you told them that in Spanish."

"Maybe." He shrugs. "Maybe not. I do not take a risk so big. Now you must tell me more of a fight you did with your woman."

"She's not my woman."

"Not already."

"I think you mean *not yet*. And it wasn't a fight. I don't know what it was, to be honest. I like this girl, Leo, and I think—I think she likes me too. I mean. We have the most insane chemistry."

Leo quirks a brow. "Chemistry?"

"You know, like—attraction. Good energy. We get along really well. And we kiss even better."

"Ah, the kiss. It does not lie."

"Exactly!" I pass in front of the first of two windows, my black shirt prickling beneath the warmth of a pale morning sun. "The kiss, Leo—the kiss was perfect. I would've kissed her all night if she'd let me."

"Just the kissing? None more of the . . ." Leo's hips buck off the couch.

"Jesus, mate, put that away," I say. "And no, no more sex. Just kissing. But this kiss, it was . . . more intense, somehow, than sex. I wanted to go slow with her this time. Make it feel less like a hookup, more like a date."

"So *you* want the dates," Leo says. "What does Maddie want?"

I shrug, letting out a sigh of defeat. "That's just it. I have no clue. One minute she was hot, and the next? Totally cold. She would hardly look at me. I mean, did I do something? Do I smell?"

Leo holds up his arm and sniffs. "No smell. I give me a shower today."

"Part of me thinks I should just let it go. She's an exchange student, for Christ's sake. She's leaving Madrid in a month. Chances are I'll never see her again, even if she does come back for her graduate studies. And her parents are going through this really terrible divorce, a divorce Maddie feels responsible for, even though it's definitely not her fault. But it's made her terrified of relationships. And you know that's what I'm looking for, Leo. A relationship. I have no business getting involved with someone who's leaving— someone who *isn't* looking for forever."

"But?"

I meet Leo's eyes. "But she's awesome. She's smart, and she's got this lovely sense of humor, and her passion—Leo, you've never met anyone as passionate as Maddie. It's exciting, being around her. She loves Madrid and our new band as much as I do. I think about her when I'm walking, when I'm in the car. I see a museum, or a restaurant, or an old church, and I want to take her there because I know she'd love it. I want to experience those things with her. I definitely want to see her again. But she thinks I'm still stuck on María Carmen—"

"Are you?" Leo asks.

I put my hands on my hips and let out a sigh of frustration. "No. I don't think so. I mean, if I hadn't met Maddie, I can't say whether or not I'd still be into Carmen. But seeing how much Maddie likes me for me—you know, she isn't all that interested in the celebrity stuff—I guess it makes me realize how much Carmen *is* into that bullshit."

"I see." Leo nods his head. "Carmen is feeling the love for the rock star, not the man."

"Yes," I say. "Exactly. And that's not who I am. Maddie knows who I am, and she likes me. At least I think she does. She makes me feel more at home in my own skin than I've ever felt before."

Leo scarfs the last of his bocadillo. "But Maddie, she is leaving very soon."

"Yeah," I say. "She leaves, and she moves five thousand miles away. Leo, what the hell do I do?"

It takes Leo a minute to process what I'm getting at. Eventually he begins to nod, holding a finger thoughtfully to his chin.

"A very confused problem it you have," he says. "How do you say . . . shit. Too much for the English I think me."

I stare at him. "What? You're killing me here, Leo."

Here's what I think, he says in Spanish. *You were gone for so long on tour, not belonging to anyone or anything, and now you're looking for your true belonging. Beyond Juan Ramos, beyond being the rock star. I believe what you're looking for is a girl to make you feel at home wherever you are. It sounds like you may have found that girl in Maddie. She's great, Javi, I'm not saying she isn't. But she is leaving Madrid. And it's hard to find a belonging with someone when you live oceans apart. She's young. She's still at university, focusing on her studies. I'm not sure she knows what she wants yet. I like her. I think she's really cool. But honestly? I think it's not meant to be. Your lives will be separated by an ocean. Which wouldn't be the biggest deal if you and Maddie wanted the same things—but you don't.*

I drop my gaze to my feet. I knew Leo was going to say something along those lines. For as much of a goob as he is, he can be surprisingly insightful.

Still. This isn't what I wanted to hear. I wanted to hear "fight for love!" and "distance be damned!" and all that *crap*, as Maddie would say.

"I know," I say, my voice a barely audible grumble. "I mean, yeah, Maddie makes me feel like home. But what does that matter when we obviously can't be together? You're right, Leo. You're so right. I was an idiot to fall for her. I just . . . I couldn't help it. She's lovely."

My advice? he says. *You have to get over her, Javi. It's time to move on.*

"I know," I repeat. But I don't want to move on.

Leo brushes the crumbs off his lap onto the floor—awesome—and grabs the guitar beside the fireplace.

"It is a thing of very great sadness," he says. "She is great girl, Maddie. I am sad for you. But in other women you will find the lovely. Much time, and you will find the others. Now we practice"—he hands me the guitar—"the music, and then maybe we drink too much cerveza and do the flirting with womens in the disco tonight?"

I sigh, rolling my eyes as I grab the guitar by the neck.

This is going to be a long day.

Maddie

A few days later

The muscles in my neck and shoulders tense, a pinch I know all too well, as I wait for Mom to pick up. The dull blare of each ring echoes in my head.

She didn't say much in her voicemail, just a quick, "Hey, Maddie, it's Mom, give me a call when you get a chance." She sounded tired. Defeated.

I work at an especially painful knot in my neck with my fingers. I've just spent the past two hours fighting panicked crowds on the Metro on my way to San Pedro. When I arrived, the building was empty. Apparently classes were cancelled earlier this morning on account of a big snowstorm we're supposed to get today and tomorrow.

Luckily I managed to hail a cab, and now I'm speeding back home, hoping to beat the blizzard.

Having a couple snow days sounds nice in theory. But considering Viv's already headed across town to shack up at Rafa's, I'm staring down the barrel of a week trapped inside my apartment with only my semi-nutty señora, her asshole dog, Chiquitin, and my ever-increasing anxiety about my thesis for company.

Also, I miss Javier. A lot.

I'm still reeling from that kiss to end all kisses. He said, point blank, that he didn't want Carmen—he said he wanted *me*. I want to believe him. Oh, how I want to believe I'm the forever girl he's looking for.

But I'm not. The fairy tale of forever doesn't exist, at least not for me. After the way I destroyed my parents' happily ever after, I hardly think I deserve one of my own.

Besides, I have to go back to Atlanta at the end of the semester. My family needs me. How could I possibly find forever with Javier if I only have a few weeks left in Madrid?

It's only ten thirty A.M. here, meaning it's still really early back home—four thirty. Who knows what's up with my parents calling me in the wee hours of the morning. Mom wouldn't call unless something was wrong. I don't know what else *could* go wrong, considering my dad tore apart our family and blamed it on me. Considering the house I grew up in is for sale because we can't afford it anymore.

But I've learned things can always, always get worse.

She picks up on the first ring.

"Hey, Maddie," she says.

"Hey, Mom," I reply. The taxi driver slams on the brakes, and I brace my hand on the passenger seat headrest. "How are you?"

"I'm okay," she says. "Sorry to bug you so early. I couldn't sleep, so I thought I'd give you a call, check in."

"No problem. Classes are actually cancelled—they're calling for a couple inches of snow today and tomorrow. Madrid is like Atlanta. When it snows even the tiniest bit, everything shuts down. I'm on my way home now."

"How cool is that! A Spanish snow day," Mom says. "Do you and Vivian have any plans? Did your señora buy extra groceries? What if you lose power? Do you have enough wine to keep you warm?"

For a second, I almost smile. She sounds like my old mom, the mom I had before shit hit the fan. She sounds like all moms, with her twenty questions, her proudly shameless desire to know everything and anything. Especially if it has to do with a natural disaster.

"We'll be fine," I say. "I have a lot of work to do on my thesis to keep me busy. Remember that dude I was telling you about—the one who got me into the monastery? He also got permission for me to take pictures inside the building. I'm hoping to go through those this week."

"Of *course* I remember that boy. Javier, right? The guitarist? Tell me more— he sounds *very* interesting."

Well, I want to say. *He's not a boy, for starters. He is a handsome-hot man, has his own plane, looks extremely sexy while plucking out tunes on his guitar, and, oh yes, he kissed me like the world was ending the other night and now all I can think about is kissing him again, even though we can't because I'm fucked up and he wants someone else.*

Also I masturbate in the shower to the memory of his body on my body. I wish he was less excellent at touching me—and at guitar, and at conversation, and at making me feel lovely—so I could stop thinking about him already.

"He's nice," I say instead. "Really nice. He's the lead guitarist in a band he started. It's pretty cool of him to let me tag along and do my research while they play. Anyway—"

"So is he your boyfriend? Are you dating? You haven't mentioned any boys this semester—not since Rafa."

"Definitely not my boyfriend," I say. "I'm not interested in Javier like that. I'm focusing on my thesis, remember? Plus I'm coming home in, what, less than four weeks? It'd be pretty pointless to start a relationship now."

"Whatever you say," Mom replies. "So is Javier tall? What languages does he—"

"Enough about me," I say. "Tell me how you are. What are you doing up so early?"

It's Mom's turn to sigh. When she speaks I can tell she's trying not to cry. "Couldn't sleep. I miss you, Madeline."

"I miss you too, Mom."

"I have some news."

My stomach does a somersault.

"We got an offer on the house." Her voice cracks. "It's such a relief, Maddie, knowing we're able to get out from under this mortgage. But I know how attached you are to the house. I keep thinking about all the memories we shared here, how many times we sang happy birthday around the kitchen table. It's just—"

The burn behind my eyes is familiar. I've felt it often enough this semester. But the pain never lessens.

I bite the inside of my cheek, take a warrior breath or two to keep from bursting into sobs. Crying isn't going to help me, and it certainly isn't going to help my mom.

Still. She's right. I am attached to our house. It's where I grew up. It's where my brother, Kevin, stabbed me with a pencil, and we both cried because we thought I'd die of lead poisoning. It's where we buried the gerbils I had to have but ended up hating because they bit me, where I got my first kiss, read my favorite books, and contemplated the mysteries of my teenage universe. I love our house. It's *home*.

And now home belongs to another family. All because my dad couldn't keep his dick in his pants.

"That's great," I manage. "I know it was stressing you out. You don't need all that space anyway. Now you can buy a sweet bachelorette pad in some swanky building closer to the city."

"I know, I know," she replies. "But I haven't even accepted the offer yet, and already I miss it—the house. Your father is going to shit a brick."

"Tough titties." Anger rises in my chest. "It's his fault we have to sell it in the first place."

It's his fault our whole family fell apart. Or maybe it's my fault. I don't know.

"Maddie," Mom says.

"Whatever." I swallow the lump in my throat. "How is he, by the way?"

Mom sighs, a heavy, trembling thing. "He's not good, Maddie. I think he's been drinking again. He's disappeared, he hasn't showed up for work. He may lose his job."

I close my eyes and let the tears fall silently down my face.

"I'm sorry to put this on you," Mom says. "But Kevin—he's too young, and I don't want to air our dirty laundry in public. I'm sorry, Maddie. I don't mean to ruin your Spanish snow day like this."

"It's all right, Mom." My throat aches with the effort of keeping my voice even. "You need to take care of yourself. Dad . . . we'll figure him out later."

"I've tried, Maddie. For years I've tried."

The taxi stops in front of a blue door. It's starting to sleet, pellets of ice that crackle against the windshield. I glance at the meter. Fourteen euro! I root around in my bag. I hope I have enough cash.

I can't see through the film of tears that blurs my vision. I shove a twenty euro bill into the driver's hand and duck out of the car, heart pounding inside my throat.

Our house. The place where I grew up.

We aren't going to live there anymore.

"Well." My hands shake as I try to shove my key into the door. "One less thing to worry about—the house, I mean."

"I'm hoping we'll close by New Year's. I'm so ready to move. Move on, you know? I have to admit it's been a little lonely, living in this big house all by myself."

It's freezing inside the lobby. I begin to climb the stairs, careful not to slip on the well-worn marble.

The thought of going home for Christmas only to pack up the house makes me feel like dying.

This sucks.

Everything fucking *sucks.*

I look up at the door to my señora's apartment. I can hear Chiquitin pacing, his nails clicking against the parquet floor as he licks his chops. I just know he's waiting to pounce on me, nip at my heels as I make a run for it to my room.

"Mom," I say. "I gotta go. I'll call you later, okay?"

"Okay, Maddie. Stay safe in that storm. Love you."

"Love you too."

I hang up my phone. My throat burns, and so do my eyes. I can't. I can't.

I just can't deal with that dickhead dog today. I can't

pretend to be in a good mood for my señora. I can't spend the next few days holed up in my tiny bedroom, hiding from them. Alone. Very, very much alone. Thinking about another family living in the house I grew up in. The house I love.

Thinking about Javier.

I turn around and bound down the steps. I need a break. I need a huge glass of wine and a comfy couch I can sit on without worrying I'm going to be attacked by a giant German Shepherd that's possessed by the devil.

I need to not be alone. I need to be with someone right now. Talk to them.

Talk to *him*.

The idea is there, fully formed in the space of a single, decisive heartbeat. It's stupid. It makes no sense. I promised myself I wouldn't, I couldn't, and I know I am not the girl he needs. We want different things, he and I. He wants the happily ever after I know doesn't exist—just look at my parents. And the last time I saw him, I ended things on a pretty sour note.

But he understands. He listens.

He's the only one who can make me feel better.

I cross the lobby, my booted footsteps clipped, and push through the door. I shiver. Squint against the thin grey light.

God, but it's cold. The air swirls with sleet, a few chunky flakes of snow.

I should probably call him first. But I'm scared he won't even answer.

I'm even more scared he will answer, and he'll tell me to never call him again.

The lump in my throat swells. Maybe if I just show up, he'll at least let me plead for his forgiveness.

I look back up at my building. Whether or not Javier hates me, I can't go back in there.

I head for the Metro.

Chapter Sixteen

MADDIE

By some miracle, I only get a little lost on my way to Javier's. After asking for directions from a twenty-something Madrileña—gorgeous, perfectly put together despite the sub-zero temperature—I find Javier's place around the corner from a pretty square.

My heart throbs as I press the buzzer for the second time. It hums beneath the pad of my thumb. I step back, looking up at the building's fashionably battered brick façade, and cross my arms.

Please, I beg. *Please be home.*

It's really snowing now, flakes dampening my eyelashes, making my sore eyes water. The cold has stirred my blood to a frenzy, a painful contrast to the heat that floods my face, radiating up my shins from the frozen sidewalk. It makes my knees ache.

I wait. The enormous windows of Javier's apartment stare back at me, blank, unblinking, their hand-blown panes waving in the fading light.

Around me the air is heavy, ominous with the coming

storm. The sky darkens, bit by bit, taking on a grey-green tint that can't be good.

I mount the step and press the buzzer one more time.

He doesn't answer.

He must really not be home.

I draw a trembling breath, closing my eyes against the sting of tears. I was really hoping he'd be here. I need—I don't know what I need.

Need to see him, I guess. Right now it's the only thing keeping my head above the water, the hope that he'll answer the door.

Only he doesn't.

My feet feel heavy and cold as stone as I turn away. The force of my disappointment knocks the breath from my lungs. I'd be more worried about the emotions he's making me feel—their strength, their lingering impression on the tender parts inside my chest—if I wasn't overwhelmed by the knowledge that *I don't have a home anymore.*

I walk away, blinking back the tears, the snow. It's starting to stick, covering the sidewalk in a thin film of slush.

"Maddie?"

My pulse trips to a stop. A familiar warm tingle moves up my spine. I know that voice.

"Maddie, is that you?"

He's home.

Halle-frickin-*lleuja,* he's home.

I look over my shoulder. Our gazes collide. He's standing on the stoop in sweats and a pair of furry-looking slippers, his hipster wave wet, like he just got out of the shower.

I can't breathe.

His handsome-hotness gets me *every*. Damn. Time.

"Were you ringing for me? Sorry, I was having a quick bath."

His breath puffs out in wispy clouds of white.

And his eyes—their amber color is piercing, even as they soften with kindness. The kindness that completely, utterly slays me.

"Maddie," he asks, his eyebrows coming together, "are you all right?"

His kindness, his loveliness, make the pain that arrows through me that much more poignant. My face crumples.

And then he's moving from the warmth of his building into the swirling snow, stepping down onto the sidewalk. He stands in front of me, his shoulders blocking out the world as he wraps a palm around the nape of my neck and pulls me into his chest. His broad, invitingly warm, well-muscled chest.

My first thought is: thank God, thank God he is here. Thank God I have him.

My second thought is ohmigod ohmigod I am going to pass out, he smells so delicious.

My tears dampen his shirt and fall onto the sidewalk between us. For a minute I let him hold me like this. It's nice, sharing my weight with him, not having to bear it on my own for once.

"I'm sorry," I say. "I'm sorry, Javier, for coming like this, especially after the other night. I just—I had nowhere else to go, and I—"

"It's all right," he says. "As long as you don't mind seeing me in my pajamas."

I look down. "Those *are* nice slippers."

"I prefer to call them foot pussies, thank you very much."

"Foot pussies?" I sniff. "Is that a British thing?"

"Nope. I don't know whose thing it is, to be honest. My roommate at university introduced me to the term and it stuck. So there you have it. Foot pussies."

"I think that's just an excuse to say the *P* word."

"It is." He grins. "And you wouldn't make fun of them if you knew how cozy they were," he says, wiggling his toes.

I meet his eyes. "Thank you."

"For what?"

"For not hating me."

He looks down at me for a long moment.

"I could never hate you," he says quietly.

Javier guides me into the crook of his arm, keeping his hand in place on the nape of my neck. His thumb glides against the sensitive skin there. A wash of heat moves through me, settling between my legs.

Already.

Not two minutes together, and already he's turning me on.

Warrior breath. *Remember your warrior breath.*

"C'mon," he says, curling his body around mine, holding me close. "Let's get you inside. It's really starting to come down, isn't it?"

Javier's bachelor pad is as swank and effortlessly cool as I (vaguely) remember it being. It's big, really big by Madrileño standards, loft-like with high-beamed ceilings. A few of the walls are exposed brick, a masculine counterpoint to the huge, Victorian-style windows.

The first floor is completely open, a mod kitchen flowing into a huge living room area. An ogre-sized leather couch beckons in front of a rough-hewn fireplace. His guitar rests against the wall beside the mantel, as if he's just been practicing. The walls are hung with all sorts of art—modern, classical landscapes, portraits—I can't wait to check them out. I imagine the space gets quite cozy, despite its size, when the lights are turned down and a fire is lit.

A super artsy staircase—iron, from what I can tell, very

industrial looking—leads to a second floor, where his bedroom is.

His bedroom.

Must. Not. Think. About. His. Bedroom.

What we did there. How good what we did was.

"May I?" he asks, tucking his fingers into the collar of my coat.

For half a second I close my eyes and revel in the feeling of his hands on me, the brush of his fingertips against my collarbones. His touch is exactly as I remember it: confident, careful. Kind.

Javier hangs up my coat, then makes his way into the kitchen. I stand at the island, watching him as he produces a corkscrew from a long, narrow drawer. Closing the drawer with his hip, he grabs a bottle of wine and two long-stemmed glasses and sets them on the counter in front of me. He pulls the cork from the bottle with a small, satisfying *pop* and then fills my glass with red wine so dark it almost looks blue in the low light.

He pours himself a glass, puts down the bottle, and sidles over to the other end of the island, facing me. After he sets down his glass, he grasps the edges of the countertop in either of his hands.

"Talk to me, Goose," he says.

A bottle and a half later, we're sitting on Javier's beast of a couch facing each other, a pile of rumpled tissues between us. The morning fades to afternoon. A cozy fire burns in the fireplace. I needed the wine more than I thought I did, the tears kept coming, and we kept drinking. The mellow buzz from the wine calms the scattershot panic of my thoughts, my pulse. I don't know if it's the wine, or Javier, or the lazy heat from the fire, but I find myself relaxing in a way I haven't in a really, really long time.

Sure, my heart and lungs are sore from a good cry. My nose is raw from wiping it so many times, and my eyes are probably so red and swollen I look like a possessed demon from the underworld. Somewhere in the back of my mind, I know my problems and all their weight will be waiting for me the second I sober up and step out of this apartment.

But it hurts less right now, the fact that I don't have a place to go home to, with Javier beside me. Listening like the champ he is. His presence makes me feel a little less lost, a little more centered.

It makes me feel *wanted*. Not in a sexual way. Just in a human way, I guess.

I look at him a long moment. I bring my glass to my lips, finish what's left of my wine. Javier grabs the bottle, ducks his head as a way of asking if I'd like more. I hold out my glass.

All the while I never stop looking at him. How is it possible I find him more attractive than ever? More hand-some-hot than I can handle?

"What?" he asks at last.

"Nothing," I say. "I'm just wondering how you do it. How you *get* me. How you understand it all so well."

"I don't know," he shrugs, pouring himself a generous glass. "Maybe because *you* get *me* so well."

I wrinkle my nose. "I do?"

"Think about it," he says. "You like my band. You like my music. You *love* my city. You appreciate me for who I am."

I look down at my glass. "Even if I keep running out on you?"

"Yes," he says, his voice soft. "Even then, I know you like me for me. Thank you for that."

"You're welcome," I say, meeting his eyes.

A shiver snakes up my spine.

"You're cold," he says. "Here, let me run upstairs and grab you some foot pussies."

"How many pussies do you have?"

"Not that many, actually. I'm pretty selective when it comes to my pussies."

"Quality over quantity," I say.

"Something like that. Why don't you get a bit closer to the fire? I've got a few songs I've been working on, and I'd love to play them for you."

A fireside jam session with more wine, more Javier, and more foot pussies?

I mean. How am I supposed to say no to that?

Chapter Seventeen

MADDIE

A few hours later, and the wind is howling outside the windows. The storm has arrived, bringing with it white-out conditions. The snow comes down so fast and so hard it got dark in the middle of the afternoon.

Every once in a while the building groans and the lights flicker. It gets progressively colder inside Javier's apartment, as the heat can't keep up with the plummeting temperature outside.

Not that we mind, or even notice. We're sitting on blankets in front of a roaring fire, warm with wine and laughter. I'm wrapped up in Javier's sweater, a chunky knit that is as soft and cozy as it gets, and a pair of foot pussies several sizes too big keeping my tootsies nice and toasty.

Javier cradles his guitar in his lap, the glossy wood shining in the fire's mellow glow. We didn't turn on the lights as the darkness fell around us, and now we're stranded, deliciously so, in the small island of light and warmth put off by the fire. He's kept it at a steady blaze, poking at it every so often, adding logs or crumpled up newspaper when the flames lag.

And he plays his songs for me. They're love songs—slow jams, if you will—and I don't think I can adequately describe how sexy Javier looks and sounds as he plays them. The songs themselves are lovely. When he apologizes for a "half-baked" chorus or a riff "that's not quite there," I tell him please, please, Javier, don't stop playing, they're so good.

"You're so good, Javi," I say.

"Thank you. I told you I've been writing a lot recently."

He meets my eyes. In the light of the fire, his are the color of molten earth, fiery browns, the slightest hint of burnt orange.

You're so beautiful, I want to say.

"Do you take requests?" I ask instead.

"I do," he says. "What would you like to hear?"

"The classical stuff—the flamenco. The stuff you started with."

He nods, sliding his fingers up the neck of his guitar. "You have good taste, Maddie. Even after all these years it's still some of my favorite stuff to play."

Javier begins with a song of swirling notes, plucking at the strings with such speed his fingers lose their shape and blur. The muscles in his forearms tighten, bulge, release, making me dizzy, making my lips swell with desire.

He doesn't sing, he just plays, the sound of the guitar filling the space between us. Shadow and light flicker across his face, his skin smooth, his stubble catching the light and burning red.

He plays.

I want.

God he's good.

And sexy.

So fucking sexy.

I am not going to make it out of here alive. He's killing me.

Javier is killing me with his forearms and his eyes and his sexy tunes of love and longing.

When the song is over, he aims a smile at me that makes my heart seize inside my chest. "D'you like it? The flamenco."

He reaches across me for my glass—his is empty—and his arm brushes against the tips of my breasts as I let him take it. He drinks.

Oh, Javier.

My pulse beats inside my head, in my lips, behind my eyes.

I never go back for seconds. Never ever ever. Doing that —letting someone in—it's dangerous. It will only hurt in the end when he finds out what a lonely, messed up loser I am. And I can't stand the thought of him knowing me like that. I can't stand the idea of him pushing me away. Of him acknowledging that I *am* a loser.

But I realize now that it's too late. I don't know when it happened, exactly, or why, but I've already let Javier in. He's in my body, in my every breath. My desire for him fills me, swims inside my skin.

I let him in, even though I'll never be his, and he'll never be mine. He wants a forever girl, and I'm leaving for the States in a few weeks.

Which means when I *do* leave, it's going to hurt.

But if it's going to hurt anyway, why shouldn't I go back for seconds? Why shouldn't we enjoy one last night together?

One more night before I go back to Atlanta, and he goes back to Carmen.

I want him, ohmi*god* I have never wanted anything or anyone as much as I want him right now.

"Javier, could I ask a favor?"

He swallows, smacks his lips. "Of course. What's up?"

"Pity fuck me," I say.

Even as the surprise registers on his face, his eyes flash with something dark.

Something like desire. The sharp, raw kind.

It's an agony, waiting one heartbeat, then another, another, another, for him to reply. I plea with him in time to my frantic pulse: *say something say something please Javier say something*.

At last he set down the wineglass. He looks down at my legs. Swallows.

Looks up at me.

And then he puts his hand on my bent leg, just above the knee, and slowly, *slowly*, drags his hand up the length of my thigh, holding me tightly between his thumb and forefinger.

Watching me all the while.

"*Pity* fuck you?" His voice is low, gravelly. He leans close.

"Yeah," I say. "Like, I've had a shitty day, take-pity-on-me-with-some-sexual-healing type of thing? It really would make me feel better."

He grins, lets out a rumble of laughter.

He leans closer, ohmigod he's so close, I can smell his skin, I am burning up, I can't take it, I want, Javier, Javier, please, I *need*—

His lips brush my jaw, just beneath my chin, and his stubble scrapes against my skin in a slow, scruffy caress.

My eyes prick at the rush of sensation that moves through me. It's terrifying.

It's wonderful.

"I won't fuck you," he murmurs. "But I will make love to you, guapa."

My heart trips to a sudden, painful stop. "I don't—you know I don't . . ."

"Humor me."

I meet his eyes. Roll my tongue between my lips. He's serious. Deadly serious.

"Let's compromise," I say. "Once my way. Once yours. Deal?"

Javier grins, revealing the comma-shaped dimples in the scruff on either side of his mouth.

"Deal." He holds out his hand. "C'mon, let's go upstairs."

Chapter Eighteen

JAVIER

I hold the blankets up, and Maddie climbs into my bed beside me, burrowing her body into the curve of my own. I've had a half-woody since Maddie said the words *pity fuck* a few minutes ago downstairs.

Now, with the warm willingness of her body pressed against me, my dick's gone full salute. And we're talking *full* salute. Like. Painfully full. I suck in a breath when she turns, her butt brushing against it.

She swallows, an enormous sound in the dark silence that surrounds us.

"Wow," she says.

"I'd say I'm sorry," I murmur. "But I'm not."

Maddie turns again so that she's facing me. The scent of her coconut shampoo fills my head. I love that smell. I even bought some coconut shampoo for myself. I smile every time I use it because it makes me think of her.

In reply she takes my hand and slowly guides it down between us. When we reach the waistband of her leggings, I freeze.

"Maddie—"

"No, Javier. My way first." Her lips brush lazily against mine as she speaks. "It's your turn to trust me. My way. Please."

I grin against her mouth. "Vale," I say. "Estoy en tus manos."

I'm in your hands.

She tugs the duvet over our heads, cloaking us in darkness. My vision goes blank. After a beat, my other senses blink alive, and I'm overwhelmed by smell and feel and taste. I'm aware of the sound of her breath, the smell of her hair, the warmth radiating off her skin.

She surrounds me, Maddie, mujer, guapa. I'm overwhelmed by the desire I have for her, the desire to touch her, possess her, make her come, make her cry out my name.

I want to do all this slowly, savoring every minute she gives me. We have all night, sure, but there's no knowing if—when—Maddie might pull away. When she might run.

I want slow, but she's in charge. For this round, anyway.

My way. She wants to do this her way. Fast, no-holds-barred pity sex. I don't mind fast, of course. I'd fuck upside-down while hanging from a circus trapeze if it meant making Maddie happy.

I only hope she gives me a chance to show her making love can be good too.

She slides our tangled fingers into the front of her leggings. My fingertips brush something that feels like lace—her underwear.

My pulse—and my dick—jump. They're tiny, her underwear, and delicate. I could rip them to shreds with a flick of my wrist.

I'm tempted. But Maddie's in the lead for this first round, so I merely follow, happy to give her what she needs.

I'm so happy she came over today.

We glide past the lacy underwear, my palm skimming the wiry surface of her pubic hair.

She lets out a long, low breath, guiding my middle finger farther, farther, her legs falling apart as we furrow between the lips of her cunt.

She's hot.

And wet. Already so. Fucking. *Wet.*

I grit my teeth. Christ, I'm going to come in my pants if I'm not careful.

In the quiet darkness, I feel the throb of her pulse inside her slick swollenness as an audible sound.

"Dios mío, mujer," I murmur. *My God, woman.*

I slide my finger farther, catching my fingertip in her entrance. She tightens around me, an invitation. I glide effortlessly into her pussy, its grip vise-like around my finger. I groan. It's going to feel so good to be inside her.

I want so badly to be inside her.

I pull out my finger, slowly, running it along the center of her slit. She guides it up, up, my fingertip working small circles into her flesh until we find her clit.

She gasps.

I grin.

Her fingers go slack as I work my way around the spot. I tease, moving my fingertip in a wide arc around the ridge of her lips; I come back to where she likes it, pressing a little harder, her soft pants filling my ears, my head.

My heart.

I try to kiss her, ducking my head so that our mouths might finally meet. But she merely bites my bottom lip and works her hips against my finger, throwing back her head so that my lips find the tender flesh of her throat.

"Off," she breathes, untangling her fingers from mine. "Take them off, Javi."

With a groan I pull my hand out from between her legs,

and then I'm tugging her leggings and her underwear off her hips, the sound of my fingers scraping against her skin, filling the small space between us. She bends her knees, helping me to pull them off her feet.

Using my foot, I shove the knot of her clothes toward the bottom of the bed.

It's completely dark beneath the covers, but my hand finds the bare length of Maddie's leg anyway. It seems like I've been waiting a lifetime to touch these otherworldly legs of hers again. It's all I can do to keep my fingers from trembling as I draw a line from her calf up to the sleek knotted lines of her knee to the softness of her thigh, inviting me to keep going, keep going—my fingers work shapes into her smooth skin, I can't believe I'm touching her like this, I can't believe she's letting me touch her again—

Her legs fall apart as my fingers part the lips of her pussy and sink into her center. Two fingers this time—middle and fourth—and she gasps as I slide into her warmth. Her fingers are there too, working at her clit while I work her center. It only takes us half a heartbeat to fall into a rhythm, and I feel her stretching around me, the first tremors of an impending orgasm.

She grabs my other hand and brings it to the hem of her shirt. Together we glide beneath it, my fingers catching on the erect pebble of her nipple.

I groan, a guttural, animal sound.

She's not wearing a bra. She must've taken it off while she was in the bathroom brushing her teeth a few minutes ago.

I press the pad of my thumb into her nipple and she gasps. I move it back and forth, the soft mound of her breast filling my palm as I work her nipple, drawing it to an even tighter—and I imagine painful—point.

Maddie's all curves and soft skin, her body so different from mine. So vulnerable, so warm, in all the right places.

I press my body against hers, closer, closer, we can never be fucking close enough. We're winding tighter, the two of us, our bodies coming together with an ease and a thumping knowledge I am not prepared for. You would think we'd have fucked dozens, hundreds of times for how comfortable this feels.

We still haven't kissed. I try to find her mouth, but then she's tugging at my tee, drawing it up over my belly and chest. I have to let go of her to take it off, and as my hands move between us I can smell the saltiness of her arousal on my fingers.

An arousal I want to bury myself in. My dick throbs. My heart beats an uneven tune inside my chest, my head, and as much as I want to take control of this moment, as much as I want to make Maddie mine in my own way, I want to give her what she needs. Control, orgasms—whatever she needs, I want to be the one to give it to her.

I'll take her any way that I can.

I take off her shirt too, letting it fall to the side. I run a hand across the skin of her belly. So much skin now between us. The tips of her nipples brush my chest as I slide my hand to the small of her back and pull her to me. I love holding her like this against me, feeling the springy press of her pubic hair against my bare hip, her breath warm on my shoulder.

Skin on skin on skin.

I go in for another kiss, but she presses a finger to my lips.

"My way," she breathes. "Remember?"

I wish I could see her eyes. *What are you feeling?* I wonder.

Is that what you really want, to keep your distance even when you're in my arms?

Her hands are moving now, down, her fingernails tracing lanes of fire across my skin.

I know where she's heading, but when she hooks her finger into the top of my sweats, I still jump. I'm ready—I am so fucking ready—but I'm not. It's happening too fast. One minute she's asking me to fuck her, and the next we're here, naked as the day we were born, and she's wet and I'm willing and we're both on the verge of losing control. We're rough with need and loud with longing. Touching each other with an urgency that is at odds with the soft, almost reverent things I feel for her.

But it's what she wants.

And I am going to give this girl what she wants.

I dig my teeth into the tender skin of her throat as Maddie's questioning finger grazes the sensitive tip of my penis.

She isn't wearing a bra.

I'm not wearing boxers.

The breath catches in her throat as lust, thick and roaring, pulverizes what's left of my senses. Maddie tugs down the fall of my pants, and—*fuck me, fuck me*—my dick surges proudly into her waiting hand.

"Wow," she repeats. "Just—wow, Javier."

She grips the shaft, gives it a slow, milking tug.

I see stars.

I'm in your hands, I repeat in Spanish. My brain has started to short-circuit; groping for words, I seem to only find the Spanish ones, my English all but forgotten.

She arches against me, pulling on my dick as she moves, running her thumb over its swollen head. It digs into her belly as I reach down and feel the pre-cum slick on her skin.

"Condom," I manage. "Now."

"Where?" she says.

"Aquí." *Here.* I duck my head out of our cocoon of blankets, gasping at the cool air. Maddie's still working at my dick, feeling, tugging, caressing. I grit my teeth. Digging into my top drawer, I grab a foil packet.

The second I'm back under the covers, Maddie climbs on top of me, her bare thighs gripping my hips.

Wait, I say, tearing at the foil with my teeth.

I don't want to wait, she replies in Spanish. *I'm ready for you now.*

I roll the condom onto my cock, Maddie's hands tangling with mine along the shaft, engorged with blood and need and arousal. I'm thankful for the condom. Without it, I'd last all of two seconds inside her.

She's sitting up now, straddling me as she grips my dick. My hands feel their way up the sides of her waist, her bones and skin so delicate, so feminine beneath my calloused fingertips, it makes my chest clench.

Maddie is smart. She's strong and she's independent and I have no doubt she's going to kill it on her own when she graduates. But knowing her like I do—touching her like I am now—I am aware that as intense as her strength is, her vulnerabilities are equally as deep.

I hate her father for hurting her. Who could ever hurt such loveliness? Who could ever take advantage of such naked passion, such strident, unabashed love for the world and all its wonders?

I'm overwhelmed by the need to protect her, to protect these bones and this enormous heart. She deserves to have her vulnerabilities protected so that her strengths might shine.

It's all I can do not to take her in my arms, and hold her, and make love to her the way I want to.

But I have to wait my turn.

This is what I agreed to give her right now. Nothing more, nothing less.

I glide my hands up to her breasts. They harden beneath my touch, filling my palms with their ripe firmness. She gasps as I thumb her nipples.

She guides my dick between her legs, her other hand braced on my chest for support. I feel her heat pressing down on me as she angles me *just* so at her entrance. She's tight; it's going to take a minute for us to figure this out, especially with her on top.

I sink into her pussy, Maddie canting her hips to help me glide more easily into her wetness. Even with the condom on, I can feel how slick she is, how ready.

Jesus. *Christ*. Have mercy. *On me*.

She lets out a moan.

She's so tight it almost hurts, so small I'm afraid I'm hurting her.

Mujer, I gasp. *Are you okay?*

In reply she sinks all the way down, swallowing my dick to the root. I gasp. She moans. She feels . . . she feels like everything. Sweetness and heartbeats and an eviscerating closeness.

I want to kiss her, badly.

I wish Maddie would let me fucking kiss her.

I also wish I could see her. See her face. See her spread-eagled on top of me, the lips of her pussy engorged around my cock. Just imagining what she'd look like is enough to make me groan.

In the dark, I can only feel her. But that's enough to know she's incredibly sexy.

It's her confidence that almost sends me over the edge. She doesn't hesitate, doesn't hide, she just *does*. And Christ does she do it well.

Both of her hands are on my chest, and she begins to move her hips. Little swivels at first, just enough movement that I glide in and out of her in short, excruciatingly delightful spurts.

I give her breasts a gentle squeeze, nipples hard against my palms, and she swivels a bit harder. Harder.

Harder.

I move my hips up to meet her. She goes still, a moan stalling in the back of her throat.

Javier, she breathes. *Javier.*

Maddie grabs one of my hands and brings it between us, just above the jointure of our bodies. Using her first two fingers, she guides my thumb in a small, slippery circle around her clit.

Touch me here, she says. *Yes—there—ah, Javier! right there—*

Her pussy contracts, another tremor, this one makes me feel the first stirrings of my own orgasm, heat spiraling tighter and tighter between my legs. I hope I can hold on long enough to let her go first.

We are, after all, doing this Maddie's way.

She's just so fucking sexy. Delicious. It's driving me crazy, not being able touch her like I want to, but if she wanted hard and fast—well, that's what we're doing. And I don't hate it.

The darkness swirls around us, and I am lost in it. I can't shake the sensation of falling through air, my stomach flipping every time Maddie breathes my name, every time she touches my skin.

She's full on riding me now, our bodies beginning to stick with sweat. Despite the pace, we manage to keep our rhythm, my hips rising to meet hers just as she falls. We're good at this thing, this pity fucking, effortlessly good at it, like this isn't our second time, like we've been at this forever and ever.

My heart is hammering in my chest and my cock is pulsing in the grip of her cunt and I can't stand it, I have to kiss her, I have to take her mouth and have it, I think it will be the thing to make her come.

It will be the thing that makes me feel less lost.

I glide my free hand from her breast to the small of her back and pull her closer to me. She's lying on top of me now, still straddled around my hips, the pebbled points of her breasts brushing my chest as she bumps up and down, up and down. It changes the angle of my dick. I'm pressing against the front wall of her pussy, hard, my thumb falling away from her clit as she massages herself against me.

"Oh," she moans. "*Oh*."

I take the back of her head in my hand and pull her to me. I don't tease her, I don't test her with a gentle press of lips. I crush my mouth to hers, my tongue as greedy as her cunt. It's a deep kiss, a messy kiss.

Best of all, Maddie kisses me back. Long, deep strokes, a tangle of lips and tongues, and she's moaning now, her pussy clenching around me. Finally touching her the way I want to makes me wild—with need, with tenderness. I have all of her right here in my arms, her mouth, her pussy, her breath, but it's not enough.

I want more. She always leaves me feeling this way—wanting *more*.

I don't know what I'm going to do when she goes back to the States.

She digs her hands into the flesh of my shoulders, clinging to me in anticipation of the rush. I hold her, wrapping my arms tightly around her, fitting her into my chest. She fits so perfectly against me, her body a compliment to my own, her soft curves a devastating foil to my sharp edges.

Guapa, I whisper in her ear, trailing my lips across her jaw. *Guapa, I know how much you like to lose gravity. Do it again. Do it again for me, Maddie.*

I take her mouth one last time, my palms gliding down the warm skin of her back, and she comes.

Great, gasping pulses that squeeze my cock so hard I have no choice but to let go, to give in to her rush.

To give into the feeling of her letting go, too, in my arms.

She's still coming around me, milking me, hurting me,

when it happens. My hips buck off the bed, the tightness between my legs bursting into a point of white-hot light. It pounds through me in time to my frantically beating heart, each pulse blaring harder, louder, pulling me inside out.

It's violent, my release.

Violent and so very sweet.

Maddie bites my lip, hard, her moan vibrating in my throat as she goes limp against me. I keep coming, and coming, holy shit, I'm *coming*, am I ever going to stop coming?

The pounding lessens, bit by bit, aftershocks wring what little energy is left in my body. I take a long, low breath, filling my lungs. Maddie's body rises with my chest, her hair tickling my nose as she moves.

I let out the breath. For a minute neither of us says a word. We just lie in my bed, our limbs tangled, not daring to break the silence. I hold her and she lets me, her arms curled between us, her head tucked into the shelter of my neck. The scents of sweat and sex hang heavy in the stuffy air underneath the blankets.

I open my eyes. The darkness is still there, but the dizziness is gone, replaced with sudden, searing clarity. Replaced with the solid weight of Maddie on top of me, her breath warm on my skin.

I felt lost before I met Maddie.

But now—now I feel *found*.

Chapter Nineteen

MADDIE

The Next Morning

I wake up to the smell of coffee.

Javier. I don't know why that homey smell makes me think of Javier, but it does. A warm rush moves through my body. My very *naked* body.

The rush pools between my legs. There's a pinch there, a small but hot hunger as I sit up and survey the cozy, fluffy expanse of Javier's massive bed.

Oh God.

I went back for seconds.

Oh *God*.

I take a warrior breath, let it out. My eyes flutter shut.

I am such an idiot.

Sleeping with Javier the first time was great.

But seconds? The seconds were fucking *amazing*. So good, so overwhelmingly delicious, that my heart's gone all soft on me. I want him. I crave him—his kindness and his body and the way he makes me feel—I like him so damn much I don't know what to do with myself.

He makes me want things, *believe* in things like happiness and hope, that I know aren't meant for me.

This is going to hurt. Leaving Javier is going to hurt so badly, I can already tell.

I should've never come here. I should've muscled out this snowstorm at my *señora*'s apartment. I should've used this time to work on my thesis.

I should've never let Javier in.

My throat tightens. I feel closer to Javier than ever before, which is all the more reason to run. I'm investing too much . . . too much emotion, I guess, too much heart and hope in a man who is much better off with someone else. Someone who will stay. Someone who is willing to put down roots here in Spain. I am not that someone. I have to go back to Atlanta, soon, and help my mom pack up the house. Even if my mom didn't need my help, there's no way my dad will pay for another semester in Madrid. I can't put down roots in a city I don't live in.

It's clear to me that Javier and I can never find forever together. We live in different cities, different countries. And we want very different things.

I'm afraid he'll hate me when I tell him we're done.

I have to get out of here. Now.

I can't find my clothes—the bed ate them, I guess—so I sneak into Javier's closet and grab a crisp white button-down. Sliding it over my head, I smell him, the scent now familiar—the cinnamon and soap. The fabric brushes against my nipples, hardening them, making the ache between my legs pulse brighter.

His shirt is huge, more like a dress on me, the starched shirt tails trailing along the middle of my thighs. I toe into my foot pussies and shuffle to the bathroom. I half expect the mirror to crack on account of my reflection, but I'm pleasantly surprised to see that I look kinda sexy in Javier's shirt, my hair a bit wild, lips still red and swollen from Javier's mouth and tongue and teeth.

I run through what I'm going to say in my head as I grasp the railing and clomp down the stairs. *We can't do this anymore, Javier. We have to stop while we're ahead. I hope you'll understand. Please, please, don't hate me for this. Also, can you help me find my clothes? I should probably head home now . . .*

I step into the living room and glance out the windows. It's a winter wonderland outside, the snow blanketing the city. There is not a soul to be seen. The sky is still grey and ominous with more snow on the way.

Javier's already lit a fire on the fireplace. It crackles and snaps, making the flat feel cozier and warmer than ever.

I turn to face the kitchen.

My heart stalls when my gaze collides with Javier's. He's more handsome-hot than ever, sleep mussed, disheveled, scruffy in sweats and a long-sleeved tee. When he smiles it's like I've been hit by a force field of kind-sexiness that is so wonderfully Javier it knocks my breath from my lungs.

Fuck fuck fuck this is going to *hurt.*

"Buenos días, guapa," he says, his voice gravelly with sleep. *Good morning, beautiful.* His gaze sharpens as it moves down the length of my body. My nipples prickle to renewed life beneath the heat of his gaze. "Holy shit, Maddie, you look . . . you look pretty amazing in my shirt. Better than I do. A lot better. Christ . . ."

"Thanks," I say, shyly. "I couldn't find my clothes, so. Um. I had to borrow yours. I hope you don't mind."

"Mind? Are you fucking kidding me?" He digs a hand into his hair. I know his eyes are still on me, and the heat is unbearable. "You are welcome to raid my closet anytime. Seriously."

I have to tell him no. No more. I have to leave, get out of here *now*, before I do something stupid.

"Listen, Javier—"

"Cappuccino with skim milk all right?" he asks, clearing his throat. "I know how much you like your caffeine. I made it extra strong."

I blink, looking up. Javier's turned his back to me, and he's messing with something that looks like a very fancy coffee maker. As he moves, the muscles in his back and shoulder bulge against the well-worn fabric of his shirt. I remember the feel of those muscles, the glide of his bare skin beneath my fingers.

Warrior breath. Must. Remember. To. Breathe.

"Yes," I manage. "Yeah, I love cappuccinos, but aren't they, like, pretty complicated to make? Really, you don't have to—"

Javier turns around, an enormous, shallow mug in his hands. A cloud of white foam spills over the side. Javier catches it with his first finger, giving his hand a shake.

"Too late. I already made you one." He meets my eyes. Grins.

He stands in front of me, tall and huge, and guides the mug into my hands.

"Shut the fuck up," I say, staring in disbelief at the gorgeous caffeinated concoction I hold between my palms. The mug is just warm enough, a pleasant sting against my skin.

He laughs, pressing his lips to the top of my head. "You're welcome."

I look up. *Tell him*. Tell him you have to go.

"Javier—"

But then he's covering my mouth with his, pulling at my lips, parting them with his tongue, and in the space of half a heartbeat I'm kissing him back, sinking into him, falling into the irresistible pull of everything Javier. His body and his barista skills and his thoughtfulness and the sensual shape of his lips and the way he smells and the way he touches me. He's impossible to resist.

I'm dizzy when he pulls away. Dizzy and turned on as hell. *Oh jeez.*

"C'mon, let's sit," he says, gesturing to a pair of stools at the island.

I'm the only one who sits, though, as Javier is busy cracking eggs into a bowl.

"Hungry?" he asks. "Thought I'd make some tortilla."

I bite my lip. "You know I don't do breakfast."

"Just try it," he says. "Please?"

I watch him move through his kitchen, opening a drawer, setting a fork in the sink. Seeing him cook is kinda sexy.

"Okay," I say. "Here, let me help."

Javier shakes his head as he whisks the eggs. "I got it. Sit. Relax. Enjoy your coffee. You sleep okay?"

I curl my hands around the mug. "Yeah, actually. You know I really haven't slept much this semester. So sleeping like I did last night—it's really nice to wake up and feel rested. Really rested."

"You should sleep with me more often then," he says with a grin.

I want to tell him that I'd like that. That I think it'd be the best thing ever, curling my body around his night after night, taking, taking, taking all he'd be willing to give me.

But whether it'd be the best thing ever or not, we both know it's not going to happen.

Maddie

"That was delish," I say when I'm finished eating. "Thank you for making it. Let me clean up."

"Absolutely not." Javier stands, but I'm already at the sink. "Just leave the dishes in there, Maddie, I'll take care of them later."

"Really, it's no big deal—"

"Really, Maddie, let me." Javier hip-checks me away from the sink, giving the plates and mugs a quick rinse before turning off the faucet.

I stand with my back against the cabinets, arms crossed. I watch as long, snaking veins pop against the tan skin of his forearms while he wipes his hands on a towel. There is something so . . . virile about him. Like he's a man, a scruffy, gravel-voiced *man*, who makes every guy I've ever been with seem like a boy.

I splay my arms out behind me, resting my hands on the cool marble countertop. I don't realize the motion reveals more thigh—a whole lotta thigh—until it's too late.

Javier's hands go still as his gaze catches on my body. His eyes darken.

"You have the nicest legs on the planet, you know that?"

My heart takes off at a sprint.

"Thank you," I say.

He drops the towel on the counter. Starts prowling toward me.

He stands in front of me, and I have to strain my neck to look up at him. God he's tall. Huge. Intimidatingly masculine.

He moves into me, gently. He doesn't press his body against mine, although our thighs brush. He just moves closer, so close he surrounds me, traps me, and the simmering desire inside my body ignites, flaring into open flame.

"My way," he murmurs. He slides his hands onto my face, fingertips tickling my ear, my scalp, and ducks his head. My eyes flutter shut as he presses a kiss onto my neck, his scruff prickling against my skin. "This time, we make love."

"Making love," I breathe. "What does that entail, exactly?"

"Going slowly," he replies, his mouth making its way along my jaw. "Taking our time. Kissing. Kissing you like I just did. Kissing you the way I want to."

He's using his hands to guide my head in time to his lips on my throat, handling me gently, knowledgeably. God he's good at this, it's only a matter of time before my knees buckle, I can't, I shouldn't, but I'm sinking into him. It's impossible not to sink into his touch and his kindness and his entirely honorable intentions.

I promise, he murmurs in Spanish. *I promise you won't regret it. I promise you'll like it.*

"*Vale,*" I whisper. *Okay.* Slowly I turn my head to face him. "But only if we play my music."

He pulls back. "Your music?"

"Country." I grin. *I promise you'll like it,* I repeat in Spanish, teasing.

Javier's grinning now, looking into my eyes. "All right. Country it is. Where's your phone? I'll plug it in to the speakers."

"Speakers?"

"I'm a musician, Maddie—if I'm not playing my own music, I'm listening to someone else's. I've got speakers installed all over the flat, upstairs and downstairs."

He puts on the playlist I tell him to—"Slow Country Jams"—and a sexy acoustic song fills the apartment.

"Happy?" Javier asks, coming back to stand in front of me.

I bite my lip. "Very."

One side of his mouth kicks up as he leans in. My stomach flips. His handsomeness his eviscerating.

He presses his lips to mine. I cling to the countertop behind me for dear life. The kiss is soft at first, tinged with the slightest hint of coffee. A sleepy, slow greeting.

But then he presses his enormous body against mine, enveloping me in the heat radiating from his limbs, and the kiss deepens of its own accord. Suddenly I'm gasping for breath, rising to meet the strokes of his tongue, the pull of his lips, pressure building between my legs. I'm going totally commando this morning on account of my MIA underwear, so Javier only needs to reach down, trail his fingers between my thighs to know that I'm already wet.

Really, really wet.

"Put your arms around my neck," he says, trailing his lips over my throat, nipping at the skin there. "Hold on to me."

I do as I'm told, crossing my wrists at the back of his neck while my fingers work their way into his hair. He lets out a groan, and before I know what he's doing he's gathering the backs of my thighs in his hands and lifting me onto the counter, using his hips to coax my legs wider.

Wide enough that he slips between them.

"Javi," I breathe as his mouth finds the hollow underneath my ear. "Javi, not here. It's too . . . too much light."

"My way," he murmurs. "Remember?"

He slides his palms up my thighs, the blood beneath my skin pumping, pumping, pumping with acute awareness. His fingers find the hem of my shirt. For a minute I think he's just going to hike it up, to bare me to him as quickly as possible.

But I forget we're doing this his way.

He takes the very last button at the bottom of the shirt in his fingers. He works at it, unbuttoning it slowly, *oh* so slowly, before moving to the one above it.

Already I want to roll my hips against him, I want to create friction, but he holds me firmly in place with his hips, unbuttoning the shirt one button at a time. I let go of his neck and brace my hands on the counter behind me, counterbalancing the press of his body with the weight of my own.

He takes my mouth with his, moving stridently but thoroughly, the kiss at once messy and tender. Parts of my body I didn't know existed prickle to life—the insides of my knees, the length of my spine, the place just inside my ribcage.

I moan. I want him to touch me. Now. I want him to put his hands on me and lower me onto his dick, quick and dirty, just how I like it.

In response, he slows his pace. Slows the kiss, long, lingering strokes of lips and tongue that leave me dizzy.

Finally, I'm naked up to my breasts. The air feels cool against my overheated skin.

The button at my breasts pops open. Javier breaks the kiss to look down. His lips part, and his eyes are dark, almost savage, when he brings them back up to meet mine. He cups my left breast, thumbing my nipple as he works at the remaining buttons with his other hand.

I arch into his hand, practically begging for more, for harder.

For pity.

Javier gives me none. He undoes the last button at my chest and parts the shirt, gently, using both hands to push it over my shoulders as he tugs at my lips with his teeth.

I am sitting on his kitchen counter, and I am completely, utterly naked, my breasts thrust in the air like an offering. I'm breathing hard, my body rising and falling in time to my ragged gasps for air.

I've never felt more vulnerable.

I've never felt more turned on.

Javier puts his hands on my bare waist. He splays his fingers around my ribcage, holding me tightly, possessively, his hands so big that his thumbs graze my bellybutton. His mouth moves from my lips to my jaw. Down, down, down the slope of my throat, I'm breathing harder now, his scruff feels deliciously rough against my chest, my nipples—ah, *ah*, now he's got one in his mouth, sucking it to a hard point, tugging at it with his teeth.

A telltale bulge begins to grow in his sweats, rubbing against my pussy. I try to reach down but he just bucks against me, holding me in place with his hands, making it impossible to reach between us.

"But I want—"

"*Yo* quiero," he replies, his breath warm on my breast. *I want.*

What do *you want*, I breathe in Spanish.

You, he murmurs. *All of you.*

No you don't, I say. *I'm too broken.*

Javier's mouth trails a line of fire down the soft slope of my belly.

"You are not broken," he says. "Bruised, maybe. But not beyond repair."

"You don't know that."

"I know you. Bad parts. Good parts. Really good parts." His hands slide down to my thighs. "I'd take them all if you'd let me."

My heart contracts. Why does he always have to say such lovely things?

Why does he always have to make me feel so at home, so *welcome* in his arms?

He dips his shoulders, grasps my ankles in his hands. One by one he sets my heels on the edge of the countertop, bending my knees. My legs are spread far—very far—apart.

For all intents and purposes, I'm spread-eagled, my lady bits on full display in the kitchen's bright light.

"You can't," I pant. "I can't."

"Oh, guapa." He gets down on his knees. Meets my eyes. "I think you can."

Chapter Twenty

MADDIE

Javier presses his palms to the very tippy-top of my inner thighs, spreading me even wider, opening me to him. Desire, searing, almost painful, pulses in the very center of my pussy.

I haven't shaved. I haven't showered. I am so wet I can smell it. If this were any other day, with any other guy, I'd be way too uncomfortable to let him go down on me.

But this is Javier. And by the look in his eyes, I can tell he doesn't give a shit about that stuff. I can tell he likes what he sees.

The fact that he finds me sexy makes me *feel* even sexier.

I fall back on my elbows, vision going dark, when he presses a soft kiss onto my clit.

Tell me where you like it, he says.

"There," I pant. "Everywhere. God, Javi—"

His tongue emerges from between his lips. He runs it up the length of my slit, a slow, hyper erotic caress.

He presses his tongue, gently, into my entrance. "There?"

"Yes."

"What about . . . here?" He licks my clit.

My head falls back. "*Yes.*"

Javier buries his mouth in the top of my pussy, his tongue working circles around the center of all this maddening sensation.

I watch him as he kisses me, his head moving between my legs. Slowly at first, he won't be rushed, he won't be hurried, even as my hips begin to roll, begging for more. His hands are warm on my thighs, holding me still when I want to jump.

It turns me on, watching him. His gaze meets mine, a knowing gleam in his eyes as he licks me, keeps licking me, licking until my eyes flutter shut and the tight pull between my legs becomes unbearable.

My hands, possessed by the throb of my pussy, find their way to my breasts. I knead each nipple, sending darts of heat through my core. I want more. I want release. I'm winding tighter, approaching the precipice, I just want to *get* there—

"That," he says. "Is hot. You're so fucking hot, mujer."

Javier begins to move more quickly, his kiss ardent now, his tongue pressing hard against my clit as he uses his thumbs to hold me open wider. My back arches off the counter as I gasp his name. I keep one hand on my breast, the other finds Javier's hair. I dig my fingers into his hipster wave, giving it a good tug.

He groans, a vibration that ricochets through my pussy, making me wild. I'm close—it hurts, I'm so close—

"I'm so close," I breathe.

Javier pulls back. *Not yet, guapa*, he says.

My eyes fly open. "What? Why—what?"

"Not yet." He stands, running a hand down his mouth.

I bolt upright, blinking against the thwarted throb of my impending orgasm. "What the hell, Javi? That's just cruel!"

"You keep forgetting," he says, putting that same hand on my thigh, "it's my turn. My call. And I want to go slow."

He slides two fingers inside my pussy, pressing his palm against my clit.

I arch against him, my lips falling apart. My knees are bunched up against his chest as I push against him, but he doesn't budge. It hurts; God, it feels so, so good.

"Tell me to stop." He's watching me, nostrils flaring. "Tell me to stop, mujer. Tell me you don't like the way I make you feel."

I meet his gaze head on. "You're such a fucking tease."

He pushes his fingers farther inside me, mouth hovering an inch above mine. "And you like it."

Before I can respond, or come, or combust, Javier loops an arm around my waist and pulls me off the counter.

"If you try to carry me anywhere," I say when he bends down to lift me, "I will literally crush you, first of all. Second, I am perfectly capable of walking, even if I'm a little—um—weak in the knees at the moment. So. Where to?"

Javier crosses to the living room. Grabbing a thick woolen blanket from the couch, he throws it on the floor in front of the fire.

"Of course," I say.

"Of course what?"

"You pick the most romantic spot. A warm blanket in front of a roaring fire."

"What?" He smirks. "The kitchen counter isn't romantic?"

I bite my lip. I wouldn't pick the kitchen counter as a romantic spot to get eaten out, no.

But with Javier's mouth on my body and my hands in his hair, it was romantic.

Intense.

But also romantic.

"Come here," he says.

And then, without preamble, he tugs his shirt over his head. The muscles in his chest and arms bulge and lengthen as he moves. My mouth goes dry.

His hands move to the drawstring at the front of his sweats. He unties it.

I hear angels singing—along with some country music in the background—as he bends down and takes off the sweats too.

He straightens, facing me, his cock jutting obscenely from between the hard angles of his hips. He is rock hard. Enormously hard.

I can't help it. My gaze rakes hungrily over the length of his body. He's sweating, his skin glistening in the light of the fire. His shoulders—the hardened muscles in his enormous thighs— the dark pinks and thick veins of his dick—the trail of wiry hair that narrows over his taut stomach into his groin—*oh*, oh, for a minute I think I might faint. My nipples prickle to renewed life. My skin feels hot, my blood rioting inside my veins.

It's an incredible turn-on, seeing him like this. Baring himself to me, completely, without question. Without hesitation. It's heady stuff.

It's also terrifying. He trusts me. I know he wants me to trust him too.

I don't trust anyone except myself.

But oh, how tempted I am to give in. To accept his unspoken invitation. He's given me every reason to trust him. He's kind and he's honest and he knows what he wants.

He wants me. I believe that.

And good Lord do I want him.

He takes his dick in his hand as I approach, giving it a lazy tug. His eyes are latched onto mine, wet and dark.

My heart is pounding. So is my pussy. I *want*. I don't think I've ever wanted something as much as I want Javier right now.

"Come *here*," he repeats.

I stand in front of him. He's almost a full head taller than

I am, and twice as broad at the shoulders. Scruffy, huge, so much strength.

And then he's sliding his hands down my back, cupping my ass as he pulls me into his body. His arms and legs curl around mine, surrounding me, the insistent jut of his dick against my tummy at once lewd and comfortable, and when he presses a kiss onto the corner of my mouth something inside my chest swells. In his arms I feel—I don't know. Cherished. Beautiful. Complete.

I can't breathe. I can't *breathe*.

And I can't resist when his lips cover mine completely, a slow, deep kiss I feel all the way to my toes. Goose bumps break out on my arms and legs. He holds me closer, tighter, his skin warm.

It's overwhelming, the need he stokes inside my body, the hungry devastation of his lips on my lips. He's turning me inside out, baring all my weaknesses, baring to the light all the things I want to hide.

I can't hide much longer. Not when Javier's kissing me like this.

I pull back, gasping for air. I feel unsteady on my feet.

I keep my eyes closed as I try to catch my breath.

"You okay?" Javier asks, putting his hands on my face. The concern in his voice is . . . it's everything.

"This," I say. "Your way—it's a lot."

His lips brush my nose, my closed eyes. "I know, guapa. Your way was a lot for me. Any time I touch you—it's a lot for me. And never enough."

I open my eyes, look into his. "Never enough," I whisper. "I'm ready, Javier."

"I know you are," he says. "I am too, Maddie."

He falls to his knees in front of me. He kisses my belly-button, his hands on my hips as his lips move to my pussy. I put my hands on his shoulders, holding on for dear life as his tongue parts my lips, finding my clit.

Lightning spikes through me, making me cry out. I'm so close, in the space of a single heartbeat I'm on the brink again, my legs beginning to shake.

He pulls me down by my hips, his mouth moving up my throat, capturing my mouth. I taste the salt of my arousal on his lips as he digs his hands into the hair at the nape of my neck, gathering it in his fists.

His touch is sweet. Unbearably sweet.

Javier kisses me, hard, and I fall on top of him, our bodies tangling on the blanket. The heat from the fire envelopes us, the campfire smell of burning wood crisp and homey.

I kiss his throat, bite the place where his pulse marks a frantic beat against his skin.

A pulse—a heart—that beats like this for me.

My heart beats like that too. So hard and so loud it blocks out everything else, everything but the smell of his skin and the feel of him all over me.

He rolls over onto his side, bringing me with him. I brush my nose against his. Javier's eyes open, reflecting the oranges and blue-reds of the fire behind me.

He looks at me, and keeps looking, his gaze intense, his eyes full. I should look away—*I need to look away*—something is happening between us, something lovely and deep and real is moving from his eyes into my skin, into my chest, my heart.

Close your eyes, he says in Spanish. *Close your eyes. Let go, Maddie. You know you're safe with me. Let go.*

And I do. Despite the thousand reasons why I shouldn't, I close my eyes and surrender.

I let go.

Javier holds me against him, one hand splayed across the small of my back as I sense him reaching over his head, toward his discarded sweats. A second later both his hands are at my back, fumbling with a foil packet.

A lick of heat burns between my legs. His penis is trapped between our bodies, warm and throbbing, its head slick with precum. I'm so hungry for him, so ready to feel him inside me, I can hardly stand it.

Javier is trying to put on the condom himself, but I reach down and take over, trapping the tip of his penis in the circle of my thumb and forefinger while I work the condom down the length of his shaft. The muscles in his stomach clench as my fingers move over him and his breath comes in hot spurts against my face.

"There," I breathe. "Ready. Oh my God, Javi, finally ready."

He presses his tongue to the sensitive skin at my throat, using the great bulk of his body to roll me onto my back. The blanket is soft against my skin, warm from our bodies. One of my favorite songs swells around us as the fire spurts, hisses.

I keep my eyes closed. Javier settles his weight over me, my legs falling apart at the urging of his hips. He covers my mouth with his, pulling, asking, the back of my head sliding against the blanket as I rise to meet his kiss.

He's reaching between us now, taking his dick in his hand. Anticipation streaks through me. He's making me wait, I know he is, taking his time with me, with my body, and it's driving me crazy in the best, *best,* way.

He guides his dick up the length of my pussy, slowly, making me cry out against his mouth. Javier swallows the sound, his penis coming to rest at the top of my sex—right on my clit. He cants his hips, pressing against me, and uses his hand to draw a small, tight circle on my slick flesh.

Bursts of light erupt behind my closed eyelids. My body bucks up, but he holds me in place, breaking the kiss to duck his head and take my nipple in his teeth.

He bites with his teeth and he circles with his dick and I am melting, I am coming—

I gasp when it happens, a full body release that is blindingly intense. My legs shake, my muscles contract. Pulse after pulse after murderous pulse move through me, making me sweat, making me curse. I hold onto Javier's hips, digging my fingernails into his skin.

I have never had an orgasm quite this intense.

Quite this lasting. It keeps going.

See, he growls, trailing his lips over my lips. *Waiting—going slow—it's worth it, isn't it?*

I don't reply—at the moment I can't summon a coherent thought—but he's right. It was an excruciating tease, doing it Javier's way.

But it just made the payoff that much sweeter.

The aftershocks of my orgasm leave me shaking as they ricochet through me, quieter now but still potent. Javier guides himself into the wet cleft of my pussy, it feels so sweet, almost a calming, joyful pressure that stills my rioting flesh.

I wrap my legs around his hips. He deepens his kiss.

Using his fingers, he holds me open, guiding himself deeper inside me. I moan, still a little sore from last night.

"You all right?" he breathes.

I nod, swallowing.

God, he says through clenched teeth. *You're unbelievably tight, Maddie. Tiny. I can still feel you coming.*

Don't come yet, I plead.

He laughs, a gruff, pained sound. *I will try, guapa.*

The pressure between my legs builds as Javier presses farther into me. He pauses, rocks back, rocks forward, the first small, pleasant thrust.

I move my hands to his ass, urging him closer. I want everything he can give me. I want all of him, his whole body, his whole being, because those are the things he took from me.

With one final, long thrust, he buries himself in me to the hilt.

And then he starts to move.

There is no preamble, no warm up. Just long, hard, gutting strokes, his body moving ardently against mine, his muscles bunching, stretching beneath my fingers. He moves like an athlete, all grace and effortless intensity.

His thrusts are unhurried, as are his lips as they trail over my throat, my face, my chest.

When he begins to swivel his hips at the end of every thrust, I think I might lose my fucking mind.

He's loving me thoroughly, he's loving me well, and I revel in the feeling of being in his arms like this, of letting myself *feel* like this. I give myself up to him, letting him do as he pleases, and good Lord does he please me.

My eyes fly open when the pressure increases. Javier is on his knees between my legs, grasping me by the waist as he maneuvers me onto his lap so that we sit, facing each other.

His hand glides up my back, curling around the nape of my neck. He meets my eyes, going still inside me as he wraps one of my legs around his waist, then the other.

He looks at me for a long, heated moment. We're both breathing hard, my nipples brushing against his broad chest. I slide my arms around his neck. He brushes his nose against mine, softly, affectionately.

Do you like my way? he asks.

I do, I say. *Too much.*

There's a tenderness between us that wasn't there before, an understanding. It terrifies me, but when he starts moving inside me again, my eyes flutter shut, a cry of submission on my lips. He guides my head into the crook of his neck, and as he glides in and out of me, in and out, he holds me against him, and I bury my teeth into the thick skin at his shoulder.

He gasps. I shake.

I'm coming, he says, taking my hand from his neck and guiding it down to my pussy. *You should too.*

My pussy is engorged and very wet, swollen with Javier inside me. I run my fingers over my clit, matching Javier's rhythm, and I can't believe it, I can't believe it, but I'm going to come again, I am defenseless against his onslaught, I am so fucking turned on by everything he does and everything he is that I can't help but come again.

It hurts this time, the orgasm. Javier's arms lock around me as it hits him at the same time. We come together, his hand fisted in my hair, his tongue in my mouth, a great rush that binds us together.

When the rush recedes, it leaves me shaking in his arms. He kisses my cheeks, my damp forehead, his scruff chafing my skin.

I curl into his chest, not wanting to open my eyes.

Not wanting this to be over.

"Maddie." Javier's breath tickles my skin.

"Javier," I sigh, grinning.

"The songs," he breathes. "The ones I've been writing—they're all about you, Maddie. The ones I played for you yesterday. Since I met you I've had this burst of creativity. It's like you turned on this spigot inside me. I've never been more inspired than when I'm writing about you."

Chapter Twenty-One

JAVIER

All morning I wondered if I should tell her. I know she's scared, but I feel like she deserves to know.

I felt telling Maddie that she's inspired me like no one else has might put to bed some of the lies she's been telling herself.

Namely, the lie that she's somehow defective and isn't special, isn't wonderful or wanted. That she isn't an incredible human being.

This morning I woke up and Maddie was in my bed, curled against me, the warmth from her skin seeping into my own. I buried my face in her hair, inhaling the scent of her coconut shampoo as I smiled, hard. And kept smiling.

Happiness filled me to the brim, until I thought I might explode. I've lived in this flat for a few months now. But it hasn't felt like home until this morning, when I woke up next to Maddie and started thinking about what I could make her for breakfast. Holding her in my arms, I felt like I was finally, finally home. Like I finally found my belonging.

I thought, over and over as I laid there next to her, about how my heart is going to break into a million fucking pieces when she leaves. She's a great girl, and I don't want to fucking let her go.

I thought about her—about us—for a long time. Maddie slept while my mind whirled. I thought and I thought, my heart swelling in my chest, I thought about kidnapping her and keeping her here in Madrid. I thought about flying across the Atlantic to see her in America. I started to think that maybe, just maybe, I don't have to let her go. Maybe there's a way we could try to make this work, even if she does have to return the States next semester and help out her mom pack up the house.

It's worth a try. This—us—it's so very good, and it's worth fighting for. I want to fight for us. She helps me feel at home, she helps me write. She helps me feel whole, like I finally found the other half of my being I didn't even know was missing.

I don't know when I began to believe that Maddie and I actually have a shot at forever, but the thought of being with her—setting down roots with her—it makes my entire being soar.

I look at her now, face flushed, bright blue eyes sated and wet. Her smile fades as her gaze searches mine. She's breathing hard, her dark hair swirled into a halo around her head.

She places the palm of her hand on my breastbone, right over my wildly beating heart.

"Say it again," she breathes.

"All those songs I've been writing," I say, brushing my lips against her collarbone. "They're about you, Maddie. All of them."

She tugs at her bottom lip with her teeth. I can tell she's trying not to smile.

"Are you saying that because we just made sweet, sweet love?"

I grin. "It was pretty sweet, wasn't it?"

"Yes," she says. "It was."

I cant my hips, pulling out of her, and she winces.

"Shit!" I say. "Shit, did I hurt you?"

"I'm just a little sore. Here, lemme get cleaned up."

"Sure," I say, rolling onto my side so she can get up. I watch her hurry to the bathroom, ducking when she runs past a window.

I hope she doesn't shut me down when I tell her what I'm thinking.

I hope she'll give us a chance.

I get up too, and make my way to the kitchen so I can toss the condom in the trash.

I hear the toilet flush, and Maddie emerges from the bathroom a second later. She smiles when she sees me.

"Hey," she says.

"Hey," I reply. I reach for her, and she lets me pull her close, her breasts pressed against my chest.

She traces a fingertip across my collarbone. I shiver.

"You okay?" she asks.

"Maddie," I say. "I want to be with you."

She looks down at her finger, her smile contracting.

"Look. I know you have to go back soon and help your mother get the house together. She needs you, and I get that. I want you to be with her. But we can still make this work."

"Javi," she says, blinking. "C'mon."

"I'm serious," I say. "Obviously we'll be together while you're still here. And when you go back to Atlanta—then we can fly back and forth. I'll pay for it. I don't mean to flaunt my money, but I've got plenty of it after touring with Juan. You can come here during your breaks, and I could fly to you between gigs with my band. Perhaps you can come back to Madrid for a semester next year? Or during the summer? And you keep saying how you'd like to come back to Spain anyway for your graduate studies. Whatever it takes, Maddie, I'll do it. I'm willing to give us a shot. It's worth it. You're worth it."

Maddie looks up at me, biting her bottom lip. The look of hope in her eyes makes me feel like I'm flying and falling, all at once.

"You really think that?" she asks.

"I do. I really do. We have to try, Maddie. This—what we have—it's too good not to. Let's see where this goes. Please."

She swallows, an audible sound. "I don't know, Javi. I mean. That's a lot of travel, and a *lot* of money. And my dad definitely won't pay for me to spend a summer or another semester here—"

"I will," I reply. "I'll pay for it. Whatever money you need, it's yours."

"That's lovely of you. Thank you, Javi. Really. But what if you invest all this time and money in me, and I end up sucking at it? The relationship stuff, I mean. You deserve the best. You deserve someone who is going to treat you well."

I tuck her hair behind her ear. "You are the best, Maddie. I think you'd be really great at the relationship stuff. You'll never know if you don't try. I'm asking you to try with me. If only because the sex is fucking hot as hell."

She scoffs. "It really is awesome, isn't it?"

"Best I've ever had."

"Me too," she says.

"So try with me," I say. I cup her face in my hand, using my thumb to wipe a stray eyelash from her cheek. "Please."

Maddie searches my eyes. Her smile, tentative, broadens, lighting up her entire face. My pulse thumps.

Holy shit.

She's actually going to say yes. Maddie Lucas, the girl who was only looking for a one-night stand, the girl who was too scared to let anyone in, is going to give me a chance to show her she deserves happily ever after. To show her that it's real.

She opens her mouth to speak at the same moment the sharp blare of my ringtone fills the kitchen.

I groan. "Sorry."

"You don't need to answer it?"

"Whoever it is can wait."

After a beat the ringing stops, thank God.

"So." I clear my throat. "What were you about to say?"

"I was going to say—"

We both start at the sound of a small, innocuous *ping*.

I glance down at the counter beside us. Maddie turns her head to look too. My phone is there, lit up with alerts.

My stomach plummets when I see María Carmen's name. Not only did she call, she also left a voicemail and sent a text.

I miss you too Javier. Too much. I broke up with Pedro last night. Call me when you get this. I need to see you.

Oh no. No no no no.

Maddie goes still in my arms.

"Maddie," I say slowly. "It's not what you think."

She blinks. Her eyes widen in horrified disbelief.

"What did you just say?" she asks.

"I swear to you, Maddie, it's not what you think. I told you before, I'm not interested in Carmen—I want try making a relationship work with *you*, not her—not Carmen—"

She puts her hands on my chest and pushes me away.

I spin around, panic hammering at my temples as I watch her mount the stairs.

"Maddie!" I shout. "Wait, please, let me explain."

"Explain what?" She leans over the handrail. "That you lied to me? Told me you wanted me instead of Carmen so you could get laid?"

I draw back. "What? That doesn't even make sense. *You* came to *me* yesterday—"

"It makes perfect sense!" she says. "Why would she be calling you and texting you and leaving you voicemails if you told her you didn't want her? Carmen isn't the kind of girl who does the chasing. She likes to be chased. And you've been chasing her this whole damn time, haven't you? Going after her while you're telling me that I'm the one who 'inspired you.' That I'm the one you want to 'try the relationship thing' with. You're a liar, Javier. A big fucking liar."

"What? Wait." I grab my sweatpants from the floor and tug them on. I head for the stairs. "Wait, Maddie. That's not true, and that's not fair. You're overreacting. That text—Carmen—she doesn't mean anything to me. If you'd just let me explain what you saw—"

I take the stairs two at a time. Maddie is in my bedroom, digging at the sheets. She finds a shirt and tugs it over her head. She grabs her leggings, one sock, her shoes.

"Please," I say, my voice cracking. "Please, Maddie, give me two minutes, I swear to you I'll make this right. Let me explain. I don't want Carmen. She doesn't—"

"Fuck you," she spits. Maddie is already moving out of the bedroom, her footsteps light on the stairs.

I follow her, shoving my arms into a sweater.

I follow her, but I know she's already gone.

I know I've lost her.

I watch the taxi's taillights disappear down the street, its tires crunching against the icy pavement. I see the back of Maddie's head sway when they hit a pothole. I hope she's warm enough; she forgot her coat.

I'm breathing hard, the frigid air knifing my lungs.

She's gone.

Maddie is really gone. Her laugh and her body are gone.

Inside my skin my blood burns. My eyes—they burn too. Closing them, I turn and ram my first into the door.

220

Pain blares from my knuckles up into my arm. I bite back a cry. I'm such an idiot. A huge fucking idiot.

I need a cigarette. Now.

I bolt upstairs and, finding my phone, shoot off a text.

I'm waiting outside my building, hands shoved in the pockets of my jacket, when Leo arrives.

"*Ha*-lo my friend," he says.

"Hey," I say. I hold out my hand. "Please."

"Is this he certain?" Leo digs around in his pocket. "You are very good of the not smoking for so many months."

I keep my hand outstretched. "I'm sure."

My fingers tremble as I place the cigarette between my lips, thumbing the strike at the top of Leo's bright orange lighter.

The familiar, pungent smell of cigarette smoke fills my head as I take a hard drag. God I've missed this.

The nicotine hits me like a ton of bricks, making me dizzy. This is the worst idea, lighting up when I've been so good since I got back to Madrid. I left that guy behind—the one who chain-smokes after a gig with all the pretty groupies.

I thought I left that guy behind. But now, with a head full of hurt and a heart so full, so swollen, it's about to burst, I wonder why I did.

So, Leo says, holding his cigarette between his thumb and forefinger, *tell me what happened with Maddie.*

I look at him from the corner of my eye. *How did you know it was Maddie?*

You couldn't stay away from her, even though you wanted to, he says.

I take a long, hard drag. Let it out.

No, I say. *I can't stay away from her. I don't want to stay away from her.*

You're in love with her, aren't you? Leo asks. *You're wanting to date her even though she's in America and you're here starting our band.*

I take another drag. The smoke gets in my eyes, making them water.

My hand hurts.

Chapter Twenty-Two

MADDIE

That Weekend

"Whoa, Mads, you think you could slow down?" Viv says, panting as she tries to keep up with me. "Why the rush?"

We carefully avoid a patch of dirty ice on the sidewalk leftover from the snowstorm. Our heels clack on the pavement, single notes in the rising cacophony of Madrid at midnight on a Saturday. Despite the cold, the streets are packed, filled with well-dressed young people intent on partying hard after being holed up at home all week.

"No rush." I huddle into my faux fur vest. "Just excited. I feel like it's been forever since we had one of our epic nights out."

"You mean since you hooked up with a random stranger you met at a discoteca?"

"Yes."

I feel the heat of Viv's gaze—and her censure—on the side of my face. "This wouldn't have anything to do with what happened between you and Javier this week, does it?"

"Yes."

Of course it does. It has everything to do with Javier. I'm

so desperate to get to this club and lose myself in men and music that I'm practically running. I need to forget the way Javier touched me and the way he tasted and the spectacular angles of his body and his kind intelligence and how at *home* I felt in his enormous arms.

Most of all, I am desperate to forget his betrayal. It was all a lie—that kindness, his interest in me, the way he made me feel. He asked me to be in a relationship with him while separated by an ocean just so he could bang me for the next few weeks. The thing I feared most, that I would let Javier in and he'd hurt me, make a fool of me the way my dad did, happened. It happened, and now I'm left reeling.

Chasing anonymous Spaniards in the hope of landing a hookup is the only way I know how to make myself forget. Because I certainly can't forgive Javier. So for now I'll settle for the forgetting.

"That's pretty dumb, you know," Viv says. "Trying to forget Javier by hooking up with some Eurotrash idiot. It's only going to make you feel worse."

We stop at a crosswalk, shivering while we wait for the light to change.

"I know it's dumb." I swallow, hard. "But what choice do I have? I'm going crazy, Viv."

"He likes you, chica. A lot. A *lot* lot. I know he's really confused—really hurt—by how things went down this week. You should unblock his number and give him a call. At least let him know you're okay."

I roll my eyes. "*He's* hurt? Do we really need to rehash this right now? He was the one who asked me to 'make love' with him. He asked me to try out a long-distance relationship. Ten minutes later, his super-hot ex—you know, the girl he swore he wasn't into—is texting him about how they miss each other? He lied to me, Viv. He used me."

Viv lets out a strangled sigh. She's frustrated, I know, but I really don't feel like talking about this right now.

"He misses you," she replies. "That's all I'm saying."

I blocked his number the second I left his apartment. The fact that he lied to me hurt enough, but I don't want to rub salt in the wound by seeing Uncle Pervy's name pop up on my phone. It's best just to cut off all contact before we do or say something we'll regret. What's done is done. I saw all I needed to in that text from Carmen.

I am so done with Javier.

When we finally get to Ático, the line to get in snakes around the corner.

"Ho-ly shit," Viv breathes.

I take a warrior breath. "The wait will be worth it, Viv."

She rolls her eyes, pulling me close.

We don't wait long. Five minutes later, there's some commotion in the line behind us. I turn to see a familiar man-bunned guy making his way across the sidewalk, his cut cheeks and intense green eyes something out of an underwear ad.

He's leading Laura by the hand.

The two of them together—just yikes. My eyeballs catch fire and burn holes into my head. Laura and her footballer bro are beyond gorgeous, perfect, sexy representations of the human species.

People gawk as they pass. Men get out their phones to take pictures, and women scream and bounce around on their heels to get a better look.

Rhys—yep, his name is Rhys, pronounced *Reese*, on top of being a super-hot celebrity soccer player, he's also Welsh—grins when he sees me and Vivian.

"Ladies." He gives each of us a quick *kiss kiss*. "Lovely to see you, as always. I reserved a table for us—let's head to the VIP line."

"Hello, handsome," I reply, wagging my eyebrows at Laura. She's flushed, her smile shy.

I sidle up beside her as we make our way to the front of the line. "You did it in the car ride over, didn't you?"

"We did," she murmurs in reply. "Is it that obvious? I think I'm still coming a little."

"I'm jealous. I'm hoping to get some action tonight myself."

Laura looks at me. "With Uncle Javier?"

The image flashes through my head: Javier naked in front of the fire, his skin glistening, eyes dark with arousal. How he'd closed those eyes as he got on his knees and slid his tongue between the lips of my pussy.

A pulse of longing rips through me. My heart stutters. The heat between my legs smarts.

Stop. I have to stop thinking about him. Missing him. He screwed me in every sense of the word, that bastard. Like an idiot, I let myself believe that he liked me. Wanted me. But he doesn't want me, he wants María Carmen. He's wanted her this whole time.

I have to stop thinking about him, or his betrayal is going to tear me apart.

I have to have many, *many* drinks, stat.

"No." I shake my head. "I'm thinking more along the lines of a drunk make-out sesh with a stranger. You know. The usual."

"The usual?" She tilts her head, dubiously. "That hasn't been the usual lately. Not for you. Everything okay?"

I roll my lips between my teeth, looking away. "Not really. But I'm trying, Laur. I have to try."

"All right." She wraps an arm around my waist. "If a sloppy bar make-out is what you need, then a sloppy bar make-out is what you'll get. Some of Rhys's teammates might meet us a little later. There's this one guy, he's obscenely hot—doesn't speak great English, but—"

"Sounds perfect. I don't plan on doing much talking anyway."

The bouncers practically bow down to Rhys when we get to the door. A pair of cocktail waitresses in ridiculous purple satin corsets magically appear. Plumping their boobs, they lead us up a winding staircase to the VIP tables.

Laura grabs my hand and I follow her, Viv a few steps behind me. We press through throngs of people, the music so loud the floor jumps in time to the bass.

Madrileños are an exceptionally good-looking crowd. Especially when they're dressed to the nines for a night out. A couple cute guys—like, *really* cute guys, with handsome smiles and come-hither eyes—check me out as a pass.

A few weeks ago, I would've returned the favor. If I was feeling especially feisty, I might wink, say hola, shimmy so that they could get a better view of my ass.

But tonight, their attention just grosses me out.

Not a good sign. I need a drink. I'm probably just out of practice. A few shots and I have no doubt I'll be back in the saddle, jonesin' for a little late night lovin'.

I just wish I could shake this feeling that something isn't right.

That where I am right now isn't at all where I should be. Where I *want* to be.

I want to be with Javier. Which, for obvious reasons, is absurd.

But there is no on/off switch for the things I feel for him. I wish there was, believe me. Then I could get on with my night, with my *life*, and never think about him again.

Despite what he did, the desire I feel for him haunts me. Even now, when I'm at my favorite discoteca surrounded by beautiful people, I want to be with him.

I close my eyes. Try another warrior breath.

We're the first ones to arrive at the table. Rhys orders a fifth of top-shelf tequila and, at my request, some salt and limes.

I knock back two shots in quick succession, hardly pausing for the lime chaser. The tequila's sour-sweet burn sears my throat as it goes down. Usually I'd gag, but tonight the fire feels good. It blocks everything else out, including thoughts of Javier. Of how cherished he made me feel.

"Whoa there," Laura says, stilling my hand when I reach for the bottle. "You know you have to be conscious for a sloppy make-out, right? Even the most dedicated guy isn't gonna want to play tongue hockey with you if you throw up on him."

"Here." Viv grabs a couple glasses and the carafe of orange juice the waitress set on the table. "How about some mixed drinks? Something a little less . . . um, potent."

"Sure," I say, and run my hands down my thighs. "Sure, that'd be great. Thank you, guys, by the way, for coming out with me tonight. I really needed this."

"Anytime, chica." Laura smiles as the three of us clank glasses. "We just want to see you happy."

But that's just it—the more I drink, the more I force myself to dance, to flirt with Rhys's ridiculously hot team-mate, Guillermo, who arrives an hour later—the more I try to party, the more miserable I become.

I've got a good buzz going: check. I feel hot in my super tight skinny jeans and teeny-weeny tank top: check. The music's great and this guy is interested: check and double check.

Why, then, is there this knot in my stomach? A knot that tightens every time Guillermo touches me, or pours me another drink.

I can't help wishing that it was Javier's hand on my hip

instead of Guillermo's. As much as I used to love hooking up with strangers, right now I am really craving the familiarity of Javier's touch.

I'm pathetic. This is pathetic. I have a hot footballer feeling me up, and I'm thinking about the guy who hurt me in the worst, the *worst* possible way.

Some sick, twisted part of me hopes Javier *does* see me tonight. Viv swore she didn't tell Rafa where we were going—girls' night out, no boys allowed—but there's always a chance she slipped up. If Rafa knew we were at Ático, and he told Javier, maybe he'd come try to find me.

I hope he does. And I hope he sees me having the best time ever making out with the hottest, most Eurotrash soccer player on the planet.

We dance, we drink. We drink some more. Rhys orders another fifth of tequila. The world starts to move a little too quickly when I turn my head or look down. I ask the waitress to bring some bottled water, but seeing as I'm not a single super-hot athlete, she ignores my request.

Guillermo and I huddle up in the corner of the velvet sofa. He palms my hips and I try not to tense at his touch. I let him pull me onto his lap. The motion makes me dizzy, and I grab onto his shoulder to stop the unpleasant spin inside my head, my stomach.

Guillermo takes that as an invitation, and slides his hand up my leg. He's so fucking hot, he'd be a prize notch on my belt. He's a famous footballer, for God's sake, rich and famous and probably an amazeballs lay.

There's no good reason why I shouldn't suck his face.

Except, of course, the fact that I keep seeing Javier's hot-handsomeness behind my closed eyes.

Stop. Stop thinking about him. Why are you thinking about him?

I don't want to think about Javier anymore.

So I wrap my arms around Guillermo's neck and open his

lips with my lips and indulge in that drunk sloppy make-out I've convinced myself I needed.

It's awful.

Guillermo is a good kisser. He's not pushy or too touchy-feely. He doesn't give me a reason, in short, to hate what we're doing.

But I do. I hate it.

I hate it because he's not Javier. Guillermo smells good, like a sexy cologne he probably does commercials for half-naked, but he doesn't smell nearly as good as Javier. He touches me with eager hands, but those hands aren't Javier's —enormous, kind, knowledgeable.

Every little thing Guillermo does is just a reminder that he isn't Javier.

It's just a reminder of how badly I wish he were.

I am so pathetic. I promised myself I would never be this girl. I promised myself I would protect my heart after my dad broke it this summer. I need to start protecting myself again.

So I force myself to keep kissing Guillermo, waiting for that wish to dissipate. Even in my drunken stupor, I know I'm being an idiot. I know I'm only making the loneliness inside me hurt that much more.

The fact that I am very, verrrrry drunk doesn't help.

When Guillermo presses his tongue inside my mouth, I recoil, a full-body shudder.

"I'm sorry," I say, scrambling upright. "Guillermo, it's not you, I just—I gotta go—"

I weave a little on my feet as I stumble across the club. I gotta get out of here. This was stupid, why am I so stupid—

I feel a hand at either of my elbows and look to see Viv and Laura half a step behind me, gently guiding me toward the exit.

"Sp-fanks," I mumble. I hang my head—the motion, the

people, the music—it's too much to take in right now. "I love you girls. Love you so much."

I make it outside before I feel like I'm going to be sick. *Fuck fuck fuck* I hate it when I get this drunk. I know better, I am such an idiot, a drunk, heartbroken idiot.

"Viv," I say. "I'm gonna puke. I think. I love you."

I hear a familiar, rumbling laugh—half amused, half sympathetic—that makes my skin prickle with awareness.

"I love you too, guapa."

I look up, the world lurching around me, but he— ohmigod it's *him*, he's here, he's so hot-handsome I can't take it—he stands tall and still in the middle of everything.

Javier is here.

Chapter Twenty-Three

MADDIE

I am so relieved that he is here I feel like crying.

Relieved and very, very angry.

I close my eyes, both to hide the tears and stop the spinning.

"I hate you," I say, swallowing. "Javi, I hate you."

I know, he says in Spanish. *I want to talk to you about it, but let's have that conversation later, okay? We'll talk when you aren't about to be sick.*

My stomach roils. *Ef* me for life, I really am going to puke.

A strong, solid warmth wraps around my torso, holding me upright, while a hand gathers my hair at the nape of my neck.

"Don't touch me," I say, but he ignores my wobbly request.

I puke all over the sidewalk, great, burning heaves that leave my throat raw. Tears stream down my cheeks. I'm so embarrassed. So ashamed of myself and the way I behaved tonight.

I am so mad at myself for letting Javier in. I'm mad at him for lying to me. Javier, who, despite everything, is rubbing my back, murmuring sweet Spanish nothings while I lose my dinner, and my lunch, and my breakfast, from the look of it, on the sidewalk outside a discoteca at three A.M.

I would sell my soul to the devil to be able to curl up and die right now.

I curl up against Javier instead as we climb into a taxi. I probably have vomit in my hair and on my clothes, but he doesn't seem to mind. He wraps me in his arms, and I rest my face against his chest, inhaling his scent. Cinnamon, soap. My pulse, sprinting since my little sidewalk episode, begins to slow.

He presses a kiss onto the top of my head and smooths back my hair. I feel so comfortable. So at home in his arms. He just saw me at my worst—I mean, I am an idiot asshole, I drank my face off and threw up in the street—but he doesn't seem put off by my behavior.

Now, more than ever, I wish he was mine to have.

But he's not. Never was.

"I told you, Javi, you can't kiss me like that," I mumble. "You want to be with someone else."

"I don't," he says. "I'm here with you now, aren't I? I want to be with you, guapa. I have since we met."

Even though in my rational brain I know he's a liar, my heart swells anyway at his kindness. He's *here*.

And he's staying by my side. My vomit-scented side.

That's no small thing, considering the smell is making me gag.

"Did Viv tell you where we were?" I murmur.

Javier laughs again. "No-o?"

Did you mean it, I want to ask. *Did you really mean that you love me?*

But then I start to get dizzy again, the taxi darting in and out of traffic with nauseating speed. I bury my face in Javier's

233

chest and pray that I make it to wherever we're going without puking again.

The Next Afternoon

I blink awake, ardent afternoon light burning through my closed eyelids.

Beside me, someone turns over, making the bed squeak.

My heart skips a beat. *Javier.*

Last night comes back in a rush that makes me cringe. Rhys and Laura, that disastrous make-out with Guillermo, Javier holding back my hair as I got sick.

The smell of his shirt as I fell asleep on his chest in the taxi.

Freaking Javier. I hate him.

I love him.

"I have to tell you something," I blurt, bolting upright.

Long blonde hair trails over the pillow as a head turns. Vivian cracks open one eye, last night's mascara making her look like a cute raccoon. "Shoot."

"Oh," I say, my heart sinking. Javier must've dropped me off at my señora's apartment last night. It's pleasantly annoying, how gentlemanly he is. "Oh, it's you."

"Don't look so thrilled to see me," she replies. "I mean, I'm not a hot naked Spaniard, so I get why you're disappointed. But I'm still your best friend."

Another head pops up over the edge of the bed. I almost jump.

"Holy shit," Laura moans, tugging at the back of her neck. "Your floor is not as soft as I thought it was last night."

I stare at her. "Wait. You slept here? What in the world—"

"Long story. Basically Rhys and I had a little disagreement

about—well, everything. Nothing. Whatever." She waves me off with a sigh. "Doesn't matter. I'm more interested in what urgent message you have for Javier. He was such a stud last night, helping us—helping you, when you got sick. He handled it like a pro."

I hide my face in my hands. "He's the best. And the worst."

Laura reaches over and tucks my hair behind my ear. "I'm sorry, chica."

"It's all right," I say.

"No it's not," Viv says. "You're not all right, and neither is Javier. He looked like shit."

"He did?" I ask, blinking. "I thought he looked hot."

"You were throwing up," she replies. "Your opinion doesn't count."

"Fair point," I say.

Laura is nodding her head. "Viv is right, now that I think about it. Javier had these big bags under his eyes. He looked . . . tired. Sad."

"If he's sad," I say, "it sure as hell isn't because he misses me. It was almost like he planned the whole thing—me seeing that text from María Carmen five minutes after we finished boning. He wanted me to leave so he could see her. He wants *her*, guys. Not me."

Laura arches a brow. "Did he say that?"

"Well . . . no. No, he didn't, like, explicitly say, 'Hey, Maddie, please leave because I like Carmen and want to hang out with her instead.' But he told me the night we met that he wanted to find his 'happily ever after' with her. He's wanted her from day one, and I was stupid to believe he'd change his mind. I mean. She's gorgeous. She's accomplished and smart. She lives in Madrid. She's the perfect girl for him."

Viv sits up. "That night Rafa and I saw you guys—the night you told me Javier kissed you after you went flying with him. You said he told you he didn't want Carmen. That he wanted you instead."

"Wait," Laura says, meeting my gaze. "He said that?"

I lift a shoulder, let it fall. "He did. He said it again last night. But how am I supposed to believe him when he's telling his smoking hot ex-girlfriend that he misses her? It's obvious he's playing me."

"Playing you?" Laura says. "I'm not saying you don't have a right to be upset, Mads. But I'm not sure if he is. Playing you, I mean. From what you've told me about Javier—he's a gentleman, he's kind, he's thoughtful—that doesn't sound like him."

I look down, picking at the coverlet. "I know. Which is why his betrayal hurts so damn much. I thought he was this great guy. Different from all the scumbags out there."

"Scumbags like your dad?" Viv asks.

"Yeah." I nod. "But turns out Javier *is* a scumbag. A giant, dickhead scumbag."

The girls pause. Exchange a look.

"Do scumbags usually hold your hair back when you're puking?" Laura asks.

"Do they help you with your thesis and take you flying on their private planes?" Viv asks.

I stare at both of them. "Well, no, but . . ."

"Did you at least let him explain himself?" Viv continues. "When you saw the text from María Carmen that morning— did you give him a chance to tell his side of the story?"

I open my mouth, close it. A lump forms in my throat, tears blur my eyes. God my head hurts.

I cover my face with my hands.

"No." My voice wavers. "I was so angry, I just—I couldn't. I thought it was happening all over again. My dad cheated on my mom, and Javier . . . we're not together, I know, but I felt like he cheated on me. And I couldn't take it. I couldn't handle being treated like shit on someone's shoe again."

Vivian gently wraps her hand around mine and pulls it away from my face. Tears roll down my cheeks onto my throat, but I don't move to wipe them away. It feels good to cry. To let it out—the sadness, the regret.

"Javier is very, very different from your dad," she says. "And the way your dad's been treating you—it's not right. It's not okay. But I think you know, deep down, that no matter what he says to you, your parents' divorce is not your fault. You're a smart girl, Maddie. Really smart—with this thesis you're writing, you're going to graduate with honors, for fuck's sake. You're smart, and you know that your dad is being a dick and taking his anger at himself out on you. It's not your fault. It's not your fault. It's *not your fault*, Mads."

The tears keep coming. I wipe them away with my shoulder.

"Maybe," I say. "I'm just so angry too, Viv. So fucking angry. At him. At myself. I just . . . I feel like I can't get past it."

The sob shakes my whole being, and letting it out feels like a knot is being pulled loose from the very center of my body. It bowls me over, my eyes burning, heart blaring.

Viv squeezes my hand. "You can carry that anger around with you for the rest of your life, Mads. You can be angry with your dad for treating you the way he did. Treating you the way he *is* treating you. You can be angry with yourself for letting him treat you that way. You can keep the fear around too, if you want. Fear of letting someone get close to you— someone like Javier. But I think it's time you let that shit *go* and live your fucking life. Make the choice now. Here. Today. Let it go, and let the good stuff in. Believe in the good stuff. Believe Javier. Let him in, Maddie, or you'll regret it for the rest of your life. You know it, and I do too."

I blink, the tears slowing their assault.

Let it go, and let the good stuff in. It plays on repeat inside my head. Over and over until, suddenly, it sticks there. No longer a sound or an idea but a fact. A solid, actionable fact. Something I know and understand with a conviction I didn't think I was capable of.

Something as sure and lovely as Javier's light brown eyes when he said *I want to be with you.*

I take a warrior breath, let it out. For the first time this semester, it genuinely seems to work. My pulse slows. My shoulders fall back from my ears.

And my heart unfurls in my chest. It seems to fill my entire chest cavity, swelling in the most wonderful, wrenching way.

Let it go. Let the good stuff in. Believe him. Believe Javier.

Viv is right. It took hearing someone else say it. But she's right nonetheless.

I have been so afraid of letting someone get close. Of sharing the barest, ugliest parts of myself. It's clear to me now that my anger toward my father has been keeping me from Javier. My anger at myself has kept me from letting Javier in. Javier, the one guy who has given me a sense of belonging and home throughout this horrible mess.

That anger isn't going to go anywhere unless I make the choice to remove it from my head and from my heart. I don't want to end up like my dad, all alone with only his bitterness for company. And I sure as hell am not going to let his deplorable actions control me or my future. Not anymore.

I deserve better.

I deserve to hope. To hope for my happily ever after with Javier Montoya.

It's time to let that shit go and *live* my life. I have three weeks left in Madrid, and I'm not going to waste them.

A little shiver of excitement darts up my spine. Yeah, I have three weeks left, but who knows how much time I'll have with Javier if I take him up on his offer to try the long-distance thing?

When I take him up on his offer.

I'm going to tell him yes. *Yes, I want you too, Javier. Yes, I want to give us a shot.* Yes to his smile and his songs and the amazing sex we have.

I don't know how Javier and I are going to make it work, not yet, but I'm willing to take a chance on us. If he still wants me—*please, please let him still want me*—then we'll bask in the bliss of having these few weeks together and then figure out the rest as we go.

I am going to say yes, and let the good stuff into my life. Good stuff like love.

Because I am in love with Javier.

"Reach out to him," Viv says, softly. "Let him explain himself. Maybe you can't trust your dad, but that doesn't mean you can't trust anyone else. I know your instinct is to keep pushing Javier away, even though all signs point to the fact that he's head over heels for *you*. Not Carmen. You. Mads, you like this guy too much to let him slip through your fingers."

"Like him?" I run a hand through my hair. It's knotted with I don't even want to know what. "I love him."

Laura gasps, leaping onto the bed. Viv claps her hands. The two of them pull me into an awkward half-hug, squealing like preteen girls.

"I'm so happy for you," Laura says.

"You smell *terrible*," Viv says.

"Sorry," I say.

"Tell me everything," she says.

"*Every*thing," Laura adds.

"But before you do, you know you have to tell him, right?"

Viv asks. "From what Rafa tells me, Javier's still confused about how you feel."

"I know," I say, slipping back under the covers.

"Are you scared?" Laura asks.

"I am," I say. "Really scared. All this time, I thought something was wrong with me. My dad treated me like shit, so I thought maybe I *was* shit. But I'm not. I deserve better. I deserve to be treated better than that. I deserve a great guy like Javier, and he deserves someone who loves him for himself. It's just gotta be the right moment. He's always been so romantic with me, and I want to return the favor."

"Fair point," Laura says.

"Something romantic," Viv says. "Hm."

After a minute, her eyes light up. "Rafa mentioned that Javier is practicing with his band tonight at the monastery," she says. "I could get the details from Rafa—on the down low, of course—and then you could surprise him there?"

"Perfect!" Laura says. "Surprises are always romantic."

"You think?" I wrinkle my nose. "I mean, I love a good surprise, but you don't think he'll be taken off guard? I haven't spoken to him since I ran out of his apartment yelling *fuck you.*"

"Even if he is taken off guard, you can make up for it with a little road head in that hot Range Rover of his afterward," Viv says. "Ooh, or better yet, on his plane."

Laura sticks out her lips. "Wouldn't that be sky head?"

"Air head, maybe?" I offer. "Pilot head? Mile-high head?"

"Whatever it's called, I'd give it a go," Viv says. "Knowing Javier, he'd give you a little mile-high head of your own too."

Javier would. Oh, he definitely, *definitely* would.

"All right," I say. "I'll do it—I'll surprise him tonight. I just gotta kick this hangover before then."

"Don't wear any underwear," Viv says.

"*Do* wear those pleather legging things," Laura adds. "They looked so hot on you."

"This is going to be epic. I wish I could be there to see his face when you tell him." Viv squeezes my arm. "I'm so happy for you, Mads."

I offer her a small smile. "Thanks Viv. I think I'm happy too."

Chapter Twenty-Four

JAVIER

That Night

I'm weirdly jittery on my drive to the monastery tonight. I can't shake the feeling that something bad is about to happen.

Something that has to do with Maddie.

My thoughts swirl as my stomach ties itself into a neat, painful little knot. I tried calling her this morning to check in, see how she was feeling. I thought, foolishly, that maybe she'd unblocked me. I imagine she had the hangover from hell, and part of me fantasized that she'd ask me over. I'd bring ibuprofen and a Gatorade, and she'd say *listen, Javi, I've thought about it and I believe what you told me, I know you don't want Carmen, I know I'm the one for you.*

She'd pause, look me in the eye. And then she'd say *you said something to me last night, and I'd like to say it back.*

But Maddie didn't unblock me. The call never went through.

I shove the Range Rover into gear. I guess I should take the hint already. She told me, in no uncertain terms, that she isn't looking for a relationship. She ran out of my flat *again*,

242

for God's sake, and aside from holding back her hair while she threw up at Ático, I haven't heard from her since.

I should take the hint and move on. But I'm in love with her. Head over heels in love with her wit and her mess, her intelligence and her passion. Her legs too.

God, I love her legs.

I'm getting hard just thinking about them.

I dig a handful of mints out of the glove compartment and chew on them five at a time. I haven't had a cigarette since Leo came over that morning. Between the two of us we smoked a pack in half an hour.

I was sick for two days afterward. As if I didn't feel miserable and lonely enough after the way Maddie left my flat.

Still. I want one very, very badly at the moment.

Very badly.

My unease only grows as I shuffle my way inside the monastery. I wanted to invite Maddie to come tonight, but for obvious reasons I couldn't. I know she only has a few weeks left until she heads back to the States. No doubt she's getting anxious to nail down some material for her thesis before she leaves.

She's leaving. I feel it like a knife shoved through my chest. If I've learned one thing about myself since I got back to Madrid, it's that I don't fall often for a girl. But when I do, I fall *hard*. Really fucking hard.

And it hurts.

Maybe Maddie has the right idea, putting up walls to protect herself, her heart. I wouldn't wish this pain on anyone.

Maybe Maddie is the smart one. She was hesitant about trying out a long-distance relationship. Flying across an ocean is no joke. It would be time consuming and hella expensive, not to mention the jet lag. Jet lag is the fucking worst.

Besides. Even in the best-case scenario, Maddie and I

would be apart more than we'd be together. The pain of that separation would be terrible, considering how much I've missed her these past few days.

Maybe Maddie was smart to think that giving us a chance was a stupid idea.

My footsteps echo off the gallery walls.

I draw up short when I enter the church. The stage lights are on, almost blinding in their intensity. It makes the rest of the soaring space feel like it's cloaked in a blanket of velvety dimness.

The church is empty, save for a woman who sits in a seat halfway up the aisle. I know that head of long, perfectly coiffed brown hair. *Shit*. It hits me with sudden, sickening force: I never responded to her text.

"María Carmen," I say, my heart beginning to pound. "I wasn't expecting to see you here so late."

She turns in her seat, bright red lips parting in a wide, lovely smile. It used to hit me squarely in the chest, the beauty of her smile, like someone landed a kick right in the center of my breastbone.

It doesn't anymore.

"I was hoping to catch you before your band arrived," she says in thick, lusciously accented English. She stands. "How are you?"

I'm surrounded in a cloud of her perfume as we exchange kisses. Her lips linger a touch too long on my cheeks, and there's something sensual about the way she pulls back, something suggestive about the way she looks at me, brown eyes soft with heat.

"I'm all right," I say. "And you?"

"I am well." She nods at her seat. "Sit with me a moment while we wait for the others."

I glance toward the stage. *Shit*. After everything that happened between me and Maddie, I completely forgot about

Carmen's text—the one she sent me. The one that sent Maddie running.

I should've turned Carmen down on the spot, I should've responded to the text straightaway with a *thanks but no thanks*, but I was too busy chasing after a certain American student to think about calling Carmen back and explaining why I don't want to be in a relationship with her.

I feel like an ass. Carmen broke up with her boyfriend for me, for God's sake. It didn't sound like she was very happy with him—it didn't sound like he treated her very well—but still, I should've had the decency to nip her feelings for me in the bud before tonight.

I should've had the decency to explain myself to her. But now that I have the chance, I'm too exhausted, and in too much pain, to rehash everything that's gone down in the past month. To tell her that I'm not in love with her, that I'm in love with someone else. Someone who doesn't want to be with me. I've barely slept, and I feel raw in every way imaginable.

What a fucking mess I've made.

"I really should set up—" I begin.

"You have the stage the rest of the night, Javier," Carmen replies. "I made sure to get you an extra few hours. Plenty of time. Please, sit."

I sit. The seats are narrow, having been installed sometime in the sixties when people were apparently much tinier than they are now. My knee brushes María Carmen's leg. I try to move it, but I don't have anywhere to move it *to*. Our thighs stick like glue.

You haven't responded to my text, she says after a beat. *I sent it four days ago.*

I swallow. Run a hand down my face.

I'm sorry, I say. Exhaustion sits like a hundred kilo weight on my chest. *Sorry about you and Pedro. Sorry for not calling you back. Listen, Carmen—*

I went to the Juan Ramos concert when you guys played here—back in March, I think?

Yes, I reply. *We played a couple shows at the beginning of March this year. Madrid has always been kind to us—a really great crowd.*

I saw you playing up there with Juan, she says. *I felt like my heart was going to burst. I was so proud of you, looking so handsome. Looking like you were having fun. I remember how we'd go to concerts together years ago, and you'd always tell me look, look, Carmen, one day I'm going to be up there on stage. And now you are. You're making your dreams come true, Javi.*

I look down at my knee. It's jumping.

Thanks, I say. *That's very kind of you to say. You're doing the same, aren't you, working at a place like this? You always loved history.*

Carmen scoffs, shaking her head. *You and I both know my parents got me this job. They give more money to the foundation each year than I get paid in my salary.*

That doesn't mean you're not good at it, I say.

I don't know, she replies. *It's hard to tell if the directors encourage me because they actually believe in my work, or because my parents are so important to them.*

You've struggled with that all your life. I look her in the eye. *You're talented, Carmen. You have a gift. With or without your parents' millions.*

Javi, she says. *What are you thinking? About us. I can't read you right now. Part of me believes you came back to Madrid so we could be together again.*

I run my tongue along my bottom lip. *I was ready to get off the road. Settle down a bit,* I say carefully.

I want to settle down too, she says. *I hope you don't mind me asking, Javi—but are you dating Maddie? You two seem to have gotten . . . close.*

I keep my gaze focused on Carmen. *No. I'm not dating her. But I should tell you—*

Vale, Carmen replies with a smile. She leans closer.

Closer. Tilts her head. Reaches out and traces a finger across my cheek.

And then she kisses me.

I freeze, dumb with shock.

I should've seen it coming. I know Carmen. I know how she operates, I know if she sees something she wants, she's going to take it. She has never been denied anything—opportunity, money, men—so why in the world would she think to ask first?

Her kiss—the way her mouth moves against mine—it's familiar.

And it's *weird*.

And it feels wrong.

Which makes me realize how *right* it felt to kiss Maddie.

Not that it matters. Maddie isn't coming back. No matter what I say or do, no matter how I feel about her, she's never going to give me a chance to explain myself. She may still be in Madrid for another few weeks, but for all intents and purposes, she's gone for good.

The girl who liked me for me—who couldn't care less about my past, who I was, what I did—the girl who felt more like home than home ever did, is gone.

When I first started dating Carmen years ago, I was so crazy about her one kiss would send me into a tailspin, making me hard as a rock in the space of two seconds.

I wait for something—anything—to stir inside my body. To make my blood rush, and appendages tingle. I wait. And wait.

Nothing.

I feel nothing.

Not a damn thing.

But I don't pull away. Instead I close my eyes and let Carmen kiss me.

Maybe her kiss won't get me all hot and bothered.

But maybe it will help me forget Maddie's kiss. *Maddie*. Guapa. How pressing her lips to mine struck a match inside me and lit me on fire and burned me from the inside out.

I'm still burning.

I still fucking burn for her, hotter than ever, even though it's obvious she's gone cold toward me.

Maddie and I don't want the same things. I'm sure, but she's scared. I want slow, she wants fast.

I've been trying to get back to the place I call home.

She's been trying to get away.

Maddie doesn't want me, that much is clear. I can't keep holding this torch for her if she won't have me.

It hurts too much.

So I take Carmen's face in my hands and kiss her back. Even though it's wrong, and even though I should pull away and tell Carmen no, no, we aren't meant to be together, I kiss her back.

My desperation to forget Maddie trumps everything else —my manners, my sense of wrong and right.

Please, I pray. *Please, God, let me forget.*

That's when I hear it—my name, spoken in a voice so tight it warbles.

"Javier?"

My blood turns to ice. It can't be. I haven't heard from her—she left me, she hates me, she's gone—

No. Oh, Christ, no.

My eyes snap open. Maddie stands in the aisle a few feet away. I see the shape of her fists, shoved into her pockets, through the shiny green fabric of that adorably ridiculous puffer jacket she wears.

A slow, splotchy creep of red spreads over her face. Her

eyes fill with tears. I'm so angry with myself for making her cry—for being such an idiot dickhead—that I can't breathe.

Maddie

So much for surprising Javier. Looks like he's the one intent on surprising *me*.

The confetti-filled joy I felt five seconds ago—*I'm in love, I was brave enough to let him in, I am brave enough to tell him, I'm in love*—turns to ash in my mouth.

The way I just saw Javier kissing María Carmen—that was no accident, no ordinary kiss. He was holding her face in his hands, his eyes clenched shut as if he were swept up in the passion of that kiss, its heat.

As if he believed in it.

He kissed me like that. How special and safe and *wanted* he made me feel with his lips on my lips.

I guess he kisses *everyone* like the world is ending.

Pain—blinding, acute—sucks the air from my lungs. For a minute I think I'm going to be sick.

I grab the back of a nearby seat. I don't trust my knees to hold me up.

I blink, trying to clear my eyes. I want so badly for this to be a dream, for this to be something other than what it clearly is, oh, God, I *want it so badly* it makes my whole being hurt.

I wanted so badly to be wrong about Carmen's text.

But I was right. Javier wants Carmen, even though he told me I was the one he wanted.

And that fact makes me feel like dying.

Javier jumps to his feet.

"Maddie," he says. His lips are swollen, red. "Oh my God, Maddie."

He moves, reaching for me, but I fall back as if he'd hit me.

The hurt in his eyes darkens them, makes them look almost black in the dim light of the theater.

"Please, guapa—"

I hold up a hand. "No. No, Javier."

María Carmen ducks her head to look at me around Javier's shoulder. Her pretty face contracts, like she's about to cry.

"It was all my fault, Maddie. I promise you, I was the one who kissed Javier. Not the other way around."

I look at Javier. When I speak, my voice is soft. Quiet. "But you kissed her back. I saw you kissing her back, Javier."

"I was trying to forget you! I kissed her back because I can't forget you, Maddie!" He spears a hand through his hair. "Fuck, Maddie, I'm going crazy thinking about you. Wanting you. I kissed Carmen because I thought I'd lost you."

I shake my head, closing my eyes.

"You just did," I say. "You just did lose me. I came to apologize for not giving you a chance to explain yourself the other morning. But now—now I'm not sorry anymore. I'm glad I left."

"You came to apologize?" he says.

I open my eyes. Meet his. "I did. I also came to tell you that I'm in love with you."

His features contort with pain.

Because I'm in love with him—because he's *home*—that pain makes my own pulse brighter.

"Maddie," he says roughly.

"Maddie," Carmen is saying, "listen to what I tell you. This was all my fault. Blame me, please, Javier is innocent."

But I'm already turning away, my steps even as I walk back up the aisle toward the doors at the back of the theater.

My heart may throb and my eyes are burning, but I walk —I don't run.

I walk away because it's clear Javier doesn't love me, and I deserve that now.

I'm done running because I know I deserve to love and be loved in return.

Chapter Twenty-Five

MADDIE

I'm hit with a rush of cold, clear night air as I step out onto the sidewalk. My eyes sting with tears—from the cold, from Javier—but I keep going, careful to stay away from the street.

I don't know what I'm going to do, how I'm going to cope. But right now I just need to put one foot in front of the other and get the *ef* out of this place.

I'll figure everything else out later.

My tears blur the world around me, dots of white, red, blue-edged darkness. It's like looking through a camera lens before it snaps into focus.

The closest Metro stop isn't far. I'll take the red line to Retiro, maybe hunker down with my thesis and a cappuccino tonight—

A hand wraps around my arm, tugging me to a stop.

I turn to see Javier, breathing hard, as huge and hand-some-hot as ever as he hovers above me, his shoulders blocking out the light from a nearby street lamp.

"For Christ's sake, Maddie, let me explain myself," he says.

His breath clouds around his head, a halo of grey against the indigo sky.

"There's nothing to explain." I offer him a tight smile. "I wish you the best, Javier, I do. I just . . . I wish you hadn't lied to me about it."

"I'm not in love with Carmen."

I roll my eyes. "That line is getting really old."

"You know what's getting old?" he asks. "You running from me every time you get scared. Stop being such a child and talk to me. Stay and fucking fight, Maddie. You say you love me, but you aren't willing to fight for it. For us."

"I'm not running from you this time," I say. "I'm walking. I'm walking away because you don't want me. You want Carmen, Javier. Or maybe you just want a bunch of women to swoon over you. Maybe you just want the attention, I don't know. Just leave me alone already."

"I don't—" He pauses, runs a hand down his face. A second later a heated torrent of Spanish escapes from his lips. I've never heard him talk like this, spitting out angry curses left and right. He speaks so quickly and with such a thick Madrileño accent I can hardly make out what he's saying. Something about fucking and Americans?

"I kissed Carmen because I'm a mess over you!" he shouts. "You have to give me a little credit here, Maddie. You've blocked my calls and my texts. I've tried calling you, a *lot*. And then all of the sudden you show up out of the blue and tell me . . . Christ. Maddie, I can't sleep. I can't think about anyone or anything else. I smoked half a pack of cigarettes . . ."

I blink. Swallow. "Well. Your choices are your own fault."

"I know." He runs a hand across his face again "I just couldn't help myself."

I look away. "You couldn't help yourself with María Carmen either."

"You're not listening to me, Maddie."

The bitterness of his betrayal—of losing him like this—

and the sad, puppy dog look on his face makes my chest burn with anger.

"You're a real piece of work," I say. "I'm supposed to be the broken one. But here you are, saying you want commitment, saying you want to find your happily ever after and make a home with someone. Saying you want all that with *me*. Then you can't even keep your dick in your pants for a fucking *week*? What the hell, Javi?"

"What about you?" Javier steps closer. He's seething now, heat radiating off his body. "Leo reads the gossip columns—"

"Of course he does."

"And apparently a 'pretty brunette' was spotted getting friendly with Guillermo Torres the other night at Ático. You wouldn't happen to know anything about that, would you? Considering Torres' friend Rhys Maddox was there too, with your girl Laura?"

I bite the inside of my bottom lip. "That's different."

"Fuck me it is!"

"I never promised you anything, Javier. I told you how I felt. I told you we couldn't be together. I've been honest with you since day one. But you—you made me feel safe. Went out of your way to make me feel like I could trust you. You said you loved me. Love is forever, Javier. But four days later you're already breaking that promise."

His shoulders rise and fall as he breathes in, breathes out. His face is so handsome and I love it so much I want to pinch it. Kiss it.

Sit on it.

But I won't. I won't spend another moment entertaining the possibility of forever with someone who doesn't want me.

"You used me," I say. "You got what you wanted. So let me go. Please, Javier, let me go."

"*I* used *you*?" He takes a step toward me. "Are you fucking serious? From the day you met me *you've* been using *me*."

My heart blares, a painful, panicked beat. "What the hell does that mean?"

"I love you, but the way you seek out random guys, doing what you do—I think you hate yourself. Maddie, you think you're garbage. I don't know why. *I* know you are passionate and generous and kind. But you don't see yourself that way. You think you need to be punished for causing your parents' divorce, even though we both know you didn't. You keep everyone at arm's length—you only go in for one-night stands —because you think you deserve to be lonely. And yet you deserve so much more than that, guapa. I hate that you used me to hurt yourself."

I close my eyes against a fresh burn of tears.

"*I* hate your implication that a girl doesn't sleep around just because she wants to," I say. "Just because it feels good. You're saying that a girl sleeps around because she must be damaged somehow. Fucked up."

Javier stares at me. "Of course a girl can sleep around if she wants to. Same as a guy. I don't hold that against you— against girls, I mean. Have all the sex you want, as long as it's *empowering*. But for you, Maddie—I don't think hooking up makes you feel any better. I think it makes you feel worse. Right now, anyway."

Of course he's right.

Hooking up used to be fun. Before shit went down with my dad, I totally enjoyed a little love 'em and leave 'em action.

But this semester? I've used sex as a weapon. Not against the guys I sleep with, but against myself.

I understand that now, and I was going to break that bad habit by giving Javier a chance.

What an idiot I was to think he'd come through.

"Well then," I say. "All the more reason for you to be with Carmen."

"Maddie," he pleads, his anger softening. "I don't know what else I can say to convince you that that kiss didn't mean *anything*. I love you. Christ, I love you."

I close my eyes again. "I want to believe you, Javier. I do. But I can't. It's done. We're done, we both know that."

A car trundles past, its muffler clanking against the cobblestone street. My head hurts. I want to go home, lick my wounds. Cry until next week. Next year, really.

I open my eyes. The car is actually a taxi, the crusty sign on its roof lit up.

I move toward it, raising my arm to hail the driver.

"Guapa," Javier is calling in Spanish. *Guapa, please don't run from me again. Please stay. Stay.*

I'm shaking so hard I can't open the car door.

Javier is at my side in half a heartbeat, opening it for me.

"You're really going home?" he says.

I look at him. "I thought my home was with you, Javi. But I guess I don't have one anymore."

You're tearing me apart, he says.

"Now you know how it feels," I say, swiping the pads of my fingers underneath my eyes.

There's nothing I can do to make you stay? he asks.

I shake my head.

He hesitates. I can smell him, the clean scent of his skin and the spice of the cinnamon on his breath.

"Fuck." He lands his fist on the roof of the cab. The driver erupts in a string of Spanish curses. Javier doesn't seem to notice.

He closes the door.

The car stalls when the driver tries to jam it into gear.

I watch as Javier walks away, his slumped shoulders limned in the yellow light put off by the street lamp. Something about the way those shoulders narrow into a taut waist

—something about the long, muscular lines of his back—makes my heart curl in on itself.

The taxi jerks into motion.

It's a long ride home.

Javier

The Next Week

I miss her.

I stare down the pack of cigarettes on my kitchen counter. I bought it yesterday, when I couldn't take it anymore and thought filling my lungs with nicotine and carbon monoxide and all that other horrible shit might empty the rest of my body of *her*.

Maddie Lucas.

The girl whose tender heart I unintentionally ripped out and stepped on. Even now the memory of her face, twisted with hurt and disbelief, makes me wince.

How could I have been so fucking stupid? She is young and hurting, vulnerable. I knew all these things.

I didn't know she was in love with me. The same kind of ardent, unconditional love I feel for her.

I don't know whose mistake that was—mine or hers. I'd take the blame, I'd apologize a thousand times, if it meant I could hold her again.

I suspected it before, but knew I was in love with Maddie the moment she stumbled out of Ático on Saturday night. She was pissed out of her mind, hanging onto her friends for support. People were staring as she stumbled past, politely stepping back like they were afraid she might vomit on their designer kicks.

She was *that* girl.

And I knew I loved her because I couldn't help but move toward her, I couldn't help but take her in my arms and hold back her hair as got sick. I wanted to comfort her. I wished it were me getting sick, I wished for nothing more than for her to feel better, a bit of the old boot and rally. Lord knows I'd done it enough myself.

Maddie was a mess, but she was *my* mess. I would do anything for her, I would sacrifice anything—that night it was my pride, and my shoes—to see her happy.

I told her I loved her while she was bent over the side-walk, my hand trailing small circles across her back. I don't think she heard me—and even if she did, she probably didn't remember it when she woke up the next morning—but I said it anyway. I wanted to let her know I was there.

I miss her.

I grab the cigarettes and head downstairs. I don't bother with a jacket. The cold feels good, a reminder that a world outside of my own—outside of Maddie—exists.

I *miss* her.

I unwrap the plastic from the pack and shove it in my pocket. I'm just about to light up when a hand materializes from the darkness and plucks the cigarette from my mouth.

I look up, and the curse on my lips—a curse that would give my mother a stroke—dies when I see Leo, a look of stern consternation on his face.

He holds up the cigarette. "What is this bullshit?"

"I'm having a bad day," I say, and try grab it from his hand.

He promptly drops it on the ground and squashes it under the heel of his boot.

"You are having the bad days for too many days currently." Leo puts his hands on his hips. "I have went to tell you no more of those days. You are a new man now. No more of the smoking. No more María Carmen. No more crazy times with many women. Not any of those things making you very happy."

I give him the side-eye. "Your English is getting better."

"Thank you," he replies. "I practice it much."

I take a breath, let it out. The pack of cigarettes is burning a hole in my back pocket, but I resist the urge to reach for it.

"I know," I sigh, digging a hand through my hair. "I know those things don't make me happy anymore. I just. I thought coming back to Madrid would make me feel more settled— more content because I was *home*. I missed that on the road —that sense of connection. Of comfort. But you know what, Leo? I felt more lost than ever when I got here. I mean, it was great having my mum around, and Carmen, and Rafa. But I still didn't feel like I was home."

Leo nods. "Not until you meet Maddie."

"Yes." I look at him. "God, since when did you develop this Jedi sixth-sense of emotional insight? It's great, really, but also a bit . . . unsettling, I guess?"

"I live," Leo shrugs. "I learn. I also read many books and love many women."

"Right. Of course."

"Madrid is the place you come from," Leo says. "But it is not your home. Home is the people, not the places. Home for you is Maddie."

I blink at the prick of tears. He's right. I've never thought about it like that, but it's true. All along I've been searching for my belonging, a sense of comfort and purpose. I thought I'd find it in a physical *place*, just like Maddie believed her home was the lovely mansion she grew up in.

Now I see that I found my belonging not in Madrid, but in Maddie.

It was always, always about Maddie.

I can't believe I didn't see it until now.

Until Leo, the guy with the errant pelvis and potty mouth, pointed it out to me.

"You're right," I say. "You're absolutely right. But it's too late, Leo. I did the worst thing I could possibly do to her—I betrayed her trust. I didn't mean to, and that kiss with Carmen—you and I both know it didn't mean anything. Still. I made Maddie a promise, and then I broke it."

Leo puts a hand on my shoulder. "Fight for the woman. One ending time."

"One *last* time."

"Yes. One last time."

"I have fought," I reply. "I've called a hundred times, texted a hundred more, but she blocked my number. I've offered Rafa more euros than I care to admit to help me see her. You know, an 'accidental' run-in at a café sort of thing. I've sent flowers. I even wrote a letter."

"And?"

"Nothing. I got nothing back. She's washed her hands of me, Leo. It's done. We're done."

Leo purses his lips, gazing out into the growing darkness.

"What is the one thing you might can do for Maddie that none other peoples can do?"

"What?" I furrow my brow. "Are you being a pervert again?"

"No, no, I do not mean it like this. I mean you are a *Madrileño*, you know the music, you play the guitar. You have a band I am in."

"What does the band have to do with Maddie?"

Leo looks at me. "Something. We figure something romantic we do for her. Maybe she misses her home? Americans, they have a love for those songs of Christmas? You know . . . como se dice . . ."

"Christmas carols."

"Yes!" Leo pokes a finger in the air. "Maybe we play the Christmas carols for Maddie, and she misses her home much less? The music, it is very much healing of the heart."

I blink. "Seriously, mate, you're starting to scare me with this self-help stuff. But that's a good idea. A really good idea. We could put on a little concert for her at the monastery—I could invite her there under the guise of doing her research— maybe on Thanksgiving, when she'll really be missing home—"

"And then, boom! We play for her."

"Yes," I say, my excitement rising. This might just actually work. "Except we're not going to play Christmas carols."

Leo blinks. "What? Then what is the thing we play?"

"I have an idea. Here, you want these?" I offer him the cigarettes.

He shakes his head. "You do the inspire me. I quit too. For one hour already!"

I pat him on the back. "Good for you, Leo. C'mon, let's get inside. We have some new songs to learn. A few favors to call in too."

Chapter Twenty-Six

MADDIE

A few days later

I set my cappuccino on the last remaining table at the café, careful not to spill the beautiful, fluffy white cloud of foam that tops the mug. I wiggle my way between tables and sit on the booth, plopping my laptop on the table.

I sip my coffee, tentatively, testing to see if it's too hot.

It's good. Not as good as Javier's. But good.

Thank God. My insomnia has returned with a vengeance, and my eyeballs hurt so badly I wish I could scoop them out of my head with a spoon.

Coffee seems to be the only thing that helps.

I open my laptop and log into my Meryton U. email account. I scroll through the usual mail—a note from the dean about finals, a corrected draft of an essay from my art history professor—but draw up short when I see María Carmen's name pop up at the top of my inbox.

My stomach does a backflip.

I wish I could say the anger I feel toward her outweighed my curiosity about what she has to say for herself.

I wish I could just delete the email without reading it, and go about my merry way.

But c'mon, who am I kidding?

Dear Madeline,

I hope this note finds you well and that your studies continue to progress. I understand you have less than three weeks until you leave Madrid, and I am sure you will make the most of them.

I confess I do not know where to begin with my apology for what happened the other night. Javier and I have not been together for some time, although we've remained friendly over the years.

I was excited when I found out Javier had returned to Madrid following his tour with Juan Ramos. I suppose I missed him more than I let on.

He's made clear to me now that he did not miss me in the same way. I don't hold this against him. But he was so charming, and I misread the signs. Being a foolish romantic, I saw interest in his friendliness when there clearly was none.

I didn't know that you and Javier were interested in each other. If I had, I would have never pursued him the way I did. I assumed he was single. I asked him if the two of you were dating. He said no; apparently he told me this right after the two of you got into an argument. He thought he would never see you again at that point.

Let me assure you that I was the one doing the pursuing, not the other way around. I was the one who kissed Javier. And he kissed me back because was trying to forget you.

It didn't work. He misses you, terribly. I have never seen him so distraught.

I would love to make this up to you in any way that I can. Perhaps you would like to conduct further research at the monastery? We have a school visit this Thursday during the day, but I am happy to open the monastery to you anytime after 5 o'clock in the afternoon.

I am deeply sorry for what happened. Javier is a wonderful man. One of the best. He would not hurt you intentionally. Not you, the woman he loves.

I hope to see you next Thursday.

Regards,

Carmen

I read the email a second time, and then a third, my heart beating faster and faster until I feel lightheaded. She's so ridiculous, María Carmen, with her stuffy tone—"I am a foolish romantic", "he's distraught"—I mean, who talks like that anymore?

She's ridiculous. But maybe she's right too.

I lean back against the booth. I don't know what to think. Oh, how I want to believe her. I want to believe that the kiss was all her fault and that Javier was, like me, very much an innocent bystander in all of this.

But believing only makes a fool out of you.

I know this now.

Regardless of my feelings towards Javier and Carmen, I still haven't gotten to a good place in my thesis. I have done plenty of research, but I can't seem to settle on a topic. The thought of leaving Spain without that all-important topic is depressing to say the least. I've already put in so much time, so much thought and effort into my ideas for the monastery.

And I love the place. Something tells me I'm not going to ever find a spot that inspires me as much as El Monasterio de los Humildes Reales.

Still. I'd rather do that thing to my eyeballs than see María Carmen again. I get it, she didn't know about Javier and me—no one did, really, except for Viv, and Laura, and Rafa I guess—but still, I can't scrub the image from my brain of her pin-up red lips moving over Javier's mouth.

I sigh, reaching for my cappuccino.
I just don't know.

Chapter Twenty-Seven

MADDIE

Thanksgiving Day

The wind, frigid, cutting, swirls around me, making my eyes water. I've given up on tucking my hair behind my ears, and now it flies wild and loose in my face.

Good thing I know my way to The Monastery of Humble Royals by heart—I can't see shit.

It's dusk, the street lamps just blinking awake. Back home, Mom is probably putting the turkey in the oven while my grandmother throws together her stuffing. Kevin will be watching football, and Dad—well, I don't know what Dad will be doing. I didn't ask, because I don't want to know.

I just hope he's not alone, wherever he is. Even he deserves a little company on what used to be an important family day.

It's hitting me especially hard today, the homesickness. The sadness and the anger and the disappointment. I miss my family, and I *really* fucking miss Javier.

I tried to get the Madrileñas together for Thanksgiving dinner, study-abroad style—my señora offered to host us— but everyone kinda crapped out, including Vivian. I'm a little miffed at her for blowing me off, because she knows how bummed I've been lately.

She knows I really need a little TLC today.

So, yeah. It's Thanksgiving, and I am alone. Not gonna lie, I'm feeling pretty sorry for myself.

My throat tightens.

Not now, I tell myself. *You can't fall apart now.*

I have so much work left to do on my thesis—mainly, I need to figure out what the hell I'm writing it on—I can't afford to fall apart today. Who knows when I'll get another chance to study the monastery?

Which is why I'm trudging through the frigid cold to accept María Carmen's invitation.

My stomach is in knots. Yeah, I'm a little nervous about seeing her.

But I'm really nervous about seeing *him*. Javier. I know he's written a lot of new material, and no doubt he and his as-yet-unnamed band are really ramping up their practice time. If some higher power takes pity on me, he won't be there tonight.

I don't know how I'm going to keep it together if I have to share a space with his deep, rumbling voice echoing off the church's frescoed walls and ceiling. It's going to kill me.

Carmen is waiting for me in the entrance hall. She's wearing skinny black slacks and high-heeled pumps, her long, shampoo-commercial hair perfectly coiffed. She looks chicer than ever.

I glance down at my jeans and scuffed boots. I let out a sigh of defeat.

As if today could get any worse.

"Maddie, I am so glad you came," she says, kissing my cheeks.

I offer her a tight smile, hoisting my backpack onto my

shoulder. "Thanks for the invite. I really appreciate your help with my thesis."

"I want to apologize again." She takes my arms in her hands and looks me in the eye. "I meant what I said in my email. Every word of it. I am aghast at myself."

Aghast. It's all I can do not to roll my eyes. This girl and her faux cut-glass English—really, it's too much.

"Javier is completely blameless," she says. "It's important that you understand that."

I look away. "Did he put you up to this?"

"No. Yes, I spoke with him after—well. After the incident. But I always intended to apologize, whether or not Javier and I talked. I'm not that sort of woman, Maddie. I'm not one of those . . . how do you call them in English?"

"Homewreckers?" I reply tartly.

She struggles not to flinch at the word. "Yes. I am not a homewrecker. I only want to see Javier happy. And from what he told me, you make him very happy indeed."

I meet her eyes. The hurt I see there only makes them more beautiful.

"Thank you," I say at last. "I appreciate that."

She gives my arm a squeeze. "Come on up, then. The church is all yours this evening."

We climb the stairs, tingly excitement spreading through me as I take in my gorgeous surroundings. The marble, the plasterwork, the tapestries that line the gallery walls—the monastery is a visual feast.

How am I ever going to narrow it down to *one* topic for my thesis?

I am beginning to despair when I smell something—a warm, familiar smell, something savory. It gets stronger the closer we get to the church.

"Are you cooking?" I ask.

Carmen's lips draw into a small smile. "You'll see."

"Carmen." I slow my gait. "What's going on?"

"You'll see."

My heart skips a beat when I hear the first notes of a song through the church's closed doors.

A *country* song. An honest-to-goodness country song.

Ohmigod.

"Ohmigod," I say.

I reach for the door, my hand trembling.

"Go in," Carmen urges. "I promise you will like what is inside."

I open the door. Javier is up on stage, leading his band in a rousing, flamenco-style remix of a country song. Leo grins as he humps the air in time to the beat.

For a minute I just stand there, dumbstruck. My pulse beats an uneven note in the back of my throat.

Javier is up on stage, and the Madrileñas—all of them, plus Rafa and Rhys and my señora, Stella—are gathered around a long table at the front of the theater.

I know what I smelled before. It's my grandmother's stuffing. I see a big casserole dish of it on the table, along with mashed potatoes and bowl of something green. Salad, maybe?

In place of a turkey, there's a giant leg of jamón íberico—Spaniards *love* their pork products—which Rafa patiently carves, handing out paper-thin slices of salty goodness as he goes.

"Mads!" Laura shouts around a mouthful of that jamón, smiling. "Happy Thanksgiving, chica!"

Viv waves at me. "Stop staring and come eat!"

But I can't. I can't stop staring.

I can't stop staring at Javier. He smiles at me, a blinding, full-face, slightly embarrassed smile that grows as he stumbles over a lyric.

He looks delicious in a (tight!) white Henley and beat-up jeans, his hipster wave of dark hair slicked back. The muscles in his thick forearms bulge against his tan skin as he plays his gleaming black acoustic guitar.

My eyes prick with tears.

Javier leaps off the stage, still playing the song as he moves up the aisle toward me, still singing about the timelessness of his love for his lady, the ease of it.

The comfort of it.

I feel faint.

María Carmen places a hand on the small of my back, urging me forward.

"Go," she murmurs. "Go to him, Madeline."

For the first time, I don't resist my need for Javier. My desire for him.

I go. I feel so light doing it, I feel such overwhelming relief, that I start to cry.

Javier finishes the song as we meet in the middle of the aisle. He's still smiling that handsome-hot smile, the one that makes me feel weak in the knees, and then he swings his guitar onto his back and reaches for my face, guitar pick still wedged between his fingers, and plants a big fat kiss on my lips.

My friends—well, *our* friends, I guess—erupt in cheers behind us. Even María Carmen gives a very uncharacteristic hoot of approval.

The kiss leaves me breathless, the way his kisses always do, and when he pulls away I am glad he presses his forehead to mine. It's the only thing that keeps me from falling over.

"Javier," I plead.

"Have I convinced you to allow me to finally explain myself?"

I scoff. "Yes. Yes."

"I've been waiting to hear that word from you," he says, and even though my eyes are closed, I can tell by the warm sound of his voice that he's grinning. "I know you're scared, mujer, you don't want to care because when you do, you always care too much. You're passionate. I've known that from the start about you. It's one of the things that made me fall so hard, and so quickly."

I swallow. "It did happen fast, didn't it?"

"Yes," he says.

"And now I care too much about you."

"Not any more than I care about you. Maddie, you're home. You're everything I've been looking for. Everything I've missed. You are my home, and I would never, *ever* betray that—the home we've begun to build together. It's too precious. María Carmen, the kiss—it was all a misunderstanding. I was an idiot. I thought kissing her back might keep me from missing you. It only made me miss you more. I'm in love with *you*. It's always been you. Only you."

I open my eyes, meet his gaze. "I've been busy making plans for us to be together," he continues. "Concrete plans, Maddie, not just ideas. I know you have to be home next semester, so I bought a plane ticket to the States at the end of January. I'll come earlier too, and help you and your mum pack up your house if you'd like. I checked out your university's schedule for next semester, and you have a nice chunk of time off in March—perhaps you might come back here? Do a little more research while you're at it? I even cleared a bit of space for your stuff in my closet. I'm willing to fly back and forth as often as you'd like until we can both be in the same city again. Even if I have to practice with the band over Skype, I'll do it if it means being with you. If one of us has to move, then so be it. I love you. You love me. We're going to make this work, come hell or high water."

There are tears in his eyes. He's trying. He's making plans for us to be together. The forever kind of together.

The happily ever after kind of together.

"I am so scared, Javi," I wheeze. "That's a lot to commit to."

He holds me closer against him, so close I can hear the dull thump of his heart. "I love all of you. The passionate parts. The pukey parts. I love all of you. Let me love you, guapa. Let me commit to you. I want you to have your own foot pussies that you keep under the bed next to mine. I want you to be happy. I want to be with you, Maddie, any way that I can. This is *our* life we're talking about—not your parents'. Our life will be different, I promise you that. I promise nothing matters more to me than your happiness."

"Say yes!" someone—I think it's Katie—shouts. "Say yes so we can eat already!"

I laugh, I let myself laugh, and then I open my eyes and look into Javier's and I kiss him, I grind my hips into his and I kiss his fucking adorable face.

When I come up for air, I glance over his shoulder. "But how did you do all this? *Why?*"

"I knew you'd be missing home today. So I had Viv get some recipes from your mum. She said your favorite was the stuffing. We couldn't find the right sausage though, so we had to use chorizo. Hope that's okay."

"Who's *we?*"

Javier looks down at me. "Leo and Rhys. You wouldn't think it, but that footballer is quite the chef."

"And the country song? What possessed you to learn that?"

He shrugs. "You've made me a convert. I'm a bit obsessed with country now. Mostly the older stuff—"

"Yeah," I say. "Nothing beats Johnny Cash."

His smile fades. "Do you forgive me?"

I wrap my arms around his neck. "I do. Of course I do. If you forgive me too."

"Vale." He bends his arm and grabs my hand, leading me toward the table. "I've got a gift for you."

"Besides the country music and the Thanksgiving dinner with my friends?"

He grins. "An early birthday present, if you will."

Of course.

Of course Javier remembered my birthday, even though I only mentioned it once, and in a text message no less.

Vivian, beaming, ducks underneath the table and produces a box, wrapped in glittery paper. She hands it to Javier, who hands it to me.

"Viv helped me with the size," he says as he watches me open it. "I hope they fit properly."

I open the box. Nestled inside is a pair of the fuzziest, coziest looking slippers I have ever seen, complete with shearling and soft, velvety suede.

"Those foot pussies I was talking about," Javier explains. "Your own pair."

"Foot pussies?" Laura wrinkles her nose.

"That sounds fun," Rachel says.

"Pussies are *always* fun," Katie says.

I bite my lip, tucking the box under my arm. "Thank you, Javi. I love them. They're perfect."

"Later," he murmurs in my ear as I lean in for a kiss. "I'd like see you in those pussies—*only* the pussies."

I grin. "Should we try the kitchen again? The island is still virgin territory."

He grins, too. "We *did* eat there together."

"Eat?" I cock a brow. "Pun intended?"

"Pun always intended. C'mon, let's try this famous stuffing and then get the hell out of here—my jeans just got tight all of the sudden."

EPILOGUE

Maddie

December

The Cessna bounces off the runway once, twice, and then we're on the ground, groaning to a stop.

My heart is in my throat and my ribs ache from laughing so hard. It never stops being a thrill, losing gravity with Javier. Sitting next to him in this tiny plane with our legs pressed together, talking, teasing, looking out the windows at the city below, the city that has become my new home.

Falling for him, with him, never stops being fun.

I look at Javier, his profile limned in the setting sun's golden light. Sharp nose, full lips, square chin. His stubble burns from black to red as he pilots the plane with confident ease. He's ridiculously handsome. Hot. Handsome-hot. I still can't believe he's my boyfriend. I still can't believe he loves me, loves me hard and thoroughly and unconditionally.

I also can't believe Javier agreed to come home with me to Atlanta for Christmas and New Year's. Mom is super excited to meet him, and of course she's excited to have the extra help packing up the house. Javier and I already have plans—like, bought our plane tickets and everything—to see each other once every two months or so next semester. If all goes well (and I think it will), I'll head back to Madrid for the whole summer—my dad has turned a new leaf and is coming around to the idea—which gives me plenty of time to continue the work on my thesis. And plenty of time, of course, to bone/hang out with my studly Spanish boytoy.

Vale. A thousand million times *vale*.

Javier turns his head. He smiles, the dimples on either side of his mouth deepening. "You get what you needed?"

"I did." I glance at the camera case, wedged between my feet. "Now that I know what I'm looking for, it's much easier to get the right shots."

"I know I've said this before, mujer, but truly, you've chosen a brilliant topic. I never would've thought of the 'celebrations' angle, even though it's right there in your face. I mean, Mass was celebrated in the church for centuries."

"And now we used the church to celebrate Thanksgiving." I smile.

"That was a good day."

"A very good day."

Not only was it the day Javier and I got together, it was also the day I was finally able to pick a topic for my thesis. Seeing the joy of everyone gathered there in the church—hearing the swell of the music around us—brought me back to the very fundamentals of architecture. I understood for the first time what the church and the monastery in general were all about.

They were spaces for celebration. Celebration of the Mass; celebration of hope, of community, of music, of belief. Celebration of *belonging*, whether it was belonging to a religious order or belonging to the passionate fandom of flamenco music.

I celebrated finding my own belonging in that church. And I decided that day that I would write my thesis on how

the church's architecture—its layout, its acoustics, its art—
fostered the sense of joy and completeness I felt there,
surrounded by my friends and my music.

It's a Saturday, and the weather is crisp and clear, so El
Aeropuerto de Cuatro Vientos is bustling. Javier guides us
past several planes being serviced. People are everywhere,
running across the wide swath of tire-scarred pavement.

At last we pull into a spot outside a massive hangar.
Several larger planes—posh private jets, as Javier calls them—
surround us. I wonder what Spanish celebrities they belong
to. Movie stars? Footballers? The King and Queen?

When we're ready to leave—tonight we have plans to
open a bottle of red wine, make paella, and watch *The Holiday*
at Javier's place (I mean, best night ever, amirite?)—I turn to
open my door, but Javier puts a hand on my thigh and gives it
a squeeze.

"Everything all right?" I ask.

His light brown eyes dance. "How about you lose gravity
one more time?"

"Here?" I look out the windshield. There are still guys
everywhere—maintenance crews, pilots in uniform, men who
drive the fuel trucks—some of them only a few feet away.

They'll be able to see everything. If, of course, they know
where to look.

"We'll be caught," I say. "They'll call the cops on us—"

My voice catches when Javier unzips my fly, one swift,
sure tug.

"Trust me," he murmurs, working the button through its
hole. "I'll make it worth the risk."

"But," I say, even as I lift my hips so he can pull my jeans
—and my underwear—over my hips. Heat spikes through my
center. "But Javier, we can't—we shouldn't, what if they see
my O-face and it scars them for life?"

"You O-face is marvelous, guapa," he replies. "In fact, I'd very much like to see it right now."

The leather seat is cool against my naked backside. Javier pulls my jeans over my knees, then hooks the back of my right knee in his fingers and tugs it away from the left. I'm practically spread-eagled now.

Spread-eagled and super turned on.

"Trust me," he says.

And I do. I don't think. I don't hesitate.

I let him duck his head and slide his fingers into my pussy, holding it open, and then his mouth is on me and my eyes flutter shut and the back of my head hits the headrest, and I am seeing stars, I am on the brink of an orgasm in two seconds flat.

Mile-high head—I mean, we're not technically in the air, but we are on a plane, and that's got to count for something, right—is the best. Thing. Ever.

I dig my fingers into his hair as he eats me out, his lips on my clit when his fingers slip inside me, stretching me, making me want to come. The idea that we could be caught—that there are people just outside my door—only adds to the excitement, the urgency I feel to let go.

My hips buck against Javier's mouth, rolling in time to his strokes. I pull his hair, I gasp as the coil between my legs winds tighter. I feel him smiling against me, caressing me with his tongue and hands and lips.

I open my eyes and watch him move between my legs, loving me like I've never been loved. Making me feel wonderful, terrifying, happy things.

Yes. I am so glad I said yes to this, to him, to myself.

"I'm almost"—I gasp—"I'm almost there, Javi."

"Dios mio, mujer, already?" he murmurs, his voice vibrating through my folds.

"You're"—another gasp—"you're really good at this. Like. Really good."

He licks my clit.

I come, a thunderous, searing orgasm that has me breathing his name, over and over, my legs shaking as Javier continues to lap at my pussy, soothing it, stoking it, making me want to laugh it feels so good.

He looks up from between my thighs. "So. Losing gravity. Do you like it?"

"I do, very much." I reach for his fly, grinning when I feel a familiar bulge in his jeans. "I like it so much that I'm willing to return the favor."

———

Javier

It's dark by the time we're finished. I help Maddie step down from the plane. She weaves a bit on her feet. No doubt her legs, like mine, are a bit unsteady after that impromptu marathon we just had.

It really was a miracle no one caught us. A couple times I thought for sure the ground crews saw us, but they all continued about their business as Maddie came in my mouth and I came in hers.

I drape my arm across her shoulders, caressing the back of her neck with my thumb. She bends her elbows and wraps her hands around my arm, and together we walk slowly toward the parking lot, our breath puffing out around us in the chill night air.

Maddie looks up at the sky—it's clear, and strewn with a thousand stars—and sighs.

"Lovely, isn't it?"

"Yes," she says. She bumps me with her hip. "Javi, I'm so happy. I love today. I love you."

I press a kiss into the top of her head. "I love you. So tell me more about this Holiday movie—"

We draw up short at the sound of voices.

Familiar voices, followed by hurried footsteps.

I glance toward the bigger planes—the private jets—and see a couple making their way toward the poshest jet at the airport.

I recognize the guy—he's tall, with a knot of hair at the crown of his head—it's Rhys Maddox. He's carrying a bright pink suitcase. A girl's suitcase.

Maddie must recognize Laura at the same time, because she shouts, "Hey! Laura! What the hell are you doing here?"

Halfway up the stairs to the plane, Laura turns, smiling. "We're headed to London for a few days."

"London?" Maddie looks at me. "That sounds . . . serious."

Rhys grabs Laura's hand. "She's my good luck charm. Can't go anywhere without her."

Laura rolls her eyes. "Rhys is convinced the only reason he's having such an awesome year is because he met me."

"It's true," Rhys says.

"It's not," Laura says.

"Sounds like you two need to go have a 'talk,'" Maddie says, curling her fingers into air quotes. "Do the pilots still close the cockpit door on private jets? You know, so you can have a little privacy?"

Rhys smiles. "They most certainly do."

"Rhys," Laura says, and the way she says it—I don't know. She sounds tired. Sad, maybe.

"Everything all right?" Maddie asks.

"Yeah," Laura says. "Yeah, we'll be fine. See you at our usual Madrileña spot next week?"

"Of course," Maddie says. "You guys have fun."

We watch them board the plane, and then Maddie and I turn and head for my truck.

"What's going on with them?" I ask.

She shrugs. "It's all very mysterious—no one really knows, not even Laura. I mean, he's a footballer, and you know how they are."

"Not all of them are like that," I say. "Into the women and the parties and the general ridiculousness. Maybe Rhys is different."

"Maybe," Maddie says. "I just hope he doesn't hurt her."

"I just hope you like my paella," I say.

Maddie smiles. My stomach flips. She's got such a beautiful smile—I'm glad I get to see it so often these days.

"I'm sure it'll be delicious," she says.

"You're delicious," I say. "Now let's get you home and into some foot pussies—you're shivering."

Thank you so much for reading Lessons in Gravity! Laura + Rhys's story is up next in Lessons in Letting Go (Study Abroad #3). Flip the page for a juicy excerpt!

LESSONS IN LETTING GO EXCERPT

Rhys

Laura's mouth is wet and warm and deliriously soft. I slide my tongue between her lips, begging entrance, and with a small moan she lets me in. She surrenders, her head falling back into my hands.

I take a step closer, nudging my body against hers. Laura isn't petite, but there's something small, almost vulnerable about her body. I hold her closer, letting the warmth of my skin seep into hers. She's covered in goosebumps.

"Are those good goosebumps?" I murmur, sliding my lips to her jaw. "Or bad goosebumps?"

Laura smiles against my mouth. "Good goosebumps. Really freaking good, Rhys."

My dick twitches inside my jeans, a hard, prickly rush of blood. I bite her bottom lip; she moans again; I go from half chub to full salute in two seconds flat. Laura must feel it, too, because she presses her belly against my erection. The heat and the pressure feel so fucking good I let out a growl.

I kiss her harder. She meets me stroke for stroke, her arms twining around my neck, pulling me close. She tastes sweet, a little fruity, like that Midori she was drinking at the bar. I like the way she tastes.

I like the way she feels even more. This girl—Christ, I needed this tonight.

I need to escape the pressure.

I am so fucking desperate to escape. For a little while, at least.

What I told Olivier at training the other day—that I don't have time for girls—is and isn't true. My football career is (hopefully) just getting started; my current contract is puny compared to those given to the big guys. Those filthy rich bastards can make upwards of fifty *million* euros a season. I make way, way less than that. *Way* less.

Which is still a lot, granted. Growing up as poor as I did, I recognize that I'm very well off. But by the time I pay taxes, an agent, a publicist, a manager, a financial manager, and an assistant, I don't have nearly enough money to support my family the way I want or need to. My sponsors make up for some of that. But to make the big bucks like the big guys, I need to up my game, and start playing like a superstar. I need to focus on footy, not on a serious relationship.

That doesn't mean I can't have a little fun with a girl every now and then—so long as it's the no-strings-attached sort of fun. I've beat myself up for months now, my thoughts a constant refrain of *you're rubbish you're rubbish you're total rubbish*. I'm under a lot of pressure to make my career work. Sex is in some ways a mute button; it gets me out of my head and into my body. It allows me to live in the moment. Which is huge, considering I spend basically all my time sweating the future.

And who better to help me live in the moment than a gorgeous, whip-smart American who laughs at my pick-up lines? Already my heartbeat is scrambling the well-worn rhythm of my thoughts, drowning out the negativity, the doubts, the fear.

It never happens this quickly with a girl. Usually it takes me a solid chunk of time to unwind from my worries. But tonight—tonight it's happening fast. Maybe because I'm all too eager to escape the crushing reality of where I am right now with my footy. Maybe because I'm so bloody attracted to Laura.

Maybe it's because I haven't had fun, just for fun's sake, in a long time. I had fun with Laura at the bar, and I hope to have even more fun with her, the naked kind, in the very near future. It's Sunday night—the night after a match—the only night of the week I can let loose. I'll never, ever be caught drinking the night before a match like my dad (that little stunt cost him his career), so I tend to be quite tame during the week. But tonight—tonight, I don't plan on wasting a single moment.

Laura slides her hands beneath the lapels of my blazer. I roll my shoulders back, helping her to take it off. Her palms whisper against the fabric of my shirt as she goes for the buttons. I laugh as she fumbles with the first one, and I cover her fingers with my own, guiding them as we unbutton it together.

"Sure you're all right, love?"

"Yes." She pulls back, just a little. She meets my eyes. "And. Um. No. I've never really hooked up with a celebrity before. The closest I ever got was my boyfriend in high school. He was the varsity lacrosse captain and was, like, this huge deal on campus. But that's seriously small beans compared to you. You're...*you*, you know? Eleven-million-Instagram-followers *you*."

I laugh again. "Wait 'til I get to twenty."

"Good thing I nabbed you when I did," she says, biting

her lip. Her hazel eyes, green in this light, dance. "I have a shot with Rhys Maddox the famous footballer. But I don't have a chance in hell with Rhys Maddox the *super* famous footballer-slash-Instagram-god."

I hook my arm around her tiny waist and crush her against me, nuzzling into the inviting curve of her neck. I inhale the smell of her perfume, something floral, a little sweet. She smells fucking delicious.

"I thought I was the one who nabbed you," I say.

She digs her fingers into the hair at the nape of my neck. My blood warms, tightens. "Not with those pick-up lines, you didn't," she says.

"Hey. They weren't all bad."

She tilts her head, spearing me with a look.

"Fine," I say. "They were terrible. But I did make you laugh."

"You did." She smiles. "Hard."

Straightening, I take her face in my hand, run my thumb along her bottom lip. Her eyes darken. "You're gorgeous when you laugh. You're gorgeous, period. This body..." I look down, devouring the curve of her breasts. "It's ridiculous."

"You're ridiculous." She fingers another button on my shirt. "But thank you."

I pull at her lips with my mine, a long, slow, lingering kiss. My body feels plugged in, lit up with the need to bury myself in her cunt that's probably as sweet as her perfume. I glide my hand underneath her shirt, skimming the smooth skin at her hip before I grab the hem and begin drawing it up over her belly. Her head falls back and she lets out a pant when I trail my mouth over her neck, my hand making steady progress up her side. Her skin is warm and soft, silky almost, so silky it makes me fantasize about how silky and warm and soft she'll be between her legs.

My dick pulses, straining against the fly of my jeans. My hand reaches her breast. I finger the lacy cup of her bra, and Laura arches into my touch.

"Rhys," she breathes.

"Hands up, love," I say, nipping at her earlobe.

Laura does as I tell her. I slip her top over her head, her long hair fanning out over her shoulders, covering her chest. I drop the shirt to the floor, ducking to kiss her, my hands roving over all this fucking *skin*. I circle my hands around her waist, my thumbs trailing over her bellybutton, the soft outline of her ribs. They come to rest at the waistband of her jeans, toying with the button of her fly. The throb between my legs heightens, starts to scream.

I begin to slowly back her up, toward the bedroom, our legs tangling as she works feverishly at the remaining buttons of my shirt. With a grunt of satisfaction she tugs it over my shoulders. I untangle my arms from the sleeves, and then I pull her close again, reveling in the feel of skin against skin, bare flesh against bare flesh. I bury my hands in her hair and cover her mouth with mine, swallowing it whole. Thrusting my hips into her groin—*gah*, the friction, it's killing me—I keep urging her backward. For the first time, I wish this suite wasn't quite as big; it's a bit of a hike from the living area to the bedroom, and I am bloody impatient to get this girl naked and get her in my bed.

Laura places her palms against my chest, like she's overwhelmed, like she's trying to shield herself from my onslaught. I hesitate, pull back. But then she's slowly moving those palms lower, exploring as she goes. She digs her fingertips into the ridges of my abs and teases her pinkies along the hard angles of my hips, dipping a questioning finger into the waistband of my jeans. I jump; she grins, making this perfect, throaty-grin-sound as her eyes flick to meet mine.

"I mean, seriously," she says, coming back to my abs. "This —these muscles—they're ridiculous. Who *are* you?"

"I'm a bloke about to go mad if I don't get you naked in the next fifteen seconds."

"Dude. Ditto." She pops open the button on my fly.

I reach around, pop open the hook on her bra.

"Whoa!" she says, clapping an arm across her chest in an attempt to catch her bra. She only half-succeeds, her bra dangling from underneath her forearm.

I hold up my hands. "I didn't hurt you, did I?"

Laura swallows and shakes her head, blond waves falling across her chest. "No. No, I just—um..."

"Listen, Laura, if you don't want to...you know. We don't have to—"

"No," she says, more firmly this time. She closes her eyes, squares her shoulders. Still holding her arm across her chest, she looks up at me and hooks her finger back into my pants, working the zipper down one centimeter at a time as she slowly begins to back into the bedroom. "I want this. I want you, before you get those twenty million followers and become *completely* unattainable. I gotta strike while the iron is hot."

"Oh, this iron's hot, all right."

She rolls her eyes, playfully. "You and the lines."

"They keep getting worse, don't they?"

"They really do."

"Sorry."

"Don't be." Laura smiles. The gathering, stretching heat low in my belly throbs.

We cross the threshold into the bedroom at the same moment my jeans slip from my hips. I pluck at Laura's lips as I shimmy them to my knees. I toe out of my sneakers and kick off my jeans, leaving them at the door. It feels so good to press the head of my dick against her belly, separated from her skin by just the flimsy jersey of my boxer briefs, that I suck in a breath.

"Christ, Laura," I say. I tug down the zipper of her jeans, kissing her hard. Kissing her like I mean it, drinking her in, running my tongue along the slick, hot inseam of her willing mouth.

I slip my hand into her open fly, her lacy underwear warm against my palm as I cup her sex. I roll my hips, impatient, as I finger aside that maddeningly tiny underwear. My finger parts her folds and meets with—fuck, oh, God, *yes*—the center of her wet, swollen pussy.

It's Laura's turn to suck in a breath. I pull back from her mouth, and watch her eyes get hazy and dark as I press that questioning finger into her wet heat. She clenches around my finger, and for a second I think I'll blow my load. She's small and tight and so wet my hand is already drenched.

I close my eyes and blow a breath through my nose. I'm going to devour this girl.

"Am I—is it—all right?" Laura stutters.

I open my eyes and look at her. Her face is flushed; her eyes glitter, her lips swollen and very pink.

I dip my head, nose her throat, her jaw. I trail my finger up the length of her slit, pressing my fingertip to her clit. She cries out.

"All right?" I murmur against her skin. "Love, you're fucking gorgeous."

I slide my other hand to her hip and begin to guide her further into the room.

"Wait," she breathes, pulling back. Her eyes flick to the door. "Hit the lights."

My eyes land on her chest; she's still clutching her bra, covering her breasts. I don't get why she'd be self-conscious about her body; I feel like I've told her ten times tonight how beautiful she is.

"What if I want to see you?" I say. "All of you. I hate having sex in the dark."

Laura ducks out of my grasp, my hand falling from between her legs, and a second later the lights overhead go out, followed by the lamps on either side of the bed. It's dark; the only light comes from faint glow of the city outside the windows at the far end of the room.

"I don't think you'll hate having sex with me," she says, turning back to me. "Even in the dark."

I grab her—I don't know how, I can't see shit, it must be instinct—but I grab her and pull her to me. Desire flashes like lightning, white-hot and loud, between our bodies. It's almost elemental, the attraction that my body feels for hers. We may only have known each other for a few hours, but the chemistry we have is insane, instinctual.

I am going to devour this girl.

I wrap my fingers around her arm. The faint, salty scent of her arousal fills the small space between us. "Drop it," I say, nodding at her bra. "If I can't see all of you, then I'm going to feel you. Every inch of this fucking incredible body of yours, I want to feel it."

Her bra falls to the floor. Then she's circling my neck in her hands, her fingers tangling in my hair, and pulling me against her. My dick surges at the press of her hard nipples against my chest. Skin on skin on *skin*.

"Oh, love," I say, trailing my hands up her sides. I take her tits in my palms, thumbing her nipples. "Oh, Laura."

She moans into my mouth, her fingers tugging at my hair, her silky skin warm against my own. She rolls her hips against mine, begging, teasing.

I fucking lose it.

Our legs hit the bottom of the bed. I take Laura's face in my hands and give her lips one last, almost violent tug. Then

I buck my hips, urging her onto the bed, and she falls onto the downy coverlet with a pleading sigh.

I can just barely see the outline of her body, the curve of her breast gleaming in the light from the window. I take off her sandals. Then I grab her jeans, her underwear, and she lifts her hips to help me tug them off. The scrape of my palms against her legs sounds above our labored breathing.

And then she's naked. Gloriously, beautifully naked.

My heart dips. She's so beautiful. Sexy.

But Laura turns her head away from me on the bed and tries to cover herself, roping her arms around her chest.

"Don't," I say, taking both her wrists in my hand. She bends one knee and I straddle the other, tangling our legs as I lay on top of her. Holding myself up on one elbow, I guide her hands above her head with my free arm, baring her to me, exposing her body to my advances.

"Rhys," she pants.

"You're all right," I say, kissing my way down her neck. "We're all right."

Her hips roll beneath me as I kiss her breast. When I take her nipple in my mouth, biting the pebbled point, she cries out, her legs falling open. I feel the heat and the wet of her exposed pussy against my thigh. *Christ*.

I settle myself between her legs, spreading her wider, opening her wider, and I roll my erection against her pussy, sucking on her nipple as I roll harder, pressing my dick to her center, wanting so badly to be buried there. Her breath is sweet and short, stalling every so often in her throat when I hit just the right spot. I dry humped practically everything when I was a randy teenager. Now I know why; as much of a tease as it is, it heightens the anticipation. And sometimes the anticipation of the act, rather than the act itself, can, frustratingly enough, be the best part.

She keeps rolling against me, me against her, the friction

making my cock pulse in agony. Her body is winding tighter, too, her pants becoming moans. She's close. Painfully close.

I give her nipple one last flick with my tongue. Then I move lower, pressing kisses into her ribs, her belly. I'm about to let go of her wrists so I can kiss her cunt when she grabs me by the hair.

I lift my head, confused. My eyes lock onto hers, shining in the darkness. She looks aroused, a little afraid.

"No," she says, breathless.

"Why not?" I cover the skin just beneath her navel with my mouth. I smell her, smell her arousal, and I want to get her there—I want to get her there before I'm inside her, because I don't think I'll be able to control my own orgasm, much less hers, once I'm sunk into her tight warmth.

"Because. I want you. I'm ready." Her fingers tighten in my hair, pulling me back up her body. "Do you have a condom?"

"You're sure?"

She offers me a grin that fades when I bite her nipple and her face contracts with pleasure. "I'm—Jesus, Rhys, I'm sure."

I climb up the length of her body and place my hands on either side of her head, my hair dangling in her face as I bend my neck to press my mouth to hers, our tongues meeting in a frantic, fractured kiss. Then I lean back, I slip an arm around her waist and lift her a bit further onto the bed. Her leg grazes my dick; my blood riots; I let out a hiss.

My hand falls heavily on the bedside table. I almost pull the drawer off its hinges as I open it and wrangle a condom from the mess of chargers and cords I've shoved inside it.

I rip open the condom with my teeth. Laura is tugging down my briefs, and then she reaches up and takes the condom from my mouth.

"Let me," she says.

I wiggle out of my underwear and hoist myself back onto my hands, lifting my hips for Laura. "I'm all yours, love."

"Love," she says, looking up at me. My arms almost buckle when she takes my cock in her hand and gives it a solid tug. "Is that what you call all the girls you sleep with?"

"No," I grunt, managing a pained smile. "Only the pretty ones."

She swirls her thumb over the head of my dick, making it slick with precum. For a minute my vision goes dim.

"I'm not—" I pant. "I'm not going to last much longer if you keep touching me like that."

"Like what?" Laura rolls on the condom slowly, very, very slowly, her thumb all the while still making circles on the head. Her touch isn't as potent as it was before the condom was on, but my body has begun to shake with impatience.

"Like *that*," I say, and then I cover her hand with mine and settle my hips between her legs. I let my weight rest on her, just a little, and she lets out a satisfied sigh.

Together we guide my dick toward her center. She arches against me when I press myself against her clit, circling, provoking, just like she did. I'm sweating now, and so is she.

"You," she pants, "are such a tease."

I kiss her neck, her ear, her chin. "Payback's a bitch, isn't it?"

When I kiss her mouth, her lips curl into a smile.

We find her center. Even through the condom she is hot and wet.

"Christ, you'll be the death of me," I say. I push—a baby push, I don't want to hurt her—and she cries out, rolling her hips against me, asking for more.

"Is this okay?" I ask.

Her eyes are closed. "Is it okay for you?"

"Pffshhhh. It's better than okay. Much, much better."

"Then give me more."

"How much more?"

"Everything."

"Like this?"

I take her leg in my hand and hitch it over my shoulder, spreading her wider. I sink a bit more inside her; I feel her stretching around me, pulsing with heat, with need.

"More, Rhys." Her free hand clutches at my chest, her nails biting into my skin. The sensation ricochets through my ribcage, my belly, landing in my cock.

I can't. I can't take it. I can't hold on anymore.

I roll back my hips and I take her mouth in mine in a bruising kiss. And then I surge forward, sinking to the hilt inside her in one swift, smooth motion.

Oh my *God.*

I see stars. She feels so bloody good I could die. She is hot and tight and wet, so tight it almost hurts.

I absorb Laura's cry with my mouth. She bites my lip; I nip at her cheek. For a minute I just stay there, filling her, holding her, possessing her. My mind is blank, my senses focused on the thrum of her pulse as I flutter my lips down her neck. Her heart is *pounding*.

So is mine.

Laura tilts her hips, looking for more friction. I grin. Sweet, sweet girl—it's like she knows what I want before I do.

"More," she whispers in my ear.

"More." I pull back, hammer forward. Our bodies make a lewd nose as mine meets with hers. "How much more can you handle?"

She opens her eyes, just a sliver. "As much as you wanna give me, fancy pants."

So I give her everything. I don't go fast; I just go hard, steady and intent and unrepentant—long, deep, gutting strokes. I circle my hips as I stroke, and she arches against me, her body rising to meet my rhythm. She loops her other leg over my other shoulder, seeking *more*, and I hold myself up on my hands and use the muscles in my lower back to go deeper. My mouth is on her mouth, my mouth is on her tits, teasing her nipples, her pussy grips me tight and wet. I don't know how, but she's getting wetter. I bloody adore it.

I close my eyes. My body goes and goes and goes. It's a workout, but one I'm really, *really* enjoying. I lose myself in the feel of Laura, the feel of taking, of having, of giving. My body is loud but my mind is quiet. I am totally present in this moment, and because I've been so distracted lately—because I've been so stressed—it's almost overwhelming, how much I *feel*. I feel her and I feel heat. I feel wound tight and I feel let go. I feel everything intensely, like I'm feeling it not only with my skin but with what's underneath it, too. Marrow and bone. Blood, sinew.

Laura's hands glide up my back. I sputter at the first stirrings of my orgasm. I'm surprised I've lasted this long. My dick almost hurts from the barrage, from her tightness. I circle my hips again, hitting her *just* there. She gasps, throwing back her head. Ecstasy is written all over her features.

Yes. So much yes.

"I'm close," I say. "I want to come together, love. Are you ready? Come for me."

She nods her head, never opening her eyes. Her forehead and cheeks are damp with sweat. "I'm close, too."

As if on cue, her cunt tightens around my dick.

This time, my arms do buckle.

I try to keep some of my weight on my elbows, but Laura drops her legs and pulls me down, pulls me against her.

"I like the feel of you," she says, then sucks in a breath, like she regrets saying it at all.

I laugh, kissing her. "I like the feel of you, too. Come, love. I want you to come."

I hit her hard where she likes it. She's breathing hard, her breasts rising and falling against my chest. I'm going fast now, unable to slow my strokes, but Laura keeps up, offering up her hips, taking what I offer.

I'm wound so tight it hurts. I'm close, I don't know how much longer—

Laura's pussy contracts, once, twice, four times. I lose count, because I lose myself in her orgasm. I surrender to my own, gasping, fireworks bursting behind my closed lids as I empty myself inside her. Every muscle in my body tightens, twists. Then they unfurl and sing, my legs shaking at the violence of my release. I'm dizzy. My chest feels hollowed out. The uneven beating of my heart drowns out everything else, Laura's skin singeing my own. It's a good singe—a welcome one.

There is so much heat between us. Me and Laura.

Laura.

"*Laura.*"

Laura. Sweet, lovely, gorgeous girl.

I open my eyes. She's opened hers, too. For several heartbeats we just look at each other. She looks...bewildered. A little scared.

"Holy fuck, Rhys," she says. She tucks an unruly curl behind my ear as I breathe above her, my nose two inches from hers.

"I know." I try to catch my breath. "That was good. It's never—it's not like that for me very often."

I watch the sinews of her throat as she swallows. "Me neither."

I nudge my nose against hers. "I'm glad you enjoyed it as much as I did."

"I did." She swallows again, turning her head away from me. "Yeah, definitely."

I pull back a little. I get the feeling something is off with Laura. But then she's grinning, rolling her hips against mine, teasing me about another a round.

I feel myself miraculously getting hard again.

Laura. Sweet, sweet girl.

Laura + Rhys's story, Lessons in Letting Go (Study Abroad #3), is available wherever books are sold!

Thank you for reading LESSONS IN GRAVITY—I hope you laughed, you cried, you got turned on by the sassy bits. If you got *especially* turned on, please consider leaving an honest review. Reviews help readers find new authors like me. I sincerely appreciate it!

Book #3 in the Study Abroad series—Lessons in Letting Go, Rhys and Laura's story—is available whoever books are sold.

I'd love to stay in touch—here are a few ways to reach me:

- Check out Jessica Peterson's City Girls, my reader group on Facebook for giveaways, serious discussions of seriously hot guys, and more
- Follow my not-so-glamorous life as a romance author on Instagram @JessicaPAuthor
- Follow me on Goodreads
- Follow me on Bookbub
- Like my Facebook Author Page
- Drop me a line at jessicapauthor@jessicapeterson.com

Dear Reader,

Thank you very much for picking up LESSONS IN GRAVITY. To say this was a tough book to write is an understatement. Maddie and Javier are perhaps the most emotionally complex couple I've ever written, and I worked really, really hard to get it right. I hope you enjoyed their angsty journey to happily ever after!

While fictional, El Monasterio de los Humildes Reales is based on a real monastery in Madrid—El Monasterio de los Descalzos Reales, or the Monastery of the Barefoot Royals. My fabulous editor came up with the idea of a church-cum-concert hall, a la the Ryman Theater in Nashville, and I gave it a Madrileño twist. I never visited the Monastery of the Barefoot Royals while I was in Madrid, but if I ever go back, I'm definitely checking it out—it looks like an incredible spot.

If you've read book #1 of the STUDY ABROAD series, LESSONS IN LOVE, you know Maddie didn't come off as an exactly sympathetic character. Relationships with your girlfriends can be complicated, especially when you're young(er), and I wanted to capture that angst in the dynamic between Vivian Bingley and her BFF Maddie. It worked (I hope!) in LESSONS IN LOVE, but that meant I had to redeem Maddie through her own story in LESSONS IN GRAVITY. I hope you have a better understanding now of where she's coming from and why she acts the way she does. She's a tough cookie, sure, and she does some pretty stupid things, but I'd like to think beneath the layers of guilt and anger she's an awesome, and awesomely relatable, human being.

Uncle Javier is actually based on a real-life Spaniard I met while studying abroad in Madrid more than ten years ago. My roommate and I went to Barcelona for a weekend early in the semester. We stayed with a friend of hers from her high school back in the States who was studying abroad there. That friend happened to have a lot of family in Barcelona. His "uncle" invited us to go on a sunset tour of the city in his plane. When said "uncle" picked us up, my roommate and I almost died. He was so. Freaking. Hot it was *unreal*. I knew I'd put him in a book if I ever wrote one—and here he is!

If you ever have the chance to study or just travel abroad, do it. Maybe you'll meet a hot Spaniard, maybe you won't— but it will change your life nonetheless.

Thanks again for reading Maddie and Javier's story. I sincerely hope you enjoyed it.

Besitos,
    Jessica

ALSO BY JESSICA PETERSON

THE SEX & BONDS SERIES

An outrageously sexy series of romcoms set in the high stakes world of Wall Street.

The Dealmaker (Sex & Bonds #1)

The Troublemaker (Sex & Bonds #2)

THE NORTH CAROLINA HIGHLANDS SERIES

Beards. Bonfires. Boning.

Southern Seducer (NC Highlands #1)

Southern Hotshot (NC Highlands #2)

Southern Sinner (NC Highlands #3)

Southern Playboy (NC Highlands #4)

Southern Bombshell (NC Highlands #5)

THE CHARLESTON HEAT SERIES

The Weather's Not the Only Thing Steamy Down South.

Southern Charmer (Charleston Heat #1)

Southern Player (Charleston Heat #2)

Southern Gentleman (Charleston Heat #3)

Southern Heartbreaker (Charleston Heat #4)

THE THORNE MONARCHS SERIES

Royal. Ridiculously Hot. Totally Off Limits...

Royal Ruin (Thorne Monarchs #1)

Royal Rebel (Thorne Monarchs #2)

Royal Rogue (Thorne Monarchs #3)

THE STUDY ABROAD SERIES

Studying Abroad Just Got a Whole Lot Sexier.

A Series of Sexy Interconnected Standalone Romances

Lessons in Love (Study Abroad #1)

Lessons in Gravity (Study Abroad #2)

Lessons in Letting Go (Study Abroad #3)

Lessons in Losing It (Study Abroad #4)

ABOUT THE AUTHOR

Jessica Peterson writes romance with heat, humor, and heart. Heroes with hot accents are her specialty. When she's not writing, she can be found bellying up to a bar in the south's best restaurants with her husband Ben, reading books with her adorable daughter Gracie, or snuggling up with her 70-pound lap dog, Martha.

A Carolina girl at heart, she fantasizes about splitting her time between Charleston and Asheville, but currently lives in Charlotte, NC. You can check out her books at www.jessicapeterson.com.